A KIM BRADY MYSTERY

# A TEMPEST DROPPING FIRE

A NOVEL BY

## EDWARD J. LEAHY

Black Rose Writing | Texas

ISBN: 978-1-68513-678-9
LIBRARY OF CONGRESS CONTROL NUMBER:
PUBLISHED BY BLACK ROSE WRITING
www.blackrosewriting.com

Printed in the United States of America
Suggested Retail Price (SRP) $22.95

*A Tempest Dropping Fire* is printed in Baskerville

*As a planet-friendly publisher, Black Rose Writing does its best to eliminate unnecessary waste to reduce paper usage and energy costs, while never compromising the reading experience. As a result, the final word count vs. page count may not meet common expectations.

# ALSO BY EDWARD J. LEAHY

## KIM BRADY MYSTERY SERIES

*Past Grief*
*Deceived By Ornament*
*Proving a Villain*
*Judgement of Beasts*

## DAN BRADY MYSTERY SERIES

*Enemies of All*
*Contagion of the Night*

# A TEMPEST
# DROPPING
# FIRE

# CHAPTER ONE

*Sunday, April 20, 11:05 a.m.*

"Go, Captain Kim!"

Detective Kim Brady was already picking up the pace as she passed Grand Army Plaza, entering the final mile of the half marathon. Prospect Park had never looked so good, and the brief concern she'd had about the twinge in her right knee back in Mile Eight faded as she checked her time.

The shout from Arman Dhillon, desk sergeant at Patrol Borough Brooklyn North, was welcome all the same, and she grinned at his reference to her having been named captain of the Brooklyn North Race Team, a group of twelve officers and detectives who'd entered the race together. As one of only two women on the team, she'd been stunned by the team's vote.

She pushed hard as she turned from West Drive onto Center Drive, with less than a tenth of a mile to go. She could see the finish line ahead and the big clock: 1:34:41… 1:34:42.

She broke into a sprint. 1:34:49… 1:34:50.

"You're gonna do it, Kim!" Jake, her husband, called out as she passed him a few yards before the finish.

She crossed the finish line, her gaze firmly on the digital clock overhead. 1:34:58.

She came through the finishing chute gasping and fighting a momentary urge to vomit. As she turned toward the open field to the right where the other finishing runners were strolling and cooling down, she caught sight of Jake running toward her, arms open.

"You did it. Sub-1:35."

"Barely." His hug was delicious. "How are the others on the team finishing?"

"Cord finished a couple of minutes ago," Jake replied. "Here he comes." Cordell Washington was a partner of hers in the PBBN Homicide Unit.

"Only a couple of minutes? I'll have to give him the business about that."

Jake handed her a fresh Gatorade. "Martin finished a minute before you." Martin Stransky was another member of the unit. "Two more team members are finishing now. Looks like you all…"

Gunshots.

Screams.

"Down!" She grabbed Jake and pulled him to the ground next to her. Instinctively, she reached for the long-nose .38 that she usually kept tucked in her waistband.

No, I left it home in the safe.

More shots, but from the opposite direction.

She waited until the shooting stopped before kneeling and looking for the nearest cops on duty. Panicked runners and spectators were dashing hither and yon in widespread panic.

Jake. She had to get him somewhere safe.

But as she glanced around, nowhere looked safe.

***

"Kim!"

The cry came from her right, further into the field.

To her horror, a growing stain of blood covered Cord's racing shirt at his lower back on the right side. He was down. She dashed to him in a crouching run, ready to dive to the ground if there were more gunshots.

She surveyed the field; many people continued hugging the ground, but a few raised their heads. Doctors and volunteers at the medical tents set up to treat running injuries peered out, undecided.

"I need a doctor," Kim yelled. "Now!"

A man, wearing a white T-shirt with "Medical Staff" written across the front, hesitated at the entrance to the tent.

Kim pulled her badge from the pocket of her running shorts. "Police! Move it!"

The man broke into a sprint. "Sorry…"

She gestured toward Cord. "He's been hit. Are you a doctor?"

"Yes." He took Cord's pulse and spoke to him. "Can you hear me?"

"I hear you just fine, Bro."

The doctor pulled out a walkie-talkie. "I have a man down, gunshot wound. I need a stretcher. And call for additional trauma support."

Stransky arrived in a crouch. "Kim, both Jackson and Galloway are down."

"Where?" Kim asked.

Stransky pointed to a spot about twenty yards from the finish line. "I checked. They're both dead."

Jake caught up to her, and she gestured for his cell.

"What's wrong with yours?" He pointed at the holder strapped to her upper left arm.

"I'm a little disoriented. Sorry." She called into the main desk at PBBN. "We've had a shooting at the race in Prospect Park. Three Members of Service down. We need backup and medical help. And send our Crime Scene Unit." She ended the call. "Martin, have you seen other members of our team?"

"Yeah, last I saw, they were over by the meeting area for families and friends."

"Good. Make sure they're okay, survey the field, and check for any additional casualties. Call my cell when you know. Then, get them to fan out and start asking questions. Where did the shots come from? Did anyone see anything?"

She stopped.

"What is it?" Stransky asked as two attendants ran over with a stretcher and proceeded to ease Cord onto it.

"Careful," the doctor said. "The wound is to his lower back."

Cord winced as they settled him on the stretcher. "Thanks, bro."

She turned to face the finish line. "Cord was walking toward me, facing this way, and he was hit in the back…" She stared at a copse of trees extending from the woods on the other side of the field. "…the shooter was in those woods."

Stransky pointed back toward the finish line. "Jackson and Galloway were over by Center Drive. He must be a crack shot to hit them from those trees."

Kim nodded. "Jake, please go home and get my piece, my wallet, a fresh T-shirt, and a pair of denim shorts."

He hesitated. "Kim, you need…"

"I'm on duty now. Please?"

He kissed her head. "I'll be back as soon as I can."

She watched him go.

"I have a bad feeling about this," Stransky said. "Cord, Galloway, and Jackson, all of them black."

"And all of them cops. Let's not jump to conclusions."

# CHAPTER TWO

Sergeant Phil Vitello of PBBN's Crime Scene Unit arrived shortly after Jake left. "Lucky for you, I was in the office today. But isn't this Brooklyn South's territory?"

"Yes. But I don't see anyone here, yet, from their shop, so I figured I'd get things rolling." Kim recapped the incident.

"Do you remember how many shots you heard?"

A question she was used to asking, not answering. And she hated the answer she had to give. "I'm not sure, Phil. I had just finished the race and was talking to my husband. I heard two distinct groups of shots." She closed her eyes and tried to force her mind back. "Five shots in the first group. I'm pretty sure of it. Then a pause, followed by several more shots, but…"

"What?"

She opened her eyes. "The sound was different. And further away. I'm certain of it." She described where Cord had been hit and pointed to the copse of trees. "Whoever shot Cord had to be in that copse of trees across the field."

"Do you recall anything else distinguishing the sound of the two groups of shots? Or only that they were further away?"

"I can't say for sure, but they sounded like different weapons."

"I'll be back." He jogged over to where Jackson and Galloway were still laying.

"Kim?" It was Captain Steve Colangelo, the supervising officer of all the detective units at PBBN.

After she brought him up to date, he asked, "Where is everyone from Brooklyn South?"

"I don't know. We decided to start, then they can take over whenever they get here. Sergeant Vitello is already here with some of our CSU group."

Stransky approached and nodded to Colangelo, under whom he, Cord, and Kim had all worked in their days at Internal Affairs. "Two more fatalities, Kim, in addition to our guys, and three more wounded."

"Any other members of service?" Kim asked.

Martin shook his head. "No, but all of them are black."

"Shit." Colangelo spat the word. "Okay, let's see what CSU comes up with. In the meantime, I'll get on the horn with Brooklyn South and see what's keeping them. Kim, you want to maybe go home and change?"

"No, thanks. Jake is bringing some things for me. Besides, what happens if Brooklyn South never shows up?"

"They'll show up."

***

She walked over to where the other two dead victims lay. Both were girls in their early-to-mid teens. CSU had already blocked off the area, and family members stood beyond, sobbing. Both had been shot in the chest and had fallen onto their backs. The shooter from the copse of trees.

Kim tried to interview the family members, but only one was able to talk to her, the father of one of the two girls. He pointed to the taller girl. "Jade just turned fifteen. She wanted to come to cheer on her brother. The other girl is Jameela, my daughter's best friend. She had a crush on my son, I think."

"Did you notice where the shots came from?"

"No, I saw both girls… get hit. Two tours in Afghanistan… saw lots of horrible things. You never get used to it. You think you do, but you don't. And you never expect…" He couldn't go on.

A veteran. "What did the shots sound like?"

"My Jade is dead. Oh, my…"

Kim decided not to press him. She touched his arm. "I'm so sorry." She started back toward Vitello when a thirtyish thin man stopped her.

"Are you with the police?" His voice was soft, with a slight hint of an accent she couldn't identify.

"Yes, I'm a detective."

"John Lodemay at your service." He gave a slight bow and then took her hand as if to kiss it, but he just held it instead.

"Nice to meet you. Did…"

"I saw everything on the field." He bowed again; his thick, bushy black brows furrowed.

She placed the accent. "Are you French?"

"I am, indeed. Descended from a long line of Frenchmen. I came to this country at an early age. I love this park, especially in the spring. Seeing the race ending was thrilling."

She asked him about the shots.

"At first, I thought they were firecrackers. A celebration for the runners, perhaps. But then there were shots fired behind me."

"That must have frightened you." Maybe he wouldn't have seen as much as he'd boasted.

He pulled himself up. "Detective, I am descended from a long line of knights. I do not frighten easily."

"Knights, huh?" Maybe he wouldn't be so helpful after all.

"Yes. The Knights Templar, to be exact."

Uh oh.

"But that's ancient history, of course. As I said, several shots came from behind me, but I believe what I thought were firecrackers were actually shots fired from the other side of the field."

"Did you see muzzle flashes?"

"No, but I detected movement in the trees."

"Where?"

"Across the field, near the finish line. There was no breeze; the movement had to be a person."

"Do you remember how many shots you heard in each group?"

"Five in what I'll call the firecracker group, about ten in the group fired from behind me."

The five shots in the first group matched her memory of it, and ten in the second sounded right.

"The shots from behind me sounded like a pistol," he added.

"What makes you say that?"

"Much louder, and, in general, pistols are louder than rifles because of the shorter barrel. The first five shots were much softer. So, I believe they were fired by a rifle."

Kim studied the densely wooded area on the opposite side of the field. "That's about a hundred yards away. The level of volume would be significantly lower."

Lodemay gave her a grin. "It would. But I still believe those shots were fired by a rifle."

"Anything else you can tell me?"

"I noticed three policemen were shot first."

"How did you know they were police?"

Lodemay pointed at her T-shirt. "The shield. It's a distinctive T-shirt. Who designed it?"

"The wife of…"

"One of the victims?"

She turned away. The paramedics had already taken Cord to the nearest medical tent. "Excuse me for a minute. Please don't leave."

She pulled her cell out of the sleeve of the holder on her arm and pulled up the number of Vera Koshkin.

Vera answered on the first ring. "Are you all right? Is Cord? Martin?"

The media must have already gotten word of the shooting. "Martin and I are fine. Cord was hit, but he's getting medical attention now. I'll let you know the moment I have news."

"Thank God. I heard two others from the command were killed."

"Yes, Jared Galloway and Mitch Jackson." She recapped the other casualties.

"Will Cord be all right?" Vera's voice cracked.

"I can't see into the medical tent, but they got to him quickly. He was shot in the lower back."

"We're not even married, yet."

"And you'll have many years, I'm sure, Vera. I promise I'll keep you informed, and if I don't, someone from the unit will. Promise."

A sniffle. "Thank you, Brilliant American Lady Detective."

Kim had to smile. "I love you, too."

Lodemay was still beside her.

Deep breath. "I'm sorry. You were saying you noticed the three members of my team were shot first?"

"Yes. The men furthest away fell in the group of shots, the ones from the woods. The third one was shot in the second group, the ones fired from back there." He pointed over his left shoulder to the copse of trees. "That's when the others were shot."

She opened the Notes App on her phone.

Lodemay turned away. "I have to go."

"Wait." She pulled the folder with her shield from a pocket in her running shorts and extracted a card. "Call me if you think of anything else. Where can I reach you?"

He took the card and rattled off a number, followed by an address.

She entered the information in her notes. "Where is…?"

But he was gone.

# CHAPTER THREE

Detective Bob Nolan was struggling to keep calm. After shouting encouragement to Kim when she ran by in the race, he'd started walking slowly toward the finish area.

And then he'd heard the shots.

The panicked crowd of people had formed a flood trying to escape from the park, and it had taken him ages to get through it. In the meantime, he'd called it into the main desk of PBBN.

When he finally reached the open field, he saw Cord Washington being carried on a stretcher. He followed it, but they wouldn't let him into the tent.

"He'll be all right," a paramedic assured him.

Don't be so sure.

"Bob!" It was Phil Vitello. "Kim's fine."

"I saw Cord. Anyone else?"

Vitello told him the rest. "No sign of Brooklyn South anywhere other than around the racecourse, so Kim's organizing the preliminary investigation. There she is."

Hearing from Vitello was one thing, seeing Kim was another. He was able to fight off the panic that had begun to grip him, and the urge to take a drink that had raised its ugly head in the last two weeks. Eight years, one month, and nine days after his last fall off the wagon, and it felt harder than ever.

"You okay, Bob?"

It was great to hear her voice. "Fine. Where the hell is Brooklyn South? Or is this our case now?"

"No one from their homicide squad is around, and several precincts of uniforms are committed to protecting the course. They've shut down the race, and the remaining runners on the course are scrambling to find their families or friends. It's a mess."

As Bob had seen for himself.

She looked him up and down. "Are you sure you're all right?"

Partner radar. Kim's was sharper than most. "Fine. I fought a human flood to get up here."

She grinned. "Now that you're here, you're senior, so…"

"No!" Oops, that came out too hard. Kim's glare showed she'd caught it. He took a deep breath. "You're better at organizing than me. And you have a head start."

She considered asking him if he was alright, but decided to let it pass for now. "Let's see if we can get any additional information from anyone who hasn't already fled."

***

Over the next hour, Kim made the rounds with CSU and the Medical Examiner's office while Bob and Martin interviewed witnesses. When Captain Colangelo called them together, she was ready.

"First," Colangelo said, "I want to thank you all for taking immediate control of a disastrous situation. The guys from Brooklyn South are on their way, and they likely won't be happy that we've already done much of the preliminary work for them. Frankly, I don't want to turn this over to them at this point. We've got a lot invested in this case."

"But," Kim said, "it *is* their jurisdiction."

Colangelo grinned at her. "Surely you're not afraid of a little turf war."

"Afraid, no. Just trying to see the conflict ahead."

"You let me worry about that. At the moment, this is our case by default, and you're lead, Detective First Grade Brady."

She'd made first grade two years earlier.

Deep breath. "Okay. Phil, what's the word on the crime scene?"

"Your witness was incredibly accurate. We found five spent .338 Lapua shell casings in the wooded area near the finish line. That's a powerful bullet designed for army snipers in Afghanistan. It's usually fired from a scoped rifle, but if the reports we have are accurate, including yours, then he fired those shots in rapid succession."

"So, possibly an AR-15." Kim thought back on the case that had first launched her to NYPD stardom, a mass shooting in the Meat Packing District, in which an AR-15, altered to full automatic, had been used to gun down three drug dealers and several innocent bystanders.

Vitello held up an evidence bag with five shells. "My thoughts, exactly. Ballistics will tell us for certain. Detectives Jackson and Galloway were both hit twice, although one would have been sufficient to kill each of them."

Kim pointed to the copse of trees across the field. "What about our second shooter?"

Vitello held up a second evidence bag. "We recovered eleven spent nine-millimeter +P shells in the copse of trees. Cord was hit once, the girls were both hit twice, the two wounded boys, once each. That's seven rounds, so there are four spent bullets somewhere around here. We'll comb all night, but I don't hold out much hope."

"Sounds like our second shooter was less accurate than our first," Kim said.

"Or maybe just less focused," Stransky added.

"We're sure the second shooter used a pistol, while the first used a rifle." Kim made a small, deferential bow to Vitello. "Although we'll wait for the final word from Ballistics."

Vitello returned the bow. "You were right, though, that the second shooter hit Cord, which was lucky for Cord."

"Yes," Colangelo added, "I've already heard he's going to be okay, although he's lost the use of his right kidney."

Kim's cell pinged. A text from Jake. *On my way back to the field. Just got off the F train at 15th Street.*

# CHAPTER FOUR

Mayor Raymond Brandt's first reaction to news of the shooting had been, "Oh, hell, not in an election year." He wasn't proud of it, but his internal polling showed that, while the city's politics on the whole had become more moderate, his disapproval ratings were slowly rising.

Then again, people these days increasingly distrusted incumbents.

He turned to his most trusted aide, Justin Cates, sitting beside him in his city-owned black Chevy Suburban. "How long before this makes it into the news cycle?"

"I expect most of the stations already have people rushing to the scene. I'd say an hour before the first 'breaking news' alerts get flashed, another hour or so before actual reporting starts."

"How's our response been?"

"My understanding is that Kim Brady had just crossed the finish line when the shooting started. She immediately organized the preliminary investigation."

"Was she hurt?" He hoped his anxiety hadn't been evident in his voice. His feelings for Kim hadn't abated in the least in the past two years. Quite the opposite. And Justin's radar for that sort of thing was keen.

Justin's expression showed he'd heard it, loud and clear. "No. But two Brooklyn North detectives were killed, and Cordell Washington was wounded. We were also lucky that other Brooklyn North personnel were already on the scene for the race."

Brandt recovered. "At least the investigation is in good hands. Kim is… excellent at her job."

"Prospect Park is in Brooklyn South's jurisdiction. Putting Kim in charge will almost certainly cause…"

"I don't care. I'm the goddamn mayor, and if I say she's in charge, then she is. If I have to promote her to captain to get it done, I'll do it."

The Suburban pulled off Prospect Park Southwest and into the park, making its way up Center Drive before stopping at a yellow tape barrier.

"Looks like CSU has blocked off the rest," Justin said. "There's Kim, Captain Colangelo, and the others."

***

Shit. Kim had been hoping Jake would arrive with some decent clothes before the mayor showed up, but those hopes were dashed by the black Suburban pulling to the edge of the field. Luckily, Stransky had lent her a sweatshirt of his, and the chill she'd felt from the April breeze against her sweat-soaked T-shirt had faded.

As the mayor approached, he was checking her out, his gaze lingering on her legs. "So glad to see you all safe."

That pissed her off. "Hardly all, Mr. Mayor. Two dead detectives and one wounded. Two dead bystanders and two wounded."

He stopped in his tracks, as if he'd been slapped. Good.

Captain Colangelo gave him the briefing. "We're just waiting to hear from Brooklyn…"

The mayor recovered. "Captain, I am ordering the commissioner to leave this investigation in the hands of Patrol Borough Brooklyn North. Detective Brady will be lead detective on the case. Any resistance that you receive from any other command will be reported to me, and I will deal with it. Am I clear, Captain?"

"Yes, sir. We will do our best."

At last, Kim spotted Jake approaching. "Excuse me a moment, please, Mr. Mayor. My husband just arrived with a change of clothes for me."

"Sorry I took so long." Jake handed over a pair of sweat pants. "I figured, under the circumstances, these would be easiest to manage."

"Thanks." With one hand on his shoulder for balance, she slipped into the sweats. Then she pulled off Stransky's sweatshirt, careful not to pull the T-shirt with it, and pulled on the one Jake had brought. Then she hugged him and let him hold her for a lingering moment.

"Are you sure you're okay? It's been years since you've been shot at."

She kissed his cheek. "They didn't shoot at me. If they had, I don't think they'd have missed. It looks like Cord's going to be okay."

He handed her a plastic bag. "It's been over three hours since the race ended. You need some quick refueling." Inside the bag were three trail mix bars and a bottle of Gatorade. "Best I could manage on the run." He gestured toward the mayor. "How's he?"

She sighed. "He wants me to lead the investigation."

A frown crossed Jake's face. "I'll bet."

No sense in denying it. Two years earlier, a news outlet had picked up on a rumor of an affair between Kim and the mayor. The rumor was false, but Kim had long been aware of his attraction to her and had rebuffed it. "I'll deal with it if I need to."

A news van pulled up with the letters "ITN" emblazoned on the side in the three primary colors.

"Well, the party's complete. Joanna's here." She kissed Jake goodbye. "I'll let you know when I'm on the way home."

Jake handed over her wallet and her second piece, a 1950 Smith and Wesson Chief's Special, a long-nose .38 that chambered five rounds. It had belonged to her grandfather, Daniel Patrick Brady, a hero detective in his day. Her father, who'd also been a detective, had presented it to Kim upon her graduation from the Police Academy. "I figured you'd want this one."

She kissed him again, then turned away before the TV reporter drew close enough so that she'd either have to talk to her or turn away in an obvious snub.

# CHAPTER FIVE

Joanna Dunbar, top political reporter for the Independent Television Network, wasn't insulted that Kim Brady had turned away. They had a long-standing agreement that Kim would keep Joanna informed so long as she obeyed the rules on what could and could not be repeated. In return, Joanna provided Kim with useful information, including leaks she received.

But as much as she wanted to talk to Kim, her immediate target was the mayor. She'd managed to reach the edge of the crime scene and found him there, and her mouth watered at the chance for an exclusive, on-site interview. While she waited for Hizzoner, her camera man got his gear ready.

As the mayor approached, he passed Kim and turned his head to follow her for a moment.

Oh, great, he still had it for her. Horny bastard.

"Mr. Mayor!" That should refocus him. "A moment, please?"

Justin Cates rushed ahead to meet her. "How'd you get in here?"

She gave him a smile that most men would have found flirtatious, but she knew Justin was immune to such advances from women. Which was okay with her. "We drove in."

"I don't know if he'll talk to you, yet. You really should wait until the department releases…"

"He's the mayor, Justin. And it's an election year. I'm sure he'll want to appear mayoral."

And as Brandt approached, his expression confirmed she was correct. "Ms. Dunbar. An unexpected pleasure."

She turned deferential. "Mr. Mayor, I know it's early, but I thought you'd want to go on the air with some initial public statement."

Just a hint of a smirk. "And an exclusive for you?"

"I'm good at this work."

"So, you are. Very well." He turned to Justin. "If Mr. Cates doesn't object."

"No, sir, you're the mayor."

Joanna waved the camera man into place with the sun at his back and the mayor facing him. She moved to the mayor's side. On the cameraman's signal, she started. "I'm here with Mayor Raymond Brandt at the scene of this morning's shooting at Brooklyn's Prospect Park. Mr. Mayor, what can you tell us about the shooting and the police investigation thus far?"

"Included among the contestants in this morning's race were three homicide detectives from North Brooklyn. They took immediate action to get medical help for the victims and to commence the investigation. Members of the Brooklyn North Crime Scene Unit also rushed to the scene. The hard work and quick thinking of these folks helped to keep the crime scene from becoming overwhelmed and unmanageable."

"What do we know at present?"

"There were two shooters, not one, and they shot from opposite sides of an open field. At least one shooter appears to have used an assault rifle, although we won't be certain until the police get reports back from Ballistics."

"What about the victims?"

"Three were members of the NYPD, two dead, one wounded. The other four were teens, two dead, two wounded. Out of respect for the families, the police have not yet released their names."

He was holding something back. She was certain of it. "Does anything link these victims together? Any common thread?"

The briefest hesitation. "I can't answer that. The police need to be able to investigate. Now, if you'll excuse me…" The mayor gave a polite nod and walked away.

Joanna gave the cameraman the "cut" sign and grabbed Cates. "What isn't he telling me? It's not like him to hold back."

Cates lowered his voice. "He doesn't want to ignite a powder keg."

"What the hell does that mean? Damnit, Justin, don't go all mysterious on me." She turned to follow his gaze. The mayor was talking with a forty-ish male in business-casual dress who appeared agitated.

"This is off the record, Joanna. You can't use it."

Deep breath. "Okay, what?"

"All the victims were black. The three detectives, the four kids, all black."

***

Kim was discussing what they knew with Captain Colangelo, Bob, and Phil Vitello. A man in his forties with the map of Ireland on his face, wearing chinos and a golf shirt, who a moment earlier had been talking with the mayor, came storming toward them from Center Drive.

"Great," Vitello said. "Here comes Driscoll."

The name rang an instant bell. Lieutenant Liam Driscoll, Brooklyn South Homicide. "This should be fun. I wonder what he and they mayor talked about."

"I'll handle this, Kim," the captain said. "Just fill in the blanks as needed."

"Lieutenant Driscoll, PBBS. Anyone want to tell me what the hell is going on?"

Colangelo extended his hand and introduced himself. "Nice to meet you, Lieutenant." He introduced the others. "Detective Brady and Sergeant Vitello were both on the scene when the shooting occurred. Recognizing that speed is essential in cases like this, they commenced the investigation immediately, since Brooklyn South appeared unable to respond."

Driscoll flushed. "We're short-staffed, and I have two detectives sick with the flu. I came as soon as I heard."

Colangelo gave him a sympathetic smile. "No explanations necessary, Lieutenant. We were fortunate to have people running the race. Kim, would you give the lieutenant a rundown on what we have thus far?"

"Glad to." She summarized everything they had, but while she mentioned what Lodemay had told her about the locations of the shooters, she didn't mention him by name.

"Sounds impressive," Driscoll said, "but I doubt anyone could have smuggled an AR-15 into the park, and if they did, I would think they would have fired more than five rounds."

"I'm not drawing any conclusions until I hear back from Ballistics," she replied.

"I'll draw my own conclusions, thank you." Driscoll turned back to the captain. "I want to thank your people for such a fine start. My guys will take it from here." Back to Kim. "I'll need the contact information for that witness you spoke with."

Colangelo's face remained pleasant. "Let's step it back a moment, Lieutenant. By your own admission, your unit is badly short-handed. So much so that you only got here…" He checked his watch. "…six hours after the shots were fired."

Driscoll's jaw was set. "This crime occurred in my jurisdiction. I'm grateful for the start your people got but…"

Colangelo cut him off. "This is Brooklyn North's case. Ms. Brady, a first grade detective, is the lead investigator. She will keep you informed of all developments in the case, and if there is an additional role your folks can perform, she will see you have the opportunity to do so. Am I clear, Lieutenant."

"Crystal, Captain. But this isn't over." Driscoll stalked away.

# CHAPTER SIX

Kim was grateful to Colangelo for the ride to Brooklyn Methodist Hospital, where Cord Washington had been taken.

"If he's had surgery, I'm sure we won't be able to see him." He cast a sidelong glance at her. "You okay? I mean, you were shot at, too."

"No, I wasn't. Vitello's guys found no additional slugs in the grass. If someone with a rifle had shot at me, they'd have hit me." The thought made her shudder, remembering the one time in her career when she had been shot, eight years earlier. She changed the subject. "You must be having some deep concerns, too. Cord was one of our guys back in Internal Affairs."

"That group we had when you, Cord, and Martin were there was the best I ever had." He turned serious as he searched for a parking space. "I'm not looking forward to the narrative on this case."

She knew what he meant. "I'm working very hard not to form an opinion on that, yet."

He found a spot, killed the engine and smiled at her. "That's why I'm making sure you stay in charge of this case."

"Before he approached us, Driscoll was talking to the mayor. I saw them."

Colangelo shrugged. "I'm sure we'll have a brawl. We'll live."

Vera was in the waiting area when they got inside, her blonde hair limp, her eyes red, her lips pale, bearing little resemblance to her usual coy, sexy self. She rushed to Kim and embraced her. "I'm so glad you're safe. Cord's still in surgery." She turned to Colangelo. "Thank you so much for coming, Captain."

He took hold of both her hands. "We're a family, Vera. We understand what others don't. Anything you need, please just ask."

Vera's eyes teared up. "I just need him to be okay."

"I'm sure he will be, but in the meantime, we're here for you."

A doctor approached and addressed Vera. "He's out of surgery and in recovery. He came through very nicely, but we couldn't save his right kidney. However, many people have only one kidney and lead perfectly normal lives."

"He'll be able to return to work?" Vera asked.

"Absolutely, after a few weeks of convalescing. We'll know better after a few days."

"Thank you, doctor. Thank you." Vera waited until he'd walked away to turn and hug Kim. "Thank God." Then she broke into a smile. "A few weeks? Cord will never sit still that long."

Colangelo placed a hand on her shoulder. "We'll work something out."

***

It was early evening when the captain dropped Kim off at the brownstone where she and Jake lived on Monroe Place in Brooklyn Heights. As soon as she closed the car door, Jake appeared in the front window, a reminder that she hadn't checked in with him once after he'd left the park.

As she entered the vestibule, he was waiting at the door to their apartment. "Have you eaten since the race?"

She had to laugh, because her head was throbbing from the low blood sugar. "Just the box lunch you gave me."

He took her in his arms. "Not enough."

"You're right. It wasn't."

"Dine out or eat in?"

"Oh, definitely eat in. Whatever you like." She let him hold her.

"Kimberly Megan Brady, didn't anyone ever tell you not to dash immediately from finishing a half marathon to a major investigation on an empty stomach?" The mention of her middle name, which she never used and had only revealed to him when they'd gotten married, was his way of chiding her with humor.

"I must have missed that section in the Patrol Guide."

"How did you come to have Megan as your middle name, anyway?"

"It was my gram's name, my dad's mother. She died when I was six but my cousin, Jim, says she was a real firecracker when she was young. I was her only granddaughter, so she always made me feel special." Memories of gram always warmed her.

Jake gave her a tight hug. "If you want to shower, I'll call out. Italian?"

"Yes, please." Then it occurred to her: Jake was a news junkie, especially after a major event, like a mass shooting. Yet the TV was off, the computer screen dark. "Why are you so anxious to get me into the shower?"

"I know you need to unwind. You must feel awfully grubby by now." But he didn't meet her gaze.

Hands on her hips. "What is it? What aren't you telling me?"

"The shooting has already hit the news cycle."

"I know. I saw Joanna Dunbar at the park. It's impossible to keep a mass shooting a secret."

"All the news stations are emphasizing the victims being black."

# CHAPTER SEVEN

*Monday, April 21, 7:45 a.m.*

"Welcome to *City News*. The city is still shaking after the mass shooting at the finish line of a half marathon in Brooklyn's Prospect Park that took the lives of two black officers and two black teen girls, and wounded a third black officer and two black teen boys. The police department has assured the public that their investigation is proceeding, but a source within the department admits they have no leads, yet. Felipe Prinz, leader of the progressive group Come Home Ernesto, issued a statement this morning calling on the New York Police Department to, in his words, 'at least take an interest in the murder of black people when two of them are members of the department. These white ultranationalists must be stopped.'

"When asked if they thought white ultranationalists were responsible, the NYPD's only response was that the investigation was proceeding and offered no alternative theory."

***

Lieutenant Adam Bostwick, a former marine who had more recently won a battle with Hodgkin's Disease, was waiting for Kim when she entered Police Borough Brooklyn North's headquarters, known as the Castle due to the building's resemblance to a battlement, on Wilson Avenue in the Bushwick section. "I'm very glad to see you well, Kim. Hell of a day, yesterday."

"I saw Vera at the hospital. Cord came through the surgery okay; he's expected to return within a month."

"He'll never stay out that long." The lieutenant gestured to the big screen TV on the wall. "They didn't waste any time. Captain Colangelo asked me to bring you up to his office as soon as you arrive."

"Anyone else from our unit here, yet?" She scanned the squad room.

"Nope, you're the first. Shall we?"

She preferred waiting for Bob, but they were rapidly approaching chaos. "Yeah, okay."

Colangelo waved them in and closed the door. "This is becoming a major shitshow."

"I know," Kim replied. "I saw the *City News* report downstairs. I guess I'm not surprised to see Prinz stirring the pot."

"What do you think of the theory?" Colangelo asked. "Based on our evidence?"

"Which is what, exactly?" She hadn't had a chance to ask about anything from Ballistics, but if they'd reported anything, the lieu would have mentioned it. "All we know is that one shooter used a rifle of some sort, possibly an AR-15, and a second shooter used a 9 millimeter, possibly a pistol. We know they shot from opposite sides of the field, and we know how many shots each fired."

"And that all the victims were black," Bostwick added.

"So," Colangelo said, "it seems the ultranationalist theory is at least viable. And, as it's already hit the airwaves, we won't be able to knock it out unless we come up with a stronger, more viable theory supported by the evidence."

"I'm not interested in popular theories, Captain. We need to look at everything with a clear, unbiased eye."

"Okay," Colangelo said. "Pretend none of us have mentioned or even heard the term, 'white ultranationalist' in connection with this shooting. What's the first fact that strikes you, Kim?"

"The first shooter—let's call him the sniper, because the power and accuracy of his shooting suggests that he may have one time been one—fired five rounds at two targets and hit both targets right in the police logo on their racing T-shirts. The first shot fired by the second shooter hit Cord just as he was turning around to face me."

"What's your point?" Bostwick asked.

"The first targets—the only targets of the sniper, and the first of the second shooter—were cops, easily identified as such by the T-shirts we all wore, and which had been featured in newspaper articles and on news programs in the days before the race." She shook her head. "Why would ultranationalists target cops first?"

"Black cops," Colangelo said. "Besides, those folks typically don't have a lot of time for police. They tend to think everyone should arm themselves to take down the government that they see as oppressive. And they see police as propping up that government."

"Also," Bostwick said, "if their target was cops, why shoot the civilians?"

She had to admit, he had a point.

Colangelo leaned forward. "Kim, I appreciate you resisting being swayed. It's why I want you to lead this investigation. Stick to your process, wait for the evidence. But this morning's report probably has DCPI up in arms and desperate for something with which to counter it." DCPI was the Deputy Commissioner for Public Information, the mouthpiece of the department.

Two sharp knocks on the door. It was the captain's civilian secretary, Therese Vargas. "Captain, Deputy Inspector Cirillo is here. He wants to see you immediately."

"Send him in." As Therese left, he added to Kim, "You know those department politics you've always hated? Brace yourself for another bout."

Deputy Inspector Andrew Cirillo hadn't changed much since leaving the office Colangelo now occupied to go work for the commissioner. He still combed his black hair, with no hint of gray, straight back and wore his uniform with impeccable neatness. Only metal-rimmed glasses, which showed in sharp contrast to his olive skin, had been added since Kim had last seen him. He was not her biggest fan, nor was she one of his.

Cirillo took the last seat. "Good morning, captain; lieutenant; detective. I assume we're discussing yesterday's shooting."

"We are," Colangelo replied. "Detective Brady was just giving us an update."

Kim repeated the facts, making no mention of the report on *City News*, nor of Mr. Lodemay.

Cirillo listened to it all before making any comment. "Thank you, Detective. I'm gratified to see you've done your usual excellent work."

"Am doing." She couldn't help herself.

Cirillo turned stone-faced. "Detective, I choose my words with care. You and your people stepped in yesterday when Brooklyn South had insufficient manpower available. That is being rectified. Once Lieutenant Driscoll informs me who he is putting on the case, he and his people will take over."

# CHAPTER EIGHT

It had been quite some time since Mayor Raymond Brandt had received his top campaign contributor, Kyle Emory, at Gracie Mansion for a breakfast conversation, and longer still since the mayor had done the summoning.

He waited until breakfast had been brought in before getting down to business. "I've pretty much decided to run this year as an independent."

Emory placed his coffee cup back on its saucer with deliberate care. "Does 'pretty much' mean that you're allowing room for me to change your mind?"

The mayor broke into a grin. "It does, if your arguments against it are superior to my reasons for it. I'll even give you the courtesy of going first."

His patron took a bite of his omelet. Good, this might be more like their discussions in the early days of their partnership, rather than the rancor of recent years. "I assume you've considered that it's rather late in the game for that. With the primary only two months away, it looks like you're afraid of Mr. Barnett."

Lawrence Barnett, Speaker of the City Council, had already announced he was challenging the mayor in the primary.

"You're also not leaving yourself much time to recruit a campaign staff," Emory continued. "In military terms, you're signaling a retreat."

The mayor waited for him to finish. "Yes, I've considered all of that. And, to keep with your military analogy, not a retreat but a redeployment. Am I concerned about Barnett's challenge in a primary? Certainly. Despite the gains we've made in the city over the past few years, the progressives continue to romanticize the bad old days, when subways were filthy, streets were unsafe, and laws were largely unenforced. Last year's national results showed the country is moving away from the extremes, but still my party refuses to read the writing on the wall."

"So, how does going it alone help you?"

The mayor was certain Emory knew; perhaps he was asking to test his response for when the press asked. "My internal polling shows that I should beat Barnett by a reasonable margin—say, about ten points. But that's close enough to give him and his progressive pals a sense that they're not that far away. Frankly, I worry about what might follow when my second full term is up."

"I hope you don't plan on saying that out loud," Emory said with a chuckle.

"Of course not. But, since I'm asking you to stick with me, and since you asked a good question, you deserve an honest answer. By running as an independent, I give myself extra time to hire staff, to raise funds, to campaign on issues and look mayoral before anyone casts a vote. Moreover, when the votes are cast, they won't be cast solely by members of my erstwhile party, but also by independent voters and members of the opposition party, who thus far have failed to nominate a viable candidate. Those two groups are almost certain to prefer me to Mr. Barnett by a substantial margin come November."

"And most of that you won't admit out loud, either. What's your spin for the press?"

The mayor spread his arms. "I'm working on it."

The intercom on the mayor's desk buzzed. "Mr. Mayor, Mr. Cates is here to see you. He says it's urgent."

A scowl crossed Emory's face at the mention of the mayor's most trusted aide, nor was the mayor unaware of the cause of his patron's animosity. But if Justin said it was urgent… "Very well, send him in."

Emory's scowl deepened as Justin entered the room.

"I'm sorry to intrude, Mr. Mayor, but if I may have a word?" Justin cast a wary eye toward Emory.

"I have no secrets from Mr. Emory. What is it?"

Justin appeared uncertain but plowed forward anyway. "I hear that Brooklyn North Homicide is being pulled off the Prospect Park shooting."

The mayor struggled to keep his temper. "Go on."

"Apparently, Lieutenant Driscoll of Brooklyn South thinks it should be their case, and it is in their jurisdiction, sir."

It was impossible to keep his temper in check. "He damned well should have gotten people over there in a timely fashion yesterday. God *damn* it, I hate these stupid turf wars. Who did Driscoll go crying to?"

"I'm not sure," Justin replied, "but all I know is that Deputy Inspector Cirillo paid a visit to the Castle this morning and laid down the law."

What the hell was Cirillo doing poking his nose into this? But he already knew the answer. Kim Brady had fixed his wagon two years earlier in the tangled web that was the Sabrina Dunn murder case. Promoting Cirillo to Deputy Inspector and moving him onto the commissioner's staff was supposed to excise the problem.

Well, best laid plans…

Emory spoke in a soft voice. "You'd best go with a light touch here, Ray."

He didn't need to hear that. "Some of these career cops are a bit like old generals—they resist bowing to civilian authority." It was a mistake to have Justin speak in front of Emory, but it was too late now.

Justin said nothing, but his expression showed the same concern as Emory.

"I'll think about it, Justin. We'll talk later."

"Very good, sir." Justin left.

Emory waited until the door closed. "I won't presume to advise you, other than to remind you that the last thing you want is to be seen as propping up a certain female detective with whom you've been linked in the past, and not in a complimentary way."

"Damn it, Kyle, that was all nonsense, and you know it."

Emory held up a hand. "Yes, I do, but you know perception trumps reality."

"Driscoll doesn't have the best reputation in the world, and on top of that he gets to the scene of the crime in the case over which he now wants control six hours late and without any resources from his borough, while members of the neighboring borough have already done the heavy lifting."

"Excuse me, but I thought both commands were in the same borough."

"Not in NYPD usage of the term. Brooklyn North and Brooklyn South are considered separate boroughs."

Emory sat back. "Would you be this pissed off if Detective Kim Brady wasn't at the center of it? Honestly?"

They both knew he wouldn't. "To answer your question, the main issue is a Deputy Inspector, a staff officer, throwing his rank around because he's trying to get even. And I'm not going to let it pass."

"Fair enough." Emory stood. "To get back to our prior conversation, I think you've thought the election issue through quite well. I'll back your independent run, and I'll raise as much as I can to assist the effort. If you'd like, you can appoint me your campaign finance chairman."

They shook hands. "Thank you, Kyle."

"But please consider my advice on the other matter."

# CHAPTER NINE

It was just before noon when Vitello presented Kim with two reports from Ballistics.

"Wow," Kim said. "That was fast. But I thought these had to be delivered to PBBS."

Vitello smirked. "There's always some guy who doesn't get the word."

"You mean because it wasn't passed on by a certain other guy?"

"I don't know what you're talking about. But I advise you to have a glance."

She read through the first report. "An AR-15. Just as we thought." She put the report down. "Damn, the shooter's aim was awfully sharp to get such concentration with an AR-15 from that range and with that crowded a field."

"Agreed. And the second." He handed her another report.

This one made her sit up and take notice. "A Glock 34? Isn't that used mostly for target shooting?"

"Once again, Kim Brady shows why she's the best, the former queen bee of the Seven-Three."

Bostwick strolled out of his office. "Whadda we got?"

Kim handed him the two ballistics reports.

"Wow. I guess you should get this to Driscoll." When Kim hesitated, he added, "I know how you feel about this case, but you need to play this one straight."

"I agree, Lieu. In fact, I thought the best thing would be to scan these and e-mail them over to him. Then, I'll give him a call and alert him to check."

Bostwick's eyes narrowed. "That's very cooperative of you. What am I missing?"

She shrugged. "Nothing. You want me to play it straight, I'm doing just that." She scanned both documents, then attached them to an e-mail to Lt. Liam Driscoll, and sent it off. "Now, if you'll excuse me, I'm going across the street to the Firehouse Deli for something for lunch. Can I get you guys coffee or a sandwich?"

"No, thanks," Vitello said with a smirk.

"Nothing for me, thanks," Bostwick said. As Kim left the Castle, she heard Bostwick ask the still-smirking Vitello, "Okay, Phil, what am I missing?"

She'd kept the originals, and she hadn't mentioned Lodemay.

***

"No, Commissioner," the mayor said into the phone, "I don't understand. It's not clear in the least. You're telling me you didn't give Cirillo authority to move the Prospect Park shooting from Brooklyn North Homicide to Brooklyn South, but that it's okay by you that he did? Here's what I want: you, Cirillo, and the Chief of Detectives are to be in my office at City Hall at three o'clock sharp, and you'd all better have some damn good answers. I will personally summon Captain Colangelo to join us, as well. The last thing I want is the police too embroiled in a stupid turf war to solve a case that must be solved quickly."

He had just ended the call when Justin Cates rushed in unannounced. "Sorry to barge in, Sir, but I think you'd better see this." He grabbed the remote for the wall screen television off the mayor's desk, and a moment later the set sprang to life, with *City News* the default station upon startup.

"Demonstrators have already stopped traffic in both directions on the Brooklyn Bridge as a group of at least three hundred demonstrators march across in protest of yesterday's mass shooting at Prospect Park. They are demanding an independent prosecutor be appointed by the Department of Justice, charging New York City Police with intentionally covering up evidence pointing to a white ultranationalist as the perpetrator."

Felipe Prinz appeared on the screen. "The police act as if they have no idea who the killer could be. But only African Americans being shot make it clear: it must be an ultra-right-wing group, many of which populate this city, but they ignore that because someone from one of those groups is doing the police department's work for them. The fact that a couple of the victims were members of the department changes nothing. These people care nothing about blue, only black."

The reporter reappeared. "So far, the police department has not commented."

"What does ITN have?" the mayor asked.

Justin changed the channel.

Joanna Dunbar was on screen. "There has been media speculation since last night that white ultranationalists might be responsible for this heinous crime, but no actual evidence has yet surfaced supporting that idea."

"Justin, tell the staff I'm holding a news conference at 3:30 this afternoon to respond to this." The mayor picked up the phone, making a call he desperately wanted to make but knew he shouldn't.

***

Kim stared at the screen of her phone as the call ended. She couldn't believe he'd called her cell. She couldn't do what he'd asked, at least not yet. And when she'd told him that it likely would not produce anything of value, he'd asked her to proceed anyway.

And then he'd made a promise that made her head spin.

He wouldn't. He couldn't. He didn't have the authority, and it was against departmental policy.

# CHAPTER TEN

The mayor glared at the men seated around his desk—the police commissioner, the Chief of Detectives, Deputy Inspector Cirillo, and Captain Colangelo. "I was at the crime scene at Prospect Park yesterday, and, with the lone exception of Captain Colangelo, I didn't see any of you there. I also saw several members of Captain Colangelo's team there, launching a complex investigation under extremely trying circumstances. As I understand it, his team located the two places the shooters occupied, recovered several slugs, and have now identified the makes and models of the two weapons used in this assault."

He paused for effect. "So, what puzzles me is why, after such a good start to a difficult investigation, you three would see fit to allowing a fifth rate pissing match to erupt. Perhaps I'm missing something—after all, I'm only the mayor—but I'm not sure what qualifies Lieutenant Driscoll's group to take over. Is it the fact that no one from that command bothered to show up for six hours, or that his short-handed staff was reduced to zero by illness?"

He let that sink in. "Finally, who gave Mr. Cirillo the authority to intervene, here?"

Cirillo spoke up. "Mr. Mayor, Lieutenant Driscoll called me and asked me to intervene. Since the crime occurred within his territory…"

The mayor leaned forward. "Is there something wrong with your hearing, Cirillo, or were you not paying attention? I asked who gave you the authority. And the only one who had that authority is sitting next to you, silent. Do I take it, Mr. Commissioner, that you did not give him the authority?"

"No, Mr. Mayor, I didn't, but when I learned of his action, I agreed with it."

"Oh, good. Then you can answer my question. Why?"

"With respect, sir, you've already said you disagree with the jurisdictional argument."

The mayor sat back. "I most certainly do. Just as I dislike the tendency to reflexively back a subordinate without knowing or considering all the facts. So, here is my decision: Deputy Inspector Cirillo's transfer of the Prospect Park shooting case is revoked. The case will remain in the capable hands of Brooklyn North Homicide. Captain Colangelo, am I correct in assuming that Detective Brady was the lead on this investigation?"

"Yes, sir."

"Good. She shall remain in that capacity. And to assure there is no further interference in her investigation, I am exercising my executive powers as mayor and promoting her to the rank of captain. Commissioner, you will see to the paperwork today."

The commissioner blanched. "Mr. Mayor, with all due respect, Detective Brady has never, to my knowledge, taken any of the exams needed for promotion up the ranks. Not for captain, lieutenant or even sergeant."

"She's a first-grade detective. Doesn't that put her on a par with a uniformed lieutenant?"

"In pay, yes, sir. But the department's regulations still require…"

The mayor stood. "You're not hearing me. She is to be promoted. You will find a way."

***

Kim waited outside the high-rise condo on Norfolk Street that Felipe Prinz had inherited when his lover, Sabrina Dunn, had been murdered two years earlier. She hoped he'd be alone when he returned, otherwise her already slim chances of success would drop to zero.

It was after nine in the evening when he finally approached.

Alone.

She stepped out of the shadows. "Good evening, Mr. Prinz. Busy day?"

He laughed. "So, they sent you? The mayor's cookie? I'd have expected an entire SWAT team, at least."

He stopped laughing when she pulled the Chief's Special. "You know what's great about revolvers? The shell casing remains in the chamber after the weapon is fired. Nothing to give me away. What's more, we're not in range of any security cameras."

"So, what, you're gonna kill me?"

"Do you want me to? Tell me now if you do."

His eyes shot in different directions, but they were alone. "Uh, no, of course not."

"Aces, because we need to have a serious conversation." She returned the pistol to the waistband of her slacks at the small of her back. "Now, to begin with, have I ever told a lie about you, either to your face or anywhere else?"

"How the fuck should I…" He froze when she reached around to her back. "Shit, no! No!"

She stopped reaching. "Good. Then you'll understand my demand that you not repeat anything you know is false, either to my face or elsewhere. The affair story was a fiction created to cripple the investigation of Sabrina's murder, a murder I ultimately solved. You might have shown a little fucking gratitude."

"Okay, okay. I'm sorry. Thank you."

"You might also recall that all you did during that investigation is try to slow us down. I realize that's a reflex for you, but it's pissing me off that you're doing it again."

"What? How?"

She nodded in the general direction of City Hall. "Your little shitshow downtown today."

He shrugged. "People want justice."

"People do, but you don't. You're stirring the pot again, getting people so riled up they'll make it impossible for us to solve this shooting, making them lose their faith in the police and in city government."

"That's nuts."

"Is it? You don't want Barnett as mayor any more than you want Brandt because he's not radical enough for you. You want slums to stay slums, law enforcement to remain lax, and the system, in general, to fail."

He glanced at her hands, as if afraid she might reach for the pistol again. "Look, I'm an activist. I fight to improve the lives of people who have it the worst. Sometimes, the rhetoric gets a little extreme because that's what energizes people."

That was easy. She smiled, which appeared to unnerve him even more than waving the pistol at him had. "Good. Then, you'll understand my request for you to lay off the rhetoric on this case. You didn't believe that I wanted to solve Sabrina's murder, but I did. And I want this one just as badly."

"Why?"

"For the same reason I want them all—to enforce the law, equally. Every time."

"You mean you're actually going to take down a bunch of white ultranationalists?"

"If white ultranationalists did it, yes."

"Who else would have…"

"That's not evidence, Felipe. That's a conjecture in search of confirmation, also known as confirmation bias. Not very helpful."

"You didn't believe the capital class had killed Sabrina, either."

"Wrong. I just didn't jump to a conclusion about it. And I'm not jumping to one here. If you genuinely care about the people, do them and us a major solid and shut the fuck up about this investigation." She handed him a card. "If you want to offer any advice, call me directly. But if I see another show like this morning…" She made a brief motion with her right hand as if reaching for the weapon, stopping when he blanched. "Just checking to make certain we understand each other, Mr. Prinz."

# CHAPTER ELEVEN

*Tuesday, April 22, 7:35 a.m.*

Kim hadn't worn her dress uniform in ages, and she was relieved that it still fit. The occasion wasn't a happy one—Jared Galloway's funeral. The unit was going together, meeting at the Castle. She was just finishing pinning her ribbons in place when Jake walked in.

"I'll drive you over this morning if you like."

"Thanks."

"All quiet on the Prinz front this morning. Perhaps your chat with him had an effect."

"Temporarily, maybe. But I doubt he'll stay quiet for long. Anything else of interest?"

"*City News* has doubled down on the white ultranationalist theory. Starting tonight, they're running a special series on white ultranationalists, American Nazis, the whole bit. I hate to say it, but they make a convincing case."

She laughed without humor. "If they present one fact linking to this case, I'll eat my hat."

He stared at her collection of ribbons—two Meritorious Duty medals, one with Honorable Mention; a Community Service medal from her days in uniform; her marksman's badge; the purple shield from when she was shot in the line of duty. "You're one hell of a cop, Kim, like your granddad was."

"Thanks, but I never stopped a band of Nazi saboteurs."

"I don't know. Preventing a church full of innocent people from being firebombed comes pretty close."

She kissed him on the cheek. "Thanks." She turned grim. "Off to bury a colleague."

***

Sergeant Dhillon, known to everyone in the command as Marshal, was at the desk when Kim entered the Castle, but the grin with which he always greeted her was nowhere to be seen. "Good morning, Kim. They're waiting for you in the lieutenant's office."

"Thanks, Marshal." They?

She stopped to leave her laptop on the docking station on her desk. Even before she reached the door of Bostwick's office, she saw Captain Colangelo.

Did Prinz file a complaint against her?

"Come in, Kim," Bostwick said. "The captain has something he needs to discuss with us."

"I was summoned to City Hall yesterday by the mayor, along with the commissioner, the chief of detectives, and Cirillo. The mayor ordered, in no uncertain terms, that the investigation of the Prospect Park shooting remain in the hands of Brooklyn North Homicide, with you as lead detective. To assure that no other tinkering with this case should occur from One Police Plaza, he is ordering that you be promoted to the rank of captain."

Calm. Remain calm. "I've never even taken the sergeant's test. I told him that…"

"You knew about this?" Bostwick asked. "Why didn't you say something?"

"Because I didn't think he'd go through with it. I told him the reason I never took any of the exams was that I had no interest in command, that I love what I do. No offense to you guys, but command just isn't for me. I'm a field person, period."

"All right, Kim," Colangelo said. "But, in the future, if you have any direct communications from the mayor, please let Lieutenant Bostwick or me know. Although it wouldn't have made much difference yesterday, aside from me being somewhat prepared when I walked in there."

But Kim's stomach was turning. "If this becomes public knowledge, my career in this department is finished. Everyone will assume that the rumors two years ago were true, and no amount of denial will change it. And there's nothing I can do about it."

***

Kim never knew Jared Galloway, other than to say hello and pass small talk. Nice guy, good cop. But now, standing by his graveside at Calvary Cemetery in Maspeth, Queens, she realized that hadn't been enough. They didn't need to have worked cases together to become friends, and yet they hadn't.

Her social group was the unit—Cord, Martin, Tim Brogan, Lieutenant Bostwick and their wives, and Bob. Although Cord and Vera weren't married, Kim thought of them that way. But as she gazed over at Marion Galloway and her two young children, she tried to think of something to offer, some connection to her deceased husband that could serve as a bond.

As the ceremony ended and the crowd dispersed, her path to the widow was suddenly blocked. "Mayor Brandt, how nice of you to come. I'm sure Marion Galloway appreciates it."

"We take care of our own in this city. I can't tell you how glad I am to see you, Captain." He offered his hand.

She didn't take it. "I'm not a captain, and I'm not eligible to be one. I heard about this stunt this morning."

"I told you yesterday…"

"I asked you not to do it. I appreciate you returning control of the park shooting to our unit. I will do my best to bring the investigation to a successful conclusion. But your stunt would destroy any chance of that happening. It will force me to resign."

He blinked. "I couldn't bear to lose you." It came out a whisper.

Oh, shit. He was lusting for her again, after all these years. "*You* would not be losing me, the department would. It would just be your fault."

"Kim, please…"

"I've told you before, it's Detective Brady."

"Brilliant detective and beautiful woman, all in one."

"If I have to slap your face to make my point, I will."

He looked as if she already had. "I… I'm sorry." He turned and walked away.

Bostwick approached her as she stormed in the opposite direction. "Was that what I think it was?"

"It was, and, if you don't mind, I'd rather not talk about it."

And she prayed no one else had noticed.

# CHAPTER TWELVE

Joanna Dunbar glanced at her watch as she stood behind the rope that had cordoned off the mayor's podium in the entrance hall of City Hall. Five after one. She'd arrived early for the one o'clock press conference, the second in as many days, knowing it wouldn't start anytime close to that.

By twelve-thirty, many of her fellow reporters had already crowded into a semi-circle radiating around her. Cameras were arrayed behind them, and arc lights raised the temperature to summer levels.

She was in her element.

Rita Henshaw of *City News*, the station Joanna had once worked for, stood next to her. "What do you think it is? Think it's about Sunday's massacre?"

Joanna fought the emerging smile from her lips. *City News,* having led the way with the assumption of white ultranationalists as the culprits, had taken to referring to the shooting as a "massacre". "I guess 'mass shooting' no longer does it for you guys, huh?"

Henshaw broke into a grin. "We use 'mass shooting' when the subject of our ire is the gun lobby. 'Massacre' is for Nazis and their ilk."

If there was one thing the city press corps all shared, it was a healthy dose of cynicism. Joanna knew it couldn't be anything about the case because Kim would have kept her informed. The only other possibility was the upcoming primary, but she couldn't imagine what would be newsworthy about that two months in advance.

The mayor's press secretary mounted the podium. "Members of the press, Mayor Brandt."

She studied him as he took his place in front of the bank of microphones. He looked older, worn. He was in his early fifties but suddenly looked all the worse for wear. Maybe the presidency wasn't the only office that ground people down.

"Good afternoon," Brandt said, his voice steady and firm.

Okay, appearances were often deceiving.

"I have an announcement to make regarding the upcoming mayoral primary."

"Think he's decided to cancel it and declare himself king?" Henshaw asked in a whisper. Joanna ignored her.

"We are," Brandt continued, "at a crossroads in this city, with a clear choice to make. We are also at a crossroads in our polity in general, with our two political parties pulling hard in opposite directions in ideological warfare while the problems that plague us in our day-to-day lives get ignored."

Joanna turned to Henshaw. "He's going to…"

"Because of this, I have decided not to run for re-election as a member of my party, but rather as an independent. My campaign has already begun the process of collecting signatures on petitions, and I have no doubt I will have enough."

A cacophony broke out from the gathered reporters. Joanna waited until it died down, but before Brandt continued to speak.

"Mr. Mayor, you realize this hands your party's nomination to Council Speaker Barnett."

"Yes, Ms. Dunbar, I do."

She followed up. "Are you prepared for him to have the resources of your party while you do not?"

"I am."

"Are you afraid of losing to Speaker Barnett in the primary?" Rita Henshaw asked.

"No." As Henshaw started to launch a follow-up, he added, "If we can have some others, please. And some order." He pointed to a reporter in the back row. "Yes?"

"*New York Times.* What's your thinking in making this move, if it isn't fear of losing the primary?"

"A desire to frame the discussion in terms of the best interests of the city, rather than the narrower interests of the party leadership." He pointed to a reporter to his right. "Yes?"

"*New York Post.* Did you consider changing parties before making this decision?"

"I didn't for the same reason. Our political parties have clustered their positions around narrower interests. What's more, the other party has failed to gain leadership strength even as many in this city have adopted more moderate views about our biggest problems. My running as an independent will focus the discussion on city-wide issues and allow it to unfold over the next six and a half months rather than two."

Joanna saw a chance. "You are on record as opposing ranked-choice voting. But in a three-way race, voters from both parties may see you as the best second choice, which could be a huge advantage for you. Has that changed your opinion about ranked-choice voting?"

Brandt broke into a grin. "A fair question, Ms. Dunbar. I still regard ranked-choice voting as a violation of the principle of one person, one vote, the same reason I support abolishing the Electoral College for presidential elections. However, ranked-choice voting is the law, and if it happens to work in my favor, then so be it. Next?"

"*Daily News*, Mr. Mayor. Do you intend to make a deal with the opposition party to support you rather than running their own candidate?"

"This is not a case of political skullduggery," Brandt replied. "If any other party decides to support me, I will welcome it, but I will not seek it. I would point out that Ms. Dunbar has already stated why that would likely be unnecessary in any event. Next?"

"*New York Workers Weekly*. Isn't this just an attempt to get Sunday's massacre by white ultranationalists out if the news cycle?"

"I doubt that anything short of a nuclear attack could get Sunday's shooting out of the news cycle, and I wouldn't even try. The police investigation is proceeding in an orderly manner. If you have hard evidence pointing to any group, including white ultranationalists, please share it with the police so they can bring the culprits to justice. Otherwise, such speculations only hinder the police. Thank you all."

***

Kim returned home to change after the funeral and saw the end of the press conference.

"He's ducking the primary," Jake said. "Smart move."

"For once." She was sorry the minute she'd said it.

Jake was instantly alert. "What do you mean?"

She explained about the proffered promotion and the confrontation she'd had with him at the cemetery.

Jake looked stunned. "Wow. Can he do that?"

"No, and I told him so."

"Why would he even want to try?" And then it hit him. "He still has a thing for you."

She couldn't deny it. "Yeah. But I don't think that's the reason, or at least not the main reason. He knows Cirillo tried to pull the rug out from under me, and he's been a problem before."

Jake's manner hardened. "Yeah, I remember. The Dunn case. He pulled you off that one, too, because of that story about you and Brandt."

"That phony story. You know all about that."

"The story was inaccurate, but in truth he had a thing for you. He still does. That's a long-lived crush if you ask me. And this latest attempt of his makes it clear he hasn't taken no for an answer."

She'd already taken off her uniform, but before she dressed for work, she went to him and draped her arms around his neck. "It's the only answer he's ever going to get. You're my guy, and I accept no substitutes."

At last, he softened. "I know. I'm not jealous, but I worry. It sounds like he's getting more insistent, even to the point of using his office to advance his… advances. You need to be careful, babe. Because, from where I'm sitting, he either doesn't know how to read the signs or doesn't care."

# CHAPTER THIRTEEN

"Ah, Detective Kim," Marshal Dhillon said as she entered the Castle. "Captain Colangelo asked that you come up as soon as you return."

Uh oh. It might be Brandt's revenge.

She stopped in the ladies room and checked herself in the mirror. She'd left in a hurry and had pulled her hair into low dog ears, a style she rarely wore these days, but she'd done it because Jake liked it.

She hadn't expected to be called in by Colangelo. But screw it. He'd seen them before.

As she approached his office, Therese Vargas saw her. "I love your hair like that, Kim. So cute."

Colangelo did a double-take when she walked in but recovered. "Thanks for coming up. You were talking to the mayor this morning at the funeral, and I just wondered if there was anything I should know."

"I told him I wouldn't accept the captaincy."

He grinned. "I expected as much." The grin vanished. "Anything else? I ask because, from where I was standing, it looked like it got intense, and…"

She waited. "And… what?"

"Personal." When she said nothing, he pressed her. "Did he hit on you, Kim? I need to know."

"Knowing won't help anything, and it may make things worse than they already are. I've made it as clear as I possibly can that I'm not interested. Anyway, can we please not talk about him?"

"Sure. What else is on your mind?"

"I appreciate that we're back on the park shooting case, but Brandt didn't do us any favors in the way he did it, even without my alleged promotion."

"Go on." She'd caught his interest.

"Now that we have the Ballistics report, it's possible that Brooklyn South could provide some leads on the weapons. Personally, I never would have locked their people out. You know I've worked with other commands before. No reason we couldn't do it again. My only beef was being cut out of it."

Colangelo chewed on that for a minute. "Interesting point. Are you asking me to request the chief of detectives…"

"No, Captain. That's sends the message that we may not know what we're doing after all. If you don't mind, I'd like to go back to Lieutenant Driscoll and work out a way to conduct this investigation together. Let him know that just because the mayor and Cirillo are ham-handed assholes doesn't mean we have to be."

A wry grin. "And very well you put it, although I'd temper it a bit when you talk to him. Go ahead but clear it with Lieutenant Bostwick first."

"Thanks, Captain."

He stopped her when she got to the door. "One thing, Kim. Are you going to keep your hair like that when you meet with him?"

"Probably. I need a new approach with this case."

***

Bostwick had been fine with it.

Kim turned off Snyder Avenue in the section of East Flatbush now called Little Caribbean and into the cramped parking lot that served the building housing Patrol Borough Brooklyn South, about a mile from the scene of the shooting. It also housed the Sixty-Seventh Precinct and FDNY Engine Company 248. As she climbed the steps, she wondered if she knew anyone from the Six-Seven.

No, not a soul. As she approached the desk, the sergeant on duty turned a malignant glare on her.

*My reputation precedes me.* "Good afternoon, Sergeant." Although she didn't need to, she presented her credentials. "I'm looking for Lieutenant Liam Driscoll. Where can I find him?"

The sergeant said nothing. He just glared.

"Sergeant," she said in as matter-of-fact tone as she could manage, "I've extended you all due courtesy, but I just came back from burying a colleague, so cut the shit and tell me where I can find Lieutenant Driscoll."

Taken aback, he pointed to a set of double doors. "Through there, second office on the right."

"Thank you." It was impossible not to sense the stares that followed her to the door, but she didn't acknowledge any of them.

She knocked once at the open door. Driscoll's jaw was already set. "Well, if it isn't Captain Brady. Shouldn't you be down at City Hall going…"

She sat. "Look Driscoll, you and I know that promotion is pure bullshit, and if Brandt ever tries to push it, I will join the PBA and the Detective Endowments Association in stopping it. You and I also know that the rumor about anything between Brandt and me is also more bullshit. My husband is Director of Analytics for the Brooklyn Nets, so who's the better catch? I've come in peace."

"What for?"

"You know as well as I do that neither of our units can solve this case on our own. I suggest we pool our resources."

"Whose idea was this? The commissioner's?"

Keep cool. In his spot, I'd be just as paranoid. "I'm here on my own, although I did get buy-in from both my lieutenant and my captain before coming. We know what weapons were used, and what ammunition was used. It's an interesting combination. I also have an eyewitness that even the mayor doesn't know about. I'm not planning to tell him."

"Why not?"

Good. Interest caught. But also decision time. "Because I don't know how much I can trust him, although everything he's told me related to the case so far has been on the money. It was because of him that our CSU people were able to recover the shells so quickly."

"So, I still don't understand the problem."

"Some things he said to me were kind of… questionable."

Driscoll cracked a smile. "Care to give me an example?"

Okay, all in. "He said he was descended from a member of the Knights Templar."

"John Lodemay." It wasn't a question.

"Yes. You know him?"

"I've run into him several times, going back to my early days in the Six-Seven. He's a real piece of work, no question."

"What kind of run-ins?"

"Various Emotional Disability episodes. There have been times he thought he *was* that knight. Some grand poobah or something. When that happens, if anyone tells him he's nuts, all hell breaks loose."

"So, you don't think he makes a credible witness?"

"Would you want him to suddenly blurt out in open court how he helped kick the infidels out of the Holy Land in 1159, or whenever it was?"

She could just picture it. "Understood. But he told us the locations of the shooters, and he knew one shooter used a rifle and the other used a pistol. I know he lives close by, so I thought I'd talk to him again."

Driscoll thought for a moment. "I know what you mean about him providing helpful information. He visits us occasionally to alert us about suspicious activity in the park. But we've never used him as a witness."

"For now, perhaps it's best to only use him to generate leads." Time to change gears. "Have you looked over the ballistics reports?"

"Yeah. An AR-15 and a Glock 34."

"I was amazed at the accuracy from the AR-15. I thought it was someone who'd been in the military." Giving him another tidbit.

Driscoll bit. "My thought as well. What about the Glock?"

"A target shooter's dream."

And then he said what she'd been thinking but resisting. "Makes you wonder if the ultranationalist theory isn't so wacky after all."

"There's only one reason I'm still not convinced: the first three victims were cops."

"Black cops. And the other victims were also black."

Her last card. "Which makes for a great misdirection play."

He extended his hand. "Detective, I think this is the beginning of a beautiful partnership."

She took it. "Call me Kim. I'll talk to Lieutenant Bostwick and Captain Colangelo to arrange for a meeting to coordinate things."

# CHAPTER FOURTEEN

*Wednesday, April 23, 1:12 p.m.*
Another day, another funeral, this one for Mitchell Jackson. This time, the mayor came, paid his respects to the grieving widow and mother, and left without so much as a glance in her direction.

"Interesting," Tim Brogan said, sidling up to her. "There are TV people here today, but they weren't at Galloway's funeral yesterday."

She hadn't noticed, but as she glanced around, she saw vans from both ITN and *City News.* "Even more interesting that Brandt didn't stop for a quick interview."

Brogan gestured toward the gravesite. "Alicia doesn't want to leave."

Brandt had kept her from offering condolences to Marion Galloway. She approached Alicia Jackson. "I'm so very sorry. I didn't get to know Mitch very well until we formed the race team."

Alicia took her hand. "Thanks, Kim. He always spoke so highly of you. He said your unit was the best in the command, and that everyone respects you."

"If there's anything I can do, please let me know." Kim hated the emptiness of that phrase. People always said it at funerals when there was rarely anything they could do.

But Alicia looked Kim in the eye, fighting back tears. "Just one thing. Hunt down whoever killed my husband and his partner. That will give me a little peace."

"That goes for me, too." A voice from behind.

Kim turned around. It was Marion Galloway.

"Marion!" Alicia said. "Thank you so much. You didn't have to come."

"Yes, I did.

Kim took her hand. "I'm sorry I didn't have a chance to talk to you yesterday."

A sad smile. "I understand. His honor demanded your time. Do us all a favor, Kim. Don't let him fuck up your investigation. Please just nail whoever did this."

"I will."

"How's Cord?" Marion asked.

"Recovering. He lost a kidney, but otherwise he'll be okay."

"Give him my best when you see him," Alicia said.

"Mine, too," Marion added.

Kim hugged them both. "Brothers in arms. Sisters, too."

***

Kim had left a change of clothes at the Castle. Not long after she changed out of her dress blues, Driscoll entered the Castle. She called the unit together and marched them upstairs to Colangelo's office, and from there moved into the conference room.

Kim took charge. "Lieutenant Driscoll agrees that the best option is for our unit and his to pool our resources and work together on this case. Lieutenant, you'd mentioned you had some people out. What's the earliest you expect to have at least some of them back?"

"The two sick detectives should be back by Monday. Meanwhile, I'll be doing some fieldwork myself. Kim and I will talk at least twice each day, more frequently if necessary."

"Did you guys decide who's in overall command?" Bostwick asked with a smirk.

Kim remained serious. "Since official control of the case lies with us, he and I agreed that Brooklyn South is assisting us."

Colangelo spoke up. "Nice work, Kim. It must have been an interesting negotiation."

She had to laugh. "What negotiation? He always wanted to be on this case."

"Yeah, can't argue with that," Driscoll added.

She turned serious. "There's one more thing. There's a great deal of speculation in the media, and there's tremendous public pressure to solve this case. Brandt has already nearly blown us off the track, and he's going to be demanding updates from the commissioner, who in turn will demand them from us. We need to be very careful what we reveal to him."

Colangelo turned sour. "Such as what?"

"Our eyewitness, for example. Lieutenant Driscoll knows him—he lives near PBBS headquarters. He's been very helpful so far, but we agree that he…" She hesitated, not wanting to sound pejorative.

"Has a screw loose?" Bob asked.

"In a nutshell. Captain, I don't want to put you in the position of lying to the commissioner, even by omission, but I also know you are keenly interested in the developments of this case, so…"

"Tell me everything, and let me know what's, shall we say, speculative? What are your next steps?"

Kim gestured to Driscoll. "I'll start checking on cases in which either an AR-15 or a Glock 34 has been involved. Since the Glock is a premier target-shooting piece, I'll check with the shooting ranges in the area to see if anyone turns up, although without a description it will be tough."

"DCPI is putting out public service announcements asking anyone who has any information on the shooting to call Crimestoppers," Colangelo said. There were groans around the room. "I know, lots of false leads. But we need to try."

"There's a precinct detective in the Six-Seven who's excellent at screening Crimestoppers calls," Driscoll said. "I can recruit him."

"Aces." Kim turned to Stransky. "In the meantime, let's review any reports we've gotten for an AR-15 or Glock 34 stolen recently. I know that's unlikely, because both shooters were quite effective, which suggests they were familiar with their weapons. Tim, you can help with that, too."

It was then she realized Nolan wasn't there. "Where's Bob?"

"He went home to change after the funeral," Bostwick said. "I'm sure he'll make up the time. In the meantime, Kim, what will you be doing?"

She faced Driscoll. "I think one of us should talk to Lodemay again."

He shook his head. "Not me, Kim. From what you told me, he trusts you. He doesn't trust me. Too many incidents. He lives alone in a nice studio apartment over by Brooklyn College, about three quarters of a mile from PBBS."

"So, he must have a job." Even studios were pricey in Brooklyn.

"He works as a delivery guy for a Caribbean place on Flatbush Avenue called the Footprints Café Express."

Hard to believe he made enough as a delivery guy to afford his own place. "Does he have any family?"

"Yes, his sister's name is Susan Garmin. She lives in that new high-rise on Cadman Plaza West, the one that caught fire several years ago when they were building it."

"You remember that, Kim?" Brogan asked.

All too well. "My neck of the woods. Do you have her address? Just in case, I mean."

"I'll dig it up when I get back."

"Anything else?" Bostwick asked.

"Yes. As much as I'd like to, we can't dismiss the ultranationalist thing. I hate that the media have jumped on it, and I doubt it's true, but we need to consider it because of the weapons and the skills of the shooters. So, in addition to seeing Mr. Lodemay, I'll call Ken Taylor over at the FBI to see what he can tell me about white ultranationalist groups."

# FIFTEEN

It was only when his cell rang that Bob Nolan realized he'd been sitting and staring for more than an hour. One look at the screen confirmed his suspicion.

It was Kim Brady calling to see where he was.

"Hello, Kim."

"Hi. We just had a meeting with Driscoll. Everything's on track, and Colangelo is pleased we've kissed and made up. Just wanted to see where you are."

"I came home after the funeral to change."

"And you're still there?"

Concern with just the hint of accusation. Kim Brady's partner radar was as keen as anyone he'd ever known. "Yeah, I was just reviewing a couple of things."

"Are you okay, Bob?"

Of course, she knew. She'd seen him the last time he'd fallen off the wagon. She'd been working with Internal Affairs but before she'd been drafted by them. It had been her partner at the time, Mike Resnick, who'd kicked his ass and told him to get back into a program. But it had been Kim who'd gone to bat for him when

Internal Affairs had interviewed him, preventing his police career from crashing.

And he'd told her everything he knew about her father's suicide.

It had only been by dumb luck that he'd been transferred from Narcotics to Brooklyn North Homicide, and that she'd been transferred there a year later.

"Bob? Are you okay?" More insistent this time.

"I'm okay. I just needed a little space. One cop's funeral is bad enough. Two on consecutive days are overwhelming. I'm still on the wagon, if that's what you mean." No need to delve into his recent agony.

"That's what I mean. We need you on this case. I think it may be the toughest you and I have ever worked together."

That was saying a lot. "Okay, Kim. Don't worry, I'm on my way in, now."

"Brothers in arms, Bob. Sisters, too."

Brothers in arms. That's what Mike Resnick had said to pull him back on track.

***

As Kim drove down to see Lodemay, dropping Driscoll off at PBBS, she couldn't shake the sense that Bob was in trouble. She hadn't heard him sound like that since the evening she and Mike had visited him at his Staten Island home. He'd answered the door holding a can of beer, and Mike had gone white.

The ensuing conversation regarding Dad had laid so much to rest and been so important to solving her first case as a lead detective that she regarded Bob as more than a partner.

Bob may not have fallen off the wagon, but she was certain he was teetering on the edge.

She couldn't afford the time for it. She found the address Driscoll had provided, and the entrance to the basement apartment that was almost certainly illegal.

Lodemay answered after the second ring. "Yes?"

Not a promising start. "Mr. Lodemay, I'm Detective Brady. We met on Sunday at the Prospect Park…"

Recognition dawned. "At the race! The shooting! Yes, I remember, now. Please come in."

She entered the kitchen, brightly lit with maple cabinets, marble countertops, white marble floor tiles, stainless steel sink, and a black and stainless steel stove and matching microwave. Across from that stood a refrigerator. He led her through to a small room with a convertible couch, one end table that looked like it had seen better days, a wall-mounted television, two bookcases crammed with books, and a small table and two chairs. A dim lamp on the end table provided the only light, plus whatever shone in from the kitchen. On the wall above one of the bookcases was a wrought-iron pentagram with a clay figure of a demon's head in the center.

Kim stared at the pentagram, which brought back memories of another case from several years earlier. She scanned the bookshelves, which held numerous works on history, particularly medieval history. There were several volumes on the Knights Templar. "Interesting place you have here."

"Do you like it? You're the only girl I've ever had here."

"I'm a married woman."

"Oh, I didn't mean to imply… I'm so sorry. But you have nothing to worry about from me. Like my ancestors, I've taken vows of poverty and celibacy."

She decided not to ask how he could have come to exist if his ancestors were all celibate. "You've read up on them, I see."

"As much as I could. They were a fascinating group, and I try to emulate them as much as I can. That's why I help the police whenever possible."

She was itching to mention the pentagram, but she worried it might be a trigger for him. If he decided to bring it up, that would be another matter. "I certainly appreciate your help on Sunday. You made it much easier for us to find the shells from the fired shots."

"Now, you need to find the shooters." His grin suggested he had more information to give her. "I'm sorry, Detective, I've forgotten my manners. Can I offer you something? Some tea, perhaps?"

"Yes, thank you. That would be very nice." She followed him back to the kitchen.

As he worked, he squinted against the bright light.

"Is the light too bright?" she asked.

"I don't like it. So powerful a light indoors is not natural. I've asked them…" he pointed toward the ceiling. "…to replace it with something less powerful, but they don't. It's not difficult to find lighting these days with lower Kelvins, which means softer light, or with lower wattage, but they insist that kitchens need bright light in order to assure there aren't any accidents. Do you think that's true?"

"I've never thought about it that way, but I do like bright light in my kitchen. Does it bother you?"

He placed tea bags in two mugs, filled them with water, and placed them in the microwave. "Yes. My eyes are too used to candlelight. Over the years, I'd always read and written by either sunlight or candlelight. We didn't have any choice."

"We?"

"My brother knights and I. Wherever we went, in France, Jerusalem, Antioch, Acre… There were no bright lights except from the sun or by fire. Our scribes wrote by what the Lord provided."

The microwave beeped. He removed the mugs and gave her one. "They didn't have microwave ovens, either. The Templars, that is. Old-fashioned fire had to do it for them."

"Have you traveled a great deal?" She hoped it was a safe question.

"Not much, lately. My vow of poverty, you see."

"I do."

They returned to the other room, sitting at opposite ends of the couch, which was lumpy.

"The news stations say the shooters were members of some ultranationalist group."

"That's just speculation," she said.

"I know. They're wrong."

"Do you know who was responsible?"

"Not specifically, but I'm sure it wasn't a white ultranationalist group."

"What makes you so certain?"

"On Sunday morning, after I decided to go watch the finish of the race, I was walking from the B41 stop at Flatbush Avenue and Parkside into the park. As I was walking around the edge of the lake, there was a guy wearing a camo T-shirt—long-sleeved—who passed me. He was walking fast, like he had someplace to be. But who would have someplace to be in Prospect Park on Sunday morning?"

"How early?"

"A little after nine. I wanted to be near the finish line. But I figured the race hadn't even started yet, so I followed the guy in the camo shirt around the lake along Wellhouse Drive. He followed it to the path that led to that field, right by the Maryland Monument, and when he reached the field, he found a nice shade tree and sat down under it. But, after I'd walked a little further and looked around, he was gone."

"Did you see his face?"

"Partially. He turned to look around before heading toward the trees. Like he wanted to make certain he wasn't being followed. He saw me and sat down. But he was wearing sunglasses, so I couldn't tell much about him, other than the front of that camo shirt had that…" He pointed to the pentagram on the wall. "…inside a circle. So, I knew."

"Knew what?"

"He was a Cathar. A sect that existed in Southern France and Northern Spain in the early Middle Ages. They were responsible for the Albigensian Heresy, which held that there was not one, but two Gods, one above, pure spirit, and one below, of all earthly things. In the Twelfth Century, the Roman Church ordered a crusade against the Cathars, and many were killed."

"And the Templars were part of that?" She wasn't sure how wise it was to pursue this, and it wasn't likely to help solve the case.

"No." He was emphatic. "Although there was a Templar castle in the region, it doesn't appear the Templars took part. They may have even helped some of the Cathars elude the crusaders. The heresy probably originated in the east, and by that time, the Templars had many dealings there. The Templars swore fealty to the church and Christ, but they were not zealots regarding tenets of the faith."

"But how are the Templars connected with the shooting?"

He grinned in triumph. "At least one shooter was a Cathar. Almost certainly from Spain." He looked at his watch. "I'm sorry, but I'm going to be late for work."

He walked her out and locked up.

"Can I drop you off?" She gestured to the car.

"No, thank you. It's only a few blocks, and I like walking. But thank you for coming by. You're very nice to talk to, and I like to help. There's a Lieutenant at the police station I talk to now and then."

"Lieutenant Driscoll?"

"That's him. He doesn't like me very much. He thinks I'm crazy." He stopped and stared at her. "Do you?"

"I like talking to you, too, John. And, no, I don't."

He grinned and walked away.

She got into the car and started the engine. "Not much, anyway."

# CHAPTER SIXTEEN

On her way back to the Castle, she activated the car's Bluetooth and called Ken Taylor at the FBI.

"I've been waiting for your call," he said, "ever since I heard 'white ultranationalists' on the news."

"Does that mean you've already done some digging?"

"Not much. I wasn't sure if you were buying it. Are you?"

Good question. "At first, I wasn't; then I had to consider it. Now, I'm doubting it. A witness who may not be playing with a full deck saw someone who may have been one of the shooters who was wearing a camo T-shirt which may have had the army's circled star insignia on it and who may have been Latino."

"Now, there's a mouthful." He took a moment, probably analyzing all the variations. "I'll start with the first one. What do you mean about the witness?"

"There are times he thinks he's a member of the Knights Templar, but most of the time he only thinks he's descended from one."

"Either way, it casts doubt on his sanity."

Precisely what she'd been struggling with. "I think he's sane, but he has moments of delusion. On things he's said with clarity and conviction, he's been right."

"So, what are you thinking, now?"

It was time to make some decisions. "I believe my witness saw one of the shooters, who was likely a Latino army veteran who was aware my witness was following him and sat under the tree to throw him off. At the first opportunity, he vanished. He could only have done so in such a short period by ducking into the copse of trees when my witness wasn't looking. Because I believe one shooter was a Latino army veteran, I do not believe this was a white ultranationalist plot. He entered the park alone from the Flatbush Avenue side and never spoke to anyone else. Because of the timing of the two sets of shots and the manner in which their lines of fire intersected, I can only conclude that this attack was carefully planned out in advance, and that the other shooter was in place around the same time as the Latino army veteran."

"Alleged."

"Don't be pedantic." She said it without a trace of humor. "The other shooter fired five shots from an AR-15 and hit two detectives square in the chest." She paused to let him form a conclusion.

"So," Taylor said, "you're thinking he might also be an army veteran. Any guess as to race?"

"No. This may not be about race."

"Every victim was black." He paused. "I agree this wasn't white ultranationalists. But you can't rule out race as a motive."

Should she argue the point? Ken Taylor was as good a friend and colleague as any she had in law enforcement, and she trusted his judgment.

"You don't agree." He didn't make it a question.

"I can't get past the fact that they were in place before the race started, and that they targeted three cops wearing T-shirts that explicitly identified them as such. The rounds from the AR-15 hit

Jackson and Galloway squarely in that police emblem. The emblem was the target. Cops were the target."

"Cord wasn't hit in the badge emblem."

"He turned to call to me just as the shooter fired. Plus, I don't know that even a Glock 34 could be that accurate from that distance."

"What about the other victims? All black."

"To throw us into this very conundrum."

"So, now your convinced?"

"I wasn't until we had this conversation. But I am, now."

***

The mayor stood at the window on the second floor of Gracie Mansion, first gazing to his far right, taking in the Roosevelt Island lighthouse, then directly across the river to Hallett's Point. Further to his left, he could see the bridge he still thought of as the Triboro, even though its name had been officially changed to the RFK Bridge years earlier. Beyond it, an Amtrak Acela was barely visible in the haze as it crossed the Hellgate Bridge.

To be on that train going somewhere, anywhere…

With her.

"Am I disturbing you?" The voice of his trusted aide, Justin Cates, coming so unexpectedly, made him jump. "I can come back later."

He shook himself. This had to stop. She was beyond his reach and would forever be so. "No, I'm grateful for the interruption, and the chance to focus." He sat, not at his desk but in the easy chair off to the side, adjacent to the small sofa where Justin sat.

"The reactions to your announcement, other than the media, who've been beside themselves, have been positive. Several members of the City Council have endorsed you."

"They're not afraid of Barnett?"

Justin broke into a grin. "They know he's term-limited, so what can he do to them? Barnett himself has said you did it because you couldn't beat him in the primary."

That made him chuckle. "He's probably right. Nice to know he's not completely dim. What else?"

"The campaign reports a surge in contributions since your announcement, mostly from individuals giving a hundred dollars or less. Oh, and Joanna Dunbar called to offer a prime-time interview. I told her I was sure you'd be interested."

"I am. Check my calendar and set a date and time."

"Oh, the state party chairman called to express his displeasure."

"Another Christmas card I won't be getting. All good news, Justin. So, then, why the long face?"

"I saw the draft of your memo to promote Kim Brady…"

"No, you were right. A bad idea, and one she refuses to go for." And, just like that, his good mood vanished, and the cloud of melancholy descended. But Justin was holding back, and he hated that. "So, what's your concern, now?"

"Not for me to say."

"It's your job to say. Spill it."

"Your confrontation with the commissioner and everyone has roiled the whole senior staff at One-PP. On the one hand, you say you're supporting the police, and on the other, you not only micromanage them, but with the worst possible ideas."

"I thought you were Kim's friend." He was sorry the moment he said it.

"I am. And I don't like seeing you paint a massive bulls-eye on her back, especially when you didn't even give her an early warning you were doing it, so she could have saved you the effort. Now, a deputy inspector has her in his crosshairs, and you can't do anything about it without everyone guessing why."

He'd suspected as much. "Can you discern where the commissioner stands?"

"What do you think?"

Okay, he'd earned that.

"The worst part," Justin went on, "is that you've managed to cement in everyone's mind at One-PP that Kim Brady is your pet. Or worse. She could single-handedly save the city from disaster, and she wouldn't get so much as a thank you from anyone at One-PP. The ribbons she's got are the only ones she'll ever get, now, and there's nothing you can do about it. She could've been more decorated than her grandfather was. And, by the way, I hear Kim went to Lt. Driscoll and worked out a partnership agreement on the park shooting case. And that's just what would have happened if you'd never opened your mouth."

He was going to resign. The mayor was sure of it. "So, what do you suggest?"

Justin stood. "Nothing. It is what it is. Have the decency to leave her alone. She deserves better. So does your wife, and don't think for a minute that she doesn't know."

# CHAPTER SEVENTEEN

Kim had just finished bringing Bob up to speed. Most of the Castle's day shift had gone home. The only thing keeping her there was Bob's glum manner.

"It's just the two of us," she said. "Do you want to tell me now what's eating you?"

"Nothing."

"Then why do you look like you just lost your best friend?"

"You don't have to lose your best friend. Two colleagues are more than enough."

Her cell pinged. A text, probably from Jake. She'd check it in a minute. "I lost them, too, Bob. We all did. And we all need to get back on the horse. I need you on this case. We're overloaded, even with the folks from PBBS." She repeated the gist of her conversation with Ken Taylor. "Coordinating this case with PBBS is going to be a bear, but we also need the FBI's help. I need you to work with Taylor and keep me and the lieu briefed. You can start by going over everything we've got on Prinz."

"You think Prinz is involved? He's more of a rally-the-masses guy, isn't he?"

True. But… "He organized that one protest on Monday, got interviewed, and got the ultranationalist theory rolling in the media. Since then, crickets."

He finally cracked a smile. "Week-old fish?"

Her favorite saying when something didn't smell right. Dad had used it all the time, and he'd claimed he got it from Granddad. "Yep. When I spoke with him, asking him to lay off, that it would hinder the investigation, I hinted that, if he didn't, we'd take a closer look at him as an accomplice. No surprise he said he'd do what he liked, but he calmed it down. That tells me he was happy just to get the ultranationalist theory out there."

"Okay, I'll see what I can find. You want me to check back with Taylor in the morning?"

"Mid-afternoon should be fine. Give the Prinz file a thorough review first."

***

The Prinz file went back seven years and contained a lot of information, including three years upstate. It began with the first case Bob had worked on with Kim, when she was still with the Internal Affairs Bureau, a year after she'd saved his career. But her run in IAB had been cut short through no fault of her own, and she'd been exiled to Brooklyn North.

The memories came flooding back. He'd been exiled, too. So, they'd made a good team.

"Hi, Bob." It was Colangelo's admin, Therese Vargas. She giggled when he started. "Sorry to spook you. Some of us are going out. Everyone's down, and there wasn't a gathering or viewing where we could all talk and grieve. You look like you could use a little companionship, so why not join us?"

Therese, a woman in her late twenties whose family was from Colombia, had attracted attention from the guys at the command from the moment she'd started working for Colangelo's predecessor as captain of all PBBN detectives, Andrew Cirillo. In those days, Therese had worn shorter skirts and higher heels, and Cirillo had gotten ideas. She'd been ready to transfer out of PBBN when Cirillo had been kicked upstairs and Colangelo had asked her to stay.

Bob glanced at the laptop screen. "Aw, you don't want an old geezer like me."

"You're not an old geezer, and we'd love to have you along." She gave him a little flirtatious smile. "Please?"

He shut the laptop down and locked it in his desk. "I am your man."

***

Kim had just finished recapping her day for Jake and hanging up her dress uniform when she realized he hadn't said much since she got home. "You alright?"

"Yeah."

"Okay, what's the matter?"

"There's talk about a shakeup at the club. The rumor is they're going to bring in a new general manager, maybe a whole new management team."

"But you're the analytics guy. You don't control the results; you just report the numbers."

"It's more complicated than that. I focus on which numbers are important and what they mean. I make recommendations about who to draft, sign, or trade for."

She sat next to him. "Do you really think your job is in jeopardy?"

"Everyone's job is. And at this level, it's a small market. I don't know what…"

The door buzzer sounded. She walked to the bay window. "It's Justin."

"What the hell does he want?" He stopped. "No, talk to him. I need a shower, and you can probably use the privacy."

She buzzed Justin in as Jake closed the bathroom door. "What's up?"

"Sorry to bother you, Kim. I just wanted to see if you were okay."

"I've been better. How are you doing?"

"I just had a major dustup with the mayor. I told him what he's doing is wrong, that it's going to end badly for him and for you, and it's bad for the department. I reminded him that his wife must know of his attentions, and I think that registered. I also told him about your treaty with Driscoll. He approved of that."

"Thanks, Justin. How's Rick?"

Rick Conti, Executive ADA in the Brooklyn DA's office, was Justin's partner. He and Kim had been through numerous cases together.

"He's fine. He's hoping you bring him some folks to try on this case."

***

The bar, a gathering spot for cops, wasn't far from the Castle. Detective Cole Rydell, who'd worked alongside Galloway and Jackson, was there with a group, so Bob and Therese joined them.

The conversation was light, mostly banter. But every time Bob stole a glance at Therese, she smiled her little flirty smile.

No, she was twenty years his junior.

But stranger things had happened. "Therese, would you like to go somewhere for dinner?"

She blinked in surprise. "Oh. Bob, that's so sweet. Thank you. But my boyfriend is meeting me here at eight. You're welcome to join us."

"No, you don't need a third wheel."

"I'm sorry if I..."

He waved it away. "No, no, I just… It's nothing. Don't give it a thought." He stared into his half-empty glass of ginger ale and tried not to think.

Rydell approached. "So, you guys gonna nail the motherfuckers who killed our brothers?"

"Brothers in arms." He said it more to the glass than to Rydell.

"Goddamn right," Rydell replied. "Do us all a favor. When you get 'em, don't arrest 'em, just gun 'em down like the dogs they are."

"Dogs are a lot nicer," Therese said.

"Got that right, honey." Rydell turned to the bartender. "Hey, another round for these good people."

"Another ginger ale for you?" the bartender asked Bob.

Time stopped.

Ask your higher power.

One day at a time.

But it really isn't. It's day after day, piling up, weeks and months and years that add up to… nothing. And does anyone really care if his streak continues?

He needed a meeting. He needed a session where he could lay it all out, speak about his fears and hurts and disappointments out loud and be understood.

He glanced one way and saw lovely Therese, beyond his reach.

In the other direction, Cole Rydell venting what he needed to vent.

Bob needed to vent.

He turned back to the bartender. "Shot and a beer chaser."

***

Jake never took long showers, a habit he claimed went back to his days in high school when they only had ten minutes after gym class to shower, change, and get to the next class. But this one was taking forever, and when he finally emerged from the bathroom, a cloud of steamy air trailed behind.

There was anger in his eyes. "Everything go okay?" The words and tone of voice didn't match.

"What's wrong?"

"For you, apparently nothing. Arrangements all made?"

"What are you talking about?"

"I heard some of what he said. He doesn't like what's going on between you and the mayor, that it's bad for both of you." He was spitting the words.

"Let me get this straight. You decide to take a shower to give us privacy, but then you eavesdrop?"

"I wasn't eavesdropping. I went back to the bedroom for a change of clothes. And I heard what I heard."

"You obviously didn't hear enough of it. Because, if you had, you would have heard how Justin's anger was directed solely at the mayor for this ridiculous obsession, how it's clouding his judgment."

"So, how is that bad for you? You should be sitting back and laughing."

"Have you forgotten about his stupid plan to order me promoted? Do you have any idea what that's done to my reputation within the department? I now have a deputy inspector who's made me his personal project. Do me a favor, next time you eavesdrop, come into the room and get it over with." She grabbed her keys off the mantel and walked out.

# CHAPTER EIGHTEEN

"Bob? Are you okay?"

Therese's voice.

He squinted. There she was. Beautiful girl, but too young for him. "Fine."

But he wasn't. Funny, he'd only had… how many drinks? He'd lost count.

"Can we drop you somewhere?"

"Car's back at the Castle."

She gasped. "You can't drive, Bob. You can't."

"I'll be okay. I'll grab some coffee at the Firehouse Deli."

"A few cups of coffee won't be nearly enough," she said.

"Hey, Bob, I thought you were on the wagon." Rydell.

"Yeah, well…"

"Tell you what," Rydell said. "Why don't you let me drive you home? Where do you live?"

"Staten Island." Despite his condition, he could see the look on Rydell's face which made it obvious he hadn't considered that a possibility. "Maybe I'll just crash at the Castle tonight."

"I'll drive you over." Rydell said.

Not a bad idea.

***

Kim had walked along Cadman Plaza West, turning at Borough Hall, where Sabrina Dunn, a gubernatorial candidate, had been assassinated, onto Fulton Avenue. It was only when she reached DeKalb Avenue that she realized she was following the course of Sunday's half marathon. She turned off Fulton, trying to force the horrific events from her mind. When she reached Flatbush Avenue, she was drawn to the bright lights of Junior's and decided she needed to sit and think.

She ordered a cup of coffee and a piece of cheesecake.

How could Jake even think she'd be interested in… She pulled out her cell. No call from Jake.

Apparently, he believed it.

She scrolled through her contact list to call him but stopped. Why should I call him? Without thinking, she scrolled up.

Jim Brady.

Cousin Jim.

After a moment's hesitation, she touched the screen on his number.

"Hey, Cuz, how're you doing?" He already sounded concerned.

"I must admit, I've been better." She described the fight with Jake and, hesitating only a moment, about the ongoing unwanted attention from the mayor.

"Geez, Kim, I figured you already had enough on your plate with the shooting. I wish I could do something."

So did she.

"Why don't you call him?"

"Because I didn't accuse him of infidelity. No, he needs to call me, and he isn't, so I need to make some plans. I can't go home with things like this." Memories of Dad's battles with Mom flashed though her mind. She'd been so certain she and Jake would never have such problems.

"I can't do anything tonight, but I have an appointment tomorrow in Queens. I know a wonderful coffeehouse where we can meet for lunch and talk. I believe it will do you good."

"Why?"

"Trust me, Kim. Meanwhile, what will you do? How far are you from the Atlantic Avenue terminal? You could take a train out here…"

"Thanks, but no. I can grab a bus to our headquarters. I've slept there before when cases got hairy. Where do you want to meet tomorrow?"

"A little place called Cool Beans in Sunnyside. Take the Seven train to the Fifty-Second Street stop and walk through the little square on the north side of Roosevelt Avenue and up Fifty-First Street, two blocks to the end. There's an Italian restaurant on the corner called Donato's. Turn left, and Cool Beans will be the first storefront after Donato's."

A ray of hope.

***

It had taken forever for the B38 bus to arrive, as service cutbacks in the evening hours were getting worse. When Kim stepped off the bus at the corner of Wilson and DeKalb, it was 9:20 and the Firehouse Deli was dark, but the Chinese restaurant opposite the Castle was open. She wasn't particularly hungry. Still, she needed nourishment and stopped in for an order of dim sum and a cup of tea.

The night desk sergeant greeted her as she walked in. He made no other comment, so she sat at her desk. Between dumplings, she powered up her laptop and updated her notes on the case.

A scattering of facts and a whole lot of speculation.

Every so often, she glanced at her cell to see if Jake had called or texted.

Nothing.

As the clock crawled past ten, she decided enough was enough and called him.

It went to voicemail. She ended the call and tried again.

Voicemail again.

Enough of this shit.

But as the beep sounded, she decided that anger wasn't her best course. "I'm sending a text. Please read it."

She finished the last of the dumplings and her tea before composing the text, all the while wondering if he'd even read it.

If he didn't, there was no hope, anyway.

*Jake. We've been through a lot together. When you proposed to me, you promised you would always be there for me. When I accepted, I promised to always be there for you. Neither of us has ever broken that promise until tonight. You broke it by believing that I would ever even look at another man, and I broke it by walking out. I'm sorry I did that, but I was afraid we would both say things we'd later regret.*

She stopped. Should she apologize when he'd been the one in the wrong?

"Never be afraid to apologize," Gram had said when Kim was a little girl. "Even if you don't mean it. Saying you're sorry soothes hurt feelings and invites the other person to do the same. It's an act of love."

They'd been sitting together on the beach at Breezy Point, by the bungalow her grandparents had bought during World War II, just after they'd been married. She longed to be back there with her.

Gram had been right. Kim returned to the text. *I'm at the Castle, and I'll stay here for the night. I'm meeting Cousin Jim for lunch tomorrow afternoon and taking the rest of the day off. I'll be home as soon as I can. Then, if you want to stay together, we have work to do.*

She was about to add, *I love you*, but decided against it, not because she didn't, but because she didn't want to risk more hurt.

Suddenly exhausted, she walked into Bostwick's office to sleep on his couch and got a shock.

Bob Nolan was asleep on it, and the office smelled like a distillery.

"Well, isn't that just peachy."

# CHAPTER NINETEEN

*Thursday, April 24, 5:35 a.m.*

Kim awoke to the ping of her cell, disoriented because she was in Colangelo's office, which had a nicer couch than the lieu's.

She'd left her phone on a charger on the captain's desk.

The text was from Jake. *I'm sorry about last night. I want to stay together.*

Gram had been right.

It was a skeleton crew after the late shift of detectives went off duty at one in the morning, so the Castle was quiet. At least the shower room would be empty.

Kim had learned long ago to keep a change of clothes in her locker, and the shower felt good. She returned to the first floor. The lieu's office was empty, although it still smelled like a distillery. She opened a window and walked out to the front desk.

"Have you seen Detective Nolan?" she asked the night desk sergeant.

"Yeah, he left a little after four. Looked like hell, but at least he was okay to drive."

She decided to answer Jake's text. *I'm glad. We'll talk later today.*

The rancid smell in the break room told her the coffee maker had remained on all night. She turned it off and left the pot in the sink to cool. Then over to the Firehouse Deli for fresh coffee and a breakfast sandwich. She hadn't had bacon, egg and cheese on a roll in ages.

This will be a busy day.

***

"Why is the window in my office open?" Bostwick asked the moment he arrived.

Kim followed him inside. First major decision of the day. "For reasons which are not relevant, I spent the night here. When I arrived, someone was sleeping in your office who'd had too much to drink, and the place smelled like it. After he left, I opened the window to air it out."

"I hope it wasn't anyone from our unit."

She didn't want to say, and she didn't want to lie. She had too much respect for this crusty ex-marine.

But when she said nothing, his eyes grew hard. "Brogan should know better than that."

He was testing her, seeing if she'd give it away. "I can't say, so please don't ask."

"It can't be Nolan, he's on the wagon."

She said nothing and kept her expression neutral.

"But it was Nolan, wasn't it? I'll give him the ultimatum when he…"

Choosing the worst alternative first. "Lieutenant, may I ask a favor? Please don't say anything unless his appearance or behavior makes it obvious, otherwise he'll assume I ran to you with it. People have been fucking up my credibility enough as it is."

"Okay, but what's your plan?"

For once, she didn't have one. "I'll let you know. In the meantime, I'll see some people. I've asked Bob to keep in touch with Ken Taylor about possible groups that could be involved in the shooting…"

"You want to rethink that?"

"Not yet. I saw John Lodemay yesterday, and today I want to see his sister, who lives near me. I also want to check in with Marisa Fuentes over at Special Victims."

"What for?"

"I'd rather not say unless it leads to something. It's about something I saw at Lodemay's place, and some things he told me. I realize you don't have much time for such things."

***

"What the fuck is the matter with you?" Bob said to his reflection in his bathroom mirror. And then he answered. "You're a fucking drunk, that's what."

In one weak moment, eight years, one month and thirteen days of progress had been lost.

Except it hadn't been one moment, it had been a bunch of them, a truckload of warning signals, screaming out that he needed to get back to the meetings, putting it all out there, getting the support and the strength that a group always gave him. But he hadn't wanted to admit it, hadn't wanted to give in to the weakness that would dog him for the rest of his days.

So, he'd given in to the bigger weakness.

He'd lost his higher power.

Now, it was back to square one. Again.

Maybe there wasn't a way out. Or maybe there was only one.

# CHAPTER TWENTY

After seeing Cord doing well and Vera looking better, Kim made her way over to the Brooklyn DA's Special Victims Unit, where Marisa Fuentes was an investigator. Now nearly thirty, Marisa could still pass for a teenager, as she had numerous times in various sting operations.

She was thrilled to see Kim and rushed over for a hug.

Kim froze. "You're pregnant? Martin didn't say a word."

"Four months. Not showing, yet. We haven't wanted to talk about it. I had some spotting, and we were worried, but it's stopped and I'm okay. I've cut back on my hours, and I'll probably go on leave by my seventh month. How can I help?"

"Is there someplace we can talk privately?"

Marisa led her to a conference room and closed the door.

"I found an eyewitness who has given me a lot of information." She described Lodemay, his apartment lent, and repeated everything he'd told her. "I know he sounds nuts, but…"

"He may be, but what he's told you about the Cathars and the Templars is accurate. Some people get fanatical about the Templars, and the line between reality and fantasy can get blurred."

"That's why I'm here." She mentioned the pentagram hanging on his wall with the demon face in the middle. "It reminded me of what you said about the five elements in pagan beliefs years ago."

Marisa grew hesitant. "That was different. Those beliefs existed long before Christianity. And early Christians often mixed old traditions with the new faith. In fact, the church established December 25th as Christmas Day because it was already a pagan feast."

"So, what does it all mean, here?"

"The Cathars didn't just believe in two deities, they believed that one of them was the devil, the god of all earthly things, and that only by rejecting, perhaps destroying, all earthly things could one attain the purely spiritual world of the heavenly god. To the Roman church, this was a heresy, but, in a way, the early monks operated on a similar principle, rejecting earthly things to attain the spiritual. As did the Templars."

"So, what was so heretical?"

"The notion that both gods were equal. Judeo-Christian tradition teaches that Lucifer was a fallen angel because he dared to claim equality to his creator. The Cathars thought otherwise."

Interesting, but of no help whatsoever.

"What you've described of his wall décor suggests something that exists in a small church in southern France, probably placed there by a priest who may not have regarded the Cathars as heretical. We'll never know. But the Cathars recognized the four earthly elements, regarding them differently than other pagan groups or Wiccans."

"Is that why he mentioned a similar symbol on the shirt of one of the possible shooters?"

"That was probably a trigger for him. It may have alerted him to danger, although for the wrong reason. It may also explain why he was kind of in and out of his fantasy world when you questioned him." Marisa changed focus. "What did you say your witness' ancestor's name was?"

"Some Templar grand master." Kim searched her notes. "De Molay, I think he said the name was."

"Jacques de Molay was the last grand master of the Templars. He was arrested in the French crackdown on the order in 1307 and was ultimately executed. And what's your witness' name?"

"Lodemay. John Lodemay."

"It's not his real name."

Kim was stunned. "How do you know that?"

Marisa laughed. "Look at the letters. Lodemay is an anagram of de Molay, and Jacques is the French version of John."

***

Susan Garmin, Lodemay's sister, wasn't home when Kim stopped by the high-rise condo on Cadman Plaza West, so she'd left her card with the doorman with her cell number and a request to call at her earliest convenience. She returned the unmarked car to the Castle.

She stopped at the desk to check with Marshal Dhillon. "Has Detective Nolan come in, yet?"

"Not yet, Detective Kim. He has also not called in."

Great. The last thing they needed was Bob off on a bender.

And now Bostwick was beckoning.

This was turning into one shitty day.

"Still no word from Nolan," Bostwick said. "I'm about to call him to roast him, but I'll give you first shot at it if you like."

You're the supervising officer, not me. But she didn't say it. "Yeah, okay, but give me a minute."

"How did your chat with Mrs. Stransky go?"

"Informative. Why do you call her that? She never changed her name."

He shrugged. "My little joke."

"Does that mean you call me Mrs. Dudek when I'm not around? I never changed my name, either."

"I wouldn't dare."

It was her first good laugh all day. She stepped outside the Castle to the parking lot in the back to call Bob but got no answer. Now, she was nervous, and she left a message for him to call her back.

"You think he's eaten his gun?" Bostwick asked.

"I can't rule it out." No choice. She had to cancel her lunch date with Cousin Jim. "I'll head over there to check on him."

She decided to text him before she trashed the rest of her day. *You're not answering your phone and you haven't returned my call. Leaving in five minutes to come check on you. Please get back to me and save me the trip.*

"Hey, Kim." It was Stransky. "Have you seen Bob?"

"Not since last night."

"Were you with Cole Rydell's bunch? He organized some folks to go for drinks."

"No, I hadn't heard." Considering that Rydell had a reputation as a world-class party animal, that would have been the worst option for Bob. She checked her watch. Decision time.

"Martin, could you do me a huge favor? I'm supposed to meet my cousin for lunch. Could you please drive over to Bob's place and check on him? No one's heard from him."

"No need. Here he is, now."

Bob approached, unshaven but dressed well enough. He no longer reeked of alcohol.

She pointed to the conference room. When he hesitated, she said, "It's me or the lieu. Take your pick."

He turned for the conference room.

She closed the door and took a deep breath. "I'm not your mother, Bob. Or your wife, or your sister, or your therapist. I'm your partner. We talk about brothers-in-arms, but last night and this morning you left me stranded in a foxhole. As it happens, I needed the lieu's couch last night, but it was already taken by someone sleeping it off."

"Why did… I'm sorry, Kim. I know I let you down…"

"You're letting this unit down and letting yourself down. I'm not going to beat you up about it. Shit like this happens more often than we like to admit. I've been getting a bad vibe from you for a while, now, even before Sunday."

"I'm getting back to the meetings, starting tonight."

"Why did you stop?"

He could only stare at her.

"You have to figure that out, Bob, otherwise you need to check yourself into a program."

Bostwick walked in, unannounced. "Kim, you said you have someplace to go?"

"I'm meeting my cousin for lunch at one." She checked her watch. Almost noon. This was going to be close.

"Where?" Bostwick asked.

"Sunnyside, in Queens. Shit, I need to get to the Seven train…"

Bostwick touched her arm. "Stay calm. Grab the L at DeKalb, change to the G at Lorimer, then the Seven at Court Square. And take the rest of the day."

"Thanks, Lieu."

# CHAPTER TWENTY-ONE

Once Kim crossed Skillman Avenue on Fifty-First Street, the canopy of green from the trees grew more dense, and the string of apartment buildings on the west side of the street gave way to clusters of attached houses. She saw the Italian restaurant Jim had mentioned a half block before she got there, its curbside seating narrowing the walk.

Her first thought as she passed it was that Jake would love it.

She turned the corner at Thirty-Ninth Avenue and stopped. Aside from the large apartment building across the street, it was all attached houses and shade trees.

"Beautiful, isn't it?"

Cousin Jim's voice from behind her made her start. She turned and embraced him. "Good to see you, Jim."

"Same here, Cuz." He gestured to the little coffeehouse next to the restaurant. A few tables and chairs were arrayed in front. "Inside or out?"

The yellow-and-white striped awning flapped in the steady breeze. "Inside, I think."

The coffeehouse was narrow but deep, with a mix of tables and chairs and a few upholstered love seats. A menu was posted by the counter, which was about halfway toward the rear.

"My treat," Jim said.

Kim ordered a turkey and pepperjack cheese sandwich and a coffee. Jim opted for roast beef and muenster and coffee. They took their coffees to a vacant table.

"What brings you to Sunnyside?" Kim asked.

"This is Sunnyside Gardens, a small subsection of Sunnyside. I have a client in Forest Hills. Whenever I'm in Queens, I try to stop by here."

"It's a lovely neighborhood, but…"

"You don't recognize it?"

What a silly question. "Why would I?"

He touched her hand. "Gram and Granddad lived a few blocks from here."

"They did? Did Gram move after he died?"

"No, but she only spent the coldest months in the apartment. Every year, she relocated to the bungalow at Breezy Point as soon as the temperatures were tolerable, and she stayed there until they weren't."

"That's where I always remember seeing her. At the bungalow. My dad would pick her up—here, I guess—for Thanksgiving and Christmas." Years earlier, Jim had given her a box of keepsakes from Granddad's days on the job, including a notebook that had gone a long way to helping her solve a case of the man who'd killed him. But it also included photos of Gram, whose memory Kim cherished, no matter how faint.

"I'll show you where she lived after lunch. But first, are you okay? I was worried sick when I heard the first reports on Sunday."

She'd known he'd ask. And she'd rehearsed in her mind what she would tell him and what she would keep to herself. But the emotional guard rail she'd constructed quickly gave way, and it all came out—the conflict with PBBS, the mayor's ridiculous idea of forcing a promotion for her, the resulting conflict, the underlying desire that drove it, and, worst of all, Jake's jealousy, and her walking out last night.

He took a thoughtful sip of coffee, and then paused to fetch their sandwiches, which the server had placed on the counter. Back at the table, he took several bites without a word.

She settled into her own lunch. "And today's only Thursday."

"Shouldn't you be with Jake instead of me? You guys have worked through some tough issues before. This is a simple misunderstanding, isn't it?"

"The irony is Jake picked up on Brandt's interest in me before I did. And we both laughed about it." She answered his quizzical look by adding, "It was when he was still a state senator. We were out for dinner one night—at Jake's insistence, I was wearing a dress, and heels—and Brandt was in the same restaurant. He came over and told us he'd paid our bill. Jake caught him staring at my legs."

"Speaking as a certified male, I can say without hesitation that you do have lovely legs, and were you not my cousin, I would find you exceptionally attractive."

"Thank you."

"So, if Jake laughed at it then, why is he angry now?"

Exactly the question she'd been asking herself. "Maybe it's the fact that it's popped up more than once. Like when Brandt sent an aide of his to Bermuda to drag me back on the assassination case two years ago. Or perhaps…" The job.

"What?"

"The Nets haven't been doing well. He thinks his job may be in jeopardy. And then the shooting on Sunday. He was frantic that I might have been hit."

"But you weren't."

"Yes, and he knew that. But when a disaster has been narrowly avoided, the tendency is to imagine the worst that might have been. I suspect that's the case with Jake."

They finished their lunch.

It was six blocks to Forty-Fifth Street. Jim pointed at the street sign. "The brown signs signify this is a historic district." They turned the corner.

"I guess the name, Packard Street, goes back to when Queens streets had names instead of numbers."

"It does, although this area didn't even begin to develop until fifteen or twenty years after they went to numbers. The only streets in this neighborhood that had names are Skillman Avenue and Barnett Avenue. I suspect that the other names refer to what the streets were called in the older neighborhoods beyond Sunnyside."

He stopped. "These are all garden apartments. In the back are the enclosed, private gardens that give the neighborhood its name." He pointed to what appeared to be a house attached to another house but abutting it and set back slightly. There was a door on the second floor leading to a small terrace with wrought-iron railings. "That's where Gram and Granddad lived, in that second-floor apartment."

Kim blinked back unexpected tears. She could almost hear Gram's voice. "It never hurts to say you're sorry." She kissed Jim on the cheek. "Thank you."

"Come on, I'll drive you home."

***

Once Bob had left the conference room after Bostwick's lecture, it was as if a wall had gone up around him. People avoided him, or so it seemed.

Bostwick's lecture had been more forceful than Kim's. He'd handed Bob the Employee Assistance Unit card. "Get help or get out." But Kim's had cut deeper, because they'd been down this road before.

Neither Kim nor the lieu had relieved the pull he was now feeling toward the abyss. Last night's episode hadn't relieved it, either. It had only made it worse. The desire to say, "Screw it; it's not worth the struggle," was becoming overwhelming.

He stared at the card. The EAU was on Church Street in Manhattan.

There were bars a lot closer.

# CHAPTER TWENTY-TWO

The apartment was still empty when Kim arrived. She walked directly to the bedroom and locked both pieces in the safe. Lying next to it on the top shelf was the box of keepsakes Jim had given her five years ago.

She retrieved it and took out the photos. Gram and Granddad out on the town. She stared at her grandfather, Daniel Patrick Brady. Jeff Daniels could have played him in a movie. In the photo, everyone had a cigarette in their hands, except him and Gram. Granddad was grinning, Gram had a huge smile on her face, and everyone else was laughing. Granddad must have just said something witty.

She loved this photo, the grandfather she never knew but had managed to avenge, and the grandmother she had only known briefly as a woman in her seventies, not the lovely young woman in the photo.

"Why did you have to die so young, Gram? You could have taught me so much."

Dad always said she lost much of her fire after Granddad's death, the fire that had once led her to spit in the face of a serial rapist. Maybe her will to live had been lost with the irreconcilable split between her sons.

Mom never liked her, and perhaps Gram had never liked mom, either.

Something else she had in common with Gram.

Megan O'Rourke Brady.

Kimberly Megan Brady.

She returned the photos to the box and returned the box to the top shelf. She stripped off the clothes she'd worn all day and took a long, hot shower. She dried her hair, polished her nails, did her makeup and got dressed. She needed to repair her marriage.

***

Captain Colangelo was on the phone with the chief of detectives, who'd called for an update on the Prospect Park shooting. The captain had held his position for two years and felt he could speak with complete candor. His background in Internal Affairs helped. "They're making some progress, but it's slow. Thanks to Brady, the two commands are now working in concert. I've gotten no updates today."

"The mayor wants constant progress reports, which means he wants to see progress."

"So do I, Chief, but we both know cases don't always cooperate. I'll check in with Bostwick and then I'll get back to you."

Two minutes later, he walked into Bostwick's office and forestalled the expected protest. "I know the case is a bitch. Just tell me what you've got."

"Brady thinks she's got a lead on something one of the shooters—suspected shooter, I should say—was wearing. A camo T-shirt with a circled star."

"She's thinking ex-military? The ultranationalist theory is viable?

"Possibly ex-military, but she doubts the theory is valid. She's focused on the fact that the first three victims were cops, and where Galloway and Jackson were shot suggests that was the main consideration. The fact that they were all black may be a misdirection play."

"That's awfully thin, even for Kim."

"Tell me about it. She's got the FBI looking for possible ultranationalist involvement…"

"So, she hasn't ruled it out."

"I think she has, and it's just a matter of getting confirmation of the negative."

***

Jake did a double take. Kim stood before him wearing a blue dress cinched at the waist, stockings and black heels. "You look fantastic."

"Thank you. Please sit." She gestured to the couch and sat next to him. "I have a lot I want to say, and I expect you do, too. If you want to go first…"

His mouth opened and closed a few times before he shook his head. "I don't know where to start."

"Then, I will. First and foremost, I'm sorry. This case may be the worst I've ever had, but that doesn't excuse me for not paying attention to your worries. I think they'd be nuts to let you go, but if they do, you will almost certainly land somewhere else. It doesn't need to be another NBA team. It could be the league office, or a sports network. I'd be willing to bet colleges are getting into analytics for their teams. So, polish up that resume and start chatting up your contacts. Maybe you'll even decide to quit rather than be fired."

He considered it. "That's not a bad idea, Kim. Thank you."

She took his hands in hers. "I love you. And we look out for each other. I'd forgotten that in the moment, but I was reminded today. I had lunch with Cousin Jim."

"So, he suggested all this?" He gestured to her dress.

"No, Gram did." She giggled at his look of astonishment. "Jim talked about Gram, and he took me to where she and Granddad had lived in Sunnyside Gardens. When I got home, I took out those old photos I have of her and Granddad. I think they loved each other the way you and I love each other. Anyway, the other thing is Brandt. I can't help what he thinks of me, or what he wants. He'll never get it, and for two reasons. One, I could never be untrue to you, and two, he could never appeal to me. So, please don't ever lose sight of that."

He turned sheepish. "I'm sorry I ever doubted you."

"Good. Now, please shave and get changed. I'm taking you out to dinner."

"Great. Where to?"

"A place I found this afternoon, next to where Jim and I had lunch. A little Italian place called Donato's." And then she fell into his arms.

He stroked the back of her dress. "Any chance of getting inside this for dessert?"

***

Bob left the Federal Office Building at 90 Church Street, which also housed the NYPD's Employee Assistance Unit. The counselor with whom he'd spoken, a young woman named Brynn who was likely no more than twenty-five, had been sweet and understanding, but had also spoken with frankness. "Since you've been through this before, you know you must want to be sober to make it happen."

"I know. I need this."

And she'd fixed upon him the sweetest, caring look. "I understand, but you need to want it. No one can give you that. Without the desire, understanding the need won't matter."

"When I came up out of the subway, I was facing the Beer Garden across the street. I came here, instead."

"That's a good start." And she'd given him a referral to a professional who could help.

He caught another glimpse of the Beer Garden as he turned for the subway. "Not today."

# CHAPTER TWENTY-THREE

*Friday, April 25, 4:08 a.m.*

"Sir, you need to wake up."

The summons, accompanied by a shove to his shoulder, dragged the mayor out of a deep sleep. Squinting against the brightness of the overhead light, he tried to orient himself.

Bedroom.

Gracie Mansion.

His wife was instantly awake. "What's wrong? What's happened?"

The fog lifted. Dominic Grayson, head of his security detail, was leaning over him. "I'm sorry sir, but there's been a shooting in Brooklyn. Two uniformed police officers were shot in their patrol car."

The last vestige of sleep fell away. "When? Where?"

"A little after two. Ferris Street in Brooklyn."

"Red Hook, by the waterfront." That made it Brooklyn South. "What were they doing there?"

"Routine patrol, sir."

"Get me the police commissioner on the…"

Grayson shoved a cell phone in his face. "Holding for you, sir."

The mayor took the phone. "I want a task force composed of people from both Brooklyn commands investigating this shooting along with the ones on Sunday, and I want Captain Colangelo heading it. Tell me about the two officers."

"Patrolman Josiah Hughes and Patrolman Will Benson of the Seven-Six, on routine patrol. We don't know, yet, if they were investigating anything specific. I've already alerted Colangelo, and he's alerting his team as we speak."

Colangelo was Brooklyn North. The Seven-Six was Brooklyn South. "How did you know to alert him? You're saying this shooting is linked to last Sunday's?"

"Yes, sir. The deceased officers were black."

***

Kim was already dressed and still apologizing to Jake for the abrupt ending to a beautiful night of lovemaking.

"At least they didn't call a few hours earlier," Jake said. "I couldn't imagine a worse form of *coitus interruptus*."

She stopped her manic dressing to kiss him one last time. It was so great to see him making light of it. "I'll check in with you later this morning."

He turned serious. "Just please watch yourself."

A patrol car from the Seven-Six was waiting for her outside with Vitello in the passenger seat.

"Colangelo got you up, too?"

He didn't laugh. "All hands on deck for this one."

"What do we know so far?"

"I already spoke with the CSU guys from Brooklyn South. The two officers, Hughes and Benson, were sitting in their patrol car, drinking coffee, on the corner of Ferris and Sullivan. They don't know how many shots were fired or the shooter's location, but the windshield was completely shot out."

The patrol car stopped at the corner of Sullivan and Conover Streets, a block from Ferris. "I can't get closer," the patrolman driving said. Police had Sullivan closed to traffic.

Kim opened her door. "Thanks, Officer."

As soon as she and Vitello were out, the driver sped up Conover Street.

"Getting out of Dodge," Vitello said.

Kim tried not to think of the bliss she'd just left, or of Jake alone in their bed. "Can't blame him. It's open season on cops."

Colangelo greeted them as they reached Ferris Street. "Until and unless evidence emerges proving otherwise, we are considering this shooting to be related to Sunday's."

Vitello excused himself to talk to the other members of CSU from both commands.

Kim examined the shot-up patrol car. "No bullet strikes on the hood, grille, bumper, or any part of the body. So, another crack shot."

Colangelo said nothing.

She stood with her legs almost touching the front of the patrol car. Both patrolmen were hit in the face and chest.

A bright flash from her left. "Excuse me, Miss. Medical Examiner's Office." He snapped several photos of the slain officers.

"No problem. Please tell me how many shots each man took when you know."

He stared in as an assistant held up an LED spotlight. "I count one head wound, one in the throat and two in the chest for the driver, and one in the head and one in the throat for the passenger."

"Hold the light, please," she said to the assistant. "I count what appear to be one… two… three strikes in the seat." But CSU would report the final count.

She turned her back on the car, which was parked halfway onto the sidewalk. Staring straight ahead, she spotted a lot surrounded by a six-foot high plywood wall—a construction site, perhaps—with a few parked cars in front of it. On the street at the corner directly across Sullivan from the patrol car was only empty space. There was an expanse of sandy dirt on the ground behind a storm drain.

Where had the shooter stood? How had he remained concealed?

She approached the expanse of dirt and pulled out her own LED flashlight.

Tire tracks. Fresh ones.

She tried to find Vitello in the swirl of investigators combing the scene. Not seeing him, she called his cell. "Phil, I'm at the corner opposite the victims' car. I need you and someone from your team."

A few moments later he was by her side. "Whaddaya got?"

She pointed to the ground. "Those tracks are fresh. The shooter must have fired from here."

"Interesting pattern. Not one I'm familiar with. I'll get one of my guys to take an impression." He was reaching for his cell when he stopped and squatted down. "This looks fresh, too."

A footprint.

Her thoughts were interrupted by a commotion up Sullivan Street.

"I believe we're about to be graced with a visit from Hizzoner," Vitello said.

"Count me out." She wasn't getting pulled into his nonsense. Focus on the case.

"Okay. What's bothering you? Besides the mayor showing up, that is."

"Does this strike you as a good spot for a coffee break? Where did they even get the coffee? I don't see any Dunkin' Donuts or Starbucks around here."

Vitello called one of his men over. "You know this neighborhood. You know of any 24-hour convenience stores around here for coffee?"

"Around here? No, Sarge, I don't. Closest place I know of is a 24-hour market over on Clinton Street, near the expressway. You want me to…"

"No, just asking. Thanks." He turned back to Kim. "Clinton by the BQE. That's not very close."

"Which makes it even weirder that they came here."

# CHAPTER TWENTY-FOUR

*There she is.*

The mayor had told himself that he'd ordered Captain Colangelo to head the task force because these murders involved both commands, and Colangelo was the most qualified to lead the effort. He'd told himself that he needed the best of both commands working in concert. And he'd nearly convinced himself that the fact that Detective Kim Brady would be front-and-center in this investigation had no bearing on his decision.

*Nearly.*

That evaporated when he saw her. She had her hair clipped back in a loose bun, as it had been when he'd seen her in a Bay Ridge restaurant with her husband five years ago. The night his passion for her had first burst into flame.

But he'd since allowed his passion to cloud his judgment, and his desires had bubbled close to the surface, the source of jokes around the water-cooler at Brooklyn North.

And now she despised him. He was certain of it.

"Good morning, Mr. Mayor." It was Captain Colangelo. "We're still making our initial investigation, but I can give you what we have so far."

"That's all right, Captain. I don't want to interrupt anyone's work, here. But on this investigation, you are to keep the Chief of Detectives informed, but you will also report to me, directly."

Colangelo frowned. "You'll forgive me, sir, but that sounds like a recipe for trouble. I'm sure the commissioner will resent it."

"I'm sure he will. Nevertheless, I want to make certain I'm getting up-to-the-minute, accurate information. I want you to call my office morning and evening, and the moment anything of significance breaks. I want to be absolutely certain that nothing is being withheld from me."

***

As soon as he left the mayor, Captain Colangelo made his way over to the patch of dirt where Kim was still standing.

"Get your marching orders?" she asked him.

"I got those earlier this morning. This was an update. He wants me to report directly to him."

"Ooh, I'm sure the commissioner will love that."

"Look at the bright side, Kim. He wants to hear it from me, not you."

"About time."

"So, what has you so deep in thought?"

"The odor of week-old fish. What were these guys doing here? Who buys coffee in the early hours of the morning and then drives to a deserted waterfront to drink it?"

Colangelo decided to play devil's advocate. "Lots of night spots around here. Gentrification and all that. Maybe they were looking for DUI busts."

"Wouldn't that be the job of Highway Patrol?"

"Buy and busts?"

"Narcotics." She hesitated. "Unless it was buy for use."

A deep sigh. "Welcome back to Internal Affairs, Kim. We have walked this road before."

"How did the shooter know they'd be here? That's what bothers me the most."

"He could have tailed them over from the grocery." Although it sounded weak the moment he said it.

"Yes, he could have. But then he would have parked in this space, directly across the street from them after passing their car. And, I'm not saying that's impossible, except that he could have stopped and opened fired right then and there, and we'd never have gotten a tire track or a footprint."

That grabbed his attention. "We got those?"

"Yes. Sorry, I thought Sergeant Vitello would have told you."

"No, I haven't spoken to him since he got back with you. Did his people take impressions?"

"They did. Excuse me, Captain."

***

The uniformed sergeant had the "76" pins on his collar. Kim introduced herself.

"Yes?"

He was already wary. Not a good sign, although everyone was shaken by this shooting. "Can you tell me why Officers Benson and Hughes were in this neighborhood, sitting in their patrol vehicle?"

His eyes narrowed. "Why do you ask?"

Not a good start. "Can you?"

"Oh, right. I forgot. You used to be in Internal Affairs, and all cops are dirty."

"Cut the shit, sergeant. I'm as upset at the loss of two more brother officers as you are, and my only concern now is to catch the motherfuckers who did it and throw their asses in jail for the rest of their lives. For that, I need everything you know about what they were doing here. Now."

He crossed his arms. "They were on routine patrol on the graveyard shift. Their patrol area includes these streets. There are several restaurants and clubs nearby, and these streets aren't the safest in the early morning hours."

"Did they radio in any problems this morning?"

"No."

"Have either of them reported any problems lately?"

"No."

"Any difficult cases?"

He shrugged. "What's difficult?"

"If you're a sergeant, you know full well what makes a difficult case." She pulled out a card and circled her departmental e-mail address. "I want a list of all the case files on which they've worked over the past six months, and I want it by the end of the day. If I don't get it, I'll go to your supervising officer, and, if necessary, to the borough commander."

***

Joanna Dunbar had her cameraman set up on Ferris Street between Dikeman and Wolcott, a block and a half from the crime scene. Not ideal, but it was closer than *City News* had gotten, so she was satisfied.

She caught a glimpse of Kim Brady, and she was dying to talk to her, but that wouldn't be possible here. Besides, Kim wouldn't give her any inside information now, anyway. Too soon, and the wounds were too raw.

She spotted the mayor, who, curiously, wasn't stopping to talk to the press. He also hadn't gone anywhere near Kim. What was that all about?

"Ready, Joanna."

"Okay." Three, two, one... "This is Joanna Dunbar reporting from the waterfront in Red Hook, where two New York City Police officers were shot and killed in their patrol car a few hours ago. Police are not releasing any details, nor the names of the victims, until the families have been notified. The mayor's office has issued a brief statement announcing the formation of a police task force to conduct the investigation, but the mayor, himself, has declined to talk to the press."

As the camera's arc light went out, her cell signaled a text.

It was from Kim Brady. *Saw your van. Can't talk now, but can we meet later this morning? Say about seven-thirty at the Korean War Veteran's Plaza at Tillary Street?*

Kim hadn't picked that spot at random. It was where they'd both witnessed a major riot several years earlier while Kim was on the case that had cemented their friendship.

Kim wasn't offering information. She was looking for it. *7:30 AM. You've got it.*

# CHAPTER TWENTY-FIVE

Joanna was sitting atop a concrete block at the entrance to the plaza. It was just where she'd been sitting on that fateful evening more than five years ago. Nice that she remembered. "Hey, you."

Joanna plopped down to ground level. "Hey, yourself. You okay?"

"As well as can be expected, considering I haven't run since the race on Sunday."

"Too nervous?"

"No, just hasn't been time. I hate when that happens. Anyway, I have a favor to ask." She started walking through the park, and Joanna followed. "You guys covered the demonstration at the Brooklyn Bridge on Monday."

"Yeah. Why?"

"How much video did you get?"

"You saw what we got. Not a lot we could use. Ed Lyons doesn't like to glorify these people, so we keep the outrageous stuff to a minimum."

The mention of the network's owner was helpful. "What about the video you didn't use?"

Joanna stopped. "What about it?"

"Do you still have it?"

"Sure, we archive everything we shoot. You never know when it will be useful."

"It may be handy, now."

"What do you need? Maybe I can help find…"

Kim halted. "No. I need it all. I can't tell you what I'm looking for. I'm prepared to get a subpoena for it, but I'd rather not." She wasn't sure she could get a subpoena, since she didn't have probable cause, but Joanna didn't know that.

"Whoa, Kim. I'm on your side, remember?"

"I know you are. That's why I'm asking you." They walked a short way in silence.

"Lyons will have to know," Joanna said.

Good. He supported the police. And he wouldn't mind nailing whoever was behind these shootings.

"He may not like it." Joanna didn't look any happier saying it than Kim felt hearing it, but then she was only doing her job.

She had to give her something she could use. "If he balks, just tell him we need to check for a match with a description we've gotten."

"Okay, but the video may not be clear enough to give you…"

"If what I'm looking for is there, I'll see it. Please let me know what he says. If it's a negative, I'll need to talk to him myself."

"Okay, I'll…"

"Thanks, Joanna. Text me when you know." Kim did an abrupt about-face and walked back the way they'd come.

***

Her next stop was just on the other side of Cadman Plaza West. Susan Garmin hadn't called—not a good sign—but she wouldn't let it go. She held her breath as she pressed the buzzer for the woman's apartment.

"Yes?"

"Police, Ms. Garmin. I need to talk to you about your brother."

A long pause.

"Ms. Garmin, I'll try not to take too much of your time, but this is important. Two more police officers were murdered early this morning."

"My brother had nothing to do with that."

"I know. That's not why I'm here. Please."

The buzzer sounded.

Ms. Garmin was waiting at her door as Kim got off the elevator. "So, what has he done, now?"

"Other than trying to help us on this investigation, nothing in particular."

"So, why are you here?"

Kim gestured to the open apartment door. "Can we talk inside?"

"Yeah, okay. But I gotta leave for work, soon."

"What do you do?"

"Office manager for a small insurance brokerage."

"Your brother was at Prospect Park on Sunday at the time of the shooting, and he gave me some good information that aided our people in finding evidence related to the crime."

"So, why are you after him?"

"I'm not. I like your brother. He's a nice guy, and he's very observant. But I need to know…"

"If he's reliable. Yeah, well, it depends. Look, cards on the table, here. My brother's experiences with the police haven't been all sunshine. I'm sure the guys in his local precinct can provide the gory details."

"I've spoken to them. I'm sympathetic. I need to have confidence I can use what he tells me and that I can rely on him as a witness, not just because I think he can help but because he'd feel like a hero if I do. He'd feel like a knight."

Ms. Garmin's widening eyes showed she'd hit her target. "He told you about that, huh?"

"Yes. And it wasn't hard to see that the name he goes by is an anagram of the last grand master of the Templars. So, which came first, his love of the Templars or his emotional disability?"

"You mean mental illness, don't you? That's what it is."

"Does that mean it came first?"

Ms. Garmin calmed down. "No. He's been fascinated by knights and the crusades since second grade. By the time he was in junior high, he knew more about the Templars than professors with doctorates in medieval history."

"When did he start…"

"Ten years ago. He suddenly was sure this de Molay guy was talking to him, and that he was descended from the guy. When he started claiming he was de Molay, I got him to a shrink, who diagnosed him as schizophrenic and prescribed medication that turned him into a zombie. That began a cycle of him coming off his meds because he hated the side-effects, followed by totally bizarre behaviors, followed by arrest and referral to a psych ward, followed by him going back onto his meds."

"Was he ever violent?"

"No. He never hurt anyone. But he scared people. The third time he repeated the cycle, I found a new shrink who referred him for an MRI. They found a small brain tumor, which turned out to be benign, and it was surgically removed. And Mr. de Molay disappeared from my life until two years ago, when the delusions returned. Not as severe, but enough to prevent him from holding any job more involved than a delivery boy."

"What do the doctors say?"

A tear tracked down her cheek. "He won't go. I can't even talk to him about it. The last time I tried, he refused to talk to me for three months. But I'm certain he has another tumor, or the old one grew back."

Kim said nothing.

"You say you like him. Does he like you?"

"I think so," Kim replied in a whisper.

"I'll make you a deal, then. If you agree to convince him to go back to the doctor, I'll help you anyway I can."

"Why would he listen to me more than his own sister?" But Susan Garmin's desperation was palpable. "I can only do my best. And I will. Is John his real first name?"

"Jonathan. But never call him that. Even in his lucid moments, he insists on John." She glanced at her watch. "I've got to go, otherwise I'll be late for work." She fished a business card out of her purse. "Call me with any other questions you have."

"Thank you. I just have one other for now."

Ms. Garmin gestured to the hallway and locked the apartment door. "Okay, walk me to the subway."

Kim waited until they were on the elevator, with no one else. "I noticed in his apartment, he…"

"He let you in his apartment? Wow. He really trusts you."

"I noticed he had a pentagram on the wall. Do you know if he holds any beliefs associated with the pentagram, such as the Cathar Heresy?"

"I don't know for certain, but I doubt it. I don't know much about the Cathars, but he's always talked about how the Templars were truly noble because they wouldn't join in persecuting them."

They reached the ground floor and left the building. Kim glanced back at it. "I remember when they built this. I live over on Monroe Place."

"They tell me it almost burned down before it was finished."

Kim had to smile at that. "A slight exaggeration. During a violent demonstration, a mob threw some Molotov cocktails and set the fire. One firefighter was shot and killed while they put it out."

"I hope they got the bastard who shot him."

"Yes, I did." Kim extended her hand. "Thank you for your help. I'll do whatever I can to convince John to see a doctor, but I'll go slow."

# CHAPTER TWENTY-SIX

Joanna hesitated before knocking on Ed Lyons' office door.

"Enter." He glanced up. "Ah, Joanna. Are you ready for the noon update on the shooting in Brooklyn?"

"Yes, although DCPI isn't saying much. I did talk to Kim Brady, but she didn't have much to say."

"Doesn't she trust you anymore? She's got to have some theories."

"She's not one to speculate, even with fellow cops. But I know she's chewing on something because she asked me for help."

Lyons sat back. "Really. What kind of help?"

"She thinks last night's shooting was linked to the Sunday attack in Prospect Park."

"The white ultranationalist theory again? I didn't think she'd buy that."

"I don't think she does. She's asked for all the video we have on Monday's protest."

"She thinks CHE did this? That's even more ludicrous than…"

Joanna plopped into a visitor's chair. "Kim's not saying what she thinks. But check it out. CHE had one protest, to stoke the ultranationalist rant, and then crickets. And there's been nothing from them today. She didn't tell me what she's looking for, but there's something she knows about Sunday that she expects to see in the video."

"I want to help the police all I can, but we can't just turn it over to them."

"They can get a subpoena. But if we make them do that, they lose time, and it also hangs on whether they get the right judge. We shot a lot of footage that day."

"Most of which was useless."

"To us, yes. But Kim thinks she might find something. I don't see the harm in giving them a copy of it."

He thought about it. "They can come here and view it. If they see something useful, we can give them a copy of whatever they find."

Joanna met his gaze. "That would give us a leg up on who they suspect. Kim probably won't like us looking over her shoulder."

Lyons spread his arms. "That's my best offer. She agrees or gets a subpoena. Her choice."

***

After stopping at the Firehouse Deli to pick up something for lunch, Kim strolled back to the Castle.

Marshal Dhillon flagged her down at the front desk as she entered. "Detective Kim, you have a visitor. He is sitting at your desk."

She was alarmed until she saw who it was. "Mr. Lodemay. This is an unexpected pleasure."

He stood immediately. "I hope you don't mind. Mr. Driscoll told me where I could find you."

It took a moment for her to realize he meant Lieutenant Driscoll. "He and I are working together on the case." She gestured to the conference room. "Let's talk inside. It's quieter."

He relaxed once they were seated at the table. "Who's the gentleman with the turban? Is that part of the official department uniform?"

"That's Sergeant Dhillon. He's Punjabi, and several years ago, the department made an official exception to the uniform regulations, adding the blue turban to the list of acceptable headwear. It must be dark blue and have the department shield on the front."

"Punjabi. From India. The Templars had dealings in the Middle East and likely extended as far as the Indian subcontinent. It's possible they brought the game of chess back to Europe."

"Do you play chess, John?"

"Yes."

"So do I. Perhaps we can play some time."

He brightened. "I'd like that. These days, I only ever play against my computer."

"I haven't played in years, but the game still fascinates me. What's your favorite opening?"

"I love playing the Alekhine Defense as black, and the Reti Opening as white. You?"

"I like the Ruy Lopez as white and the French Defense as black. What can I do for you today?"

"I saw the news reports about those two police officers last night. Do you suspect the Cathars were responsible for this, too?"

Dangerous ground. She needed to step very lightly. "We don't know who was responsible. We're still gathering information."

"Good. Because I think I may have been wrong. The Cathars were not the only ones who used the pentagram for their beliefs. Many pagan sects do the same. The shooting in the park may not have been Cathars. But the same group, whoever they are, is responsible for both attacks."

"Why are you so sure?" She'd had the same thought.

"They attacked our modern-day knights, the police. A despicable thing." He paused. "Do you mind if I ask you something else? What is your full name?"

"Kimberly Brady. Why?"

"You don't have a middle name?"

"I do. It's Megan. After my paternal grandmother."

He sat back. "Astonishing."

"What's so astonishing about it?"

"Megan is a diminutive of Margaret. There are two St. Margarets—St. Margaret of Scotland and St. Margaret of Antioch. Antioch was one of the last strongholds of the Templars in the middle east, and Scotland is often rumored as the destination of the Templars when France banned the order in the early 1300s. Margaret of Scotland is known as the Pearl of Scotland, and the name has come to mean 'pearl'. Which I believe you are."

"Thank you, John. And thanks for coming to see me. I will keep your suspicions in mind as I continue to investigate last night's shooting."

"So, you agree with me that they're related."

"I believe they are, yes. But please don't…"

"Don't worry, I never discuss these matters with anyone."

***

"What did Mr. Nutbar want?" Bostwick asked after Lodemay left the Castle.

"He's not a 'nut bar'." It was a reflex.

"Don't tell me you're becoming emotionally attached to this guy. Sounds to me like he's crazy as a loon."

"I spoke with his sister this morning, and she gave me some background. Anyway, to answer your question, he didn't have anything new, but he believes the two shootings are connected. I also saw Joanna Dunbar this morning."

"Oh? What did she want?"

"She didn't want anything. I did. I asked to see the footage they shot of the demonstration on Monday. She said she'd…"

Her cell pinged with a new text. It was from Joanna. *Spoke to Lyons. You may view our tapes but it must be here; won't release a copy to you unless you find something specific.*

She read it aloud to Bostwick. "Crafty bastard, wants to see what we're looking for."

"You could get a subpoena. Just stay away from Let 'em Run Ron." Judge Ronald C. Vickers, who had a reputation for being soft on criminals. Kim had crossed swords with him a few times in recent years.

"With only an army insignia on a camo T-shirt to go on, we don't have probable cause. I doubt even Judge Castellano over in Manhattan would go for it."

"And we don't want a scuffle about judge-shopping. Okay, go see what you can find. Bob's taking the day, so take Martin with you. Second set of eyes."

# CHAPTER TWENTY-SEVEN

Bob stared at his reflection in the mirror. "What the fuck is wrong with you?"

He looked like hell. He hadn't made it past the Beer Garden on Church Street. Just one last one, a little Mardi Gras before the permanent Lent. An alcohol-free Lent.

Somehow, he'd made it home without killing anyone or destroying his car.

His appointment with the shrink was set for 11:30. It was now after ten. Not much time.

Why not cancel and reschedule?

No. Bostwick would have his ass. And Kim… shit, that didn't even bear thinking about.

He stared at his reflection. "Why the hell is it so much harder this time than last time?"

***

"Cord went home this morning," Martin said as they approached the offices of the Independent Television Network. "Vera's finally relaxing."

"I'll try to stop in to see them in the next few days. I spoke to him last night. He's already itching to get back."

"Maybe you can convince the lieu to allow him to come back, light duty only."

As if she didn't already have enough on her plate. Once inside, Joanna met them and led them to a small viewing room with a large screen TV.

Ed Lyons was waiting for them. "Pleasure to meet you, Detective Brady. Any objection if I sit in?"

"Since it's your film and your theater, I guess I can't. But I must insist that you share nothing about what we see or discuss with anyone for any reason. This is strictly police business."

"Understood. We're on your side."

For now. "All right." She nodded to Joanna, and they all sat.

The screen sprang to life. Joanna held the remote and narrated what they were seeing. "This is our first shot of the protesters coming off the Brooklyn Bridge. Do you want sound, as well?"

"Not yet," Kim said. "I'm more interested in visuals."

"Which visuals?" Lyons asked.

"Not sure. I'll know it if I see it."

Joanna continued as the scene changed. The marchers were now piling into City Hall Park. "They didn't have a permit, but the police declined to challenge them about it."

"Inmates running the asylum." Lyons again.

Kim didn't comment.

The scene changed to a scanning of the crowd as Prinz began speaking. Individuals were now clearly visible. The segment lasted about ten seconds, but nothing popped out at Kim. "Joanna, could you please go back and run that again, in slow-motion this time?"

"How slow?"

Martin spoke up. "Frame by frame, if you can manage it."

"I can."

But even frame by frame, it was difficult to follow because the cameraman was panning the crowd. Until…

"Freeze it," Kim called out. The image froze. Kim walked over to the screen and pointed. A young man with shoulder-length black hair and wearing sunglasses and a mottled khaki shirt was yelling with his arm raised with a fist. On his shirt's the left breast was a lighter-colored circle around a shape Kim couldn't discern. "Martin, tell me what you think."

"That could be an army insignia. Joanna, is there any way we can get better definition?"

Joanna glanced at Lyons, who shook his head. "I don't think so, no."

"Can we get a screenshot?" Kim asked.

This time, Lyons answered. "Yes, we can do that."

Kim nodded to Joanna when she'd saved the screenshot. "Okay, keep going."

A short while later, Kim again called a halt—another young man in a similar shirt, black hair down to his neck, wearing sunglasses, yelling and shaking his fist. "That's definitely camo, and that sure looks like a star inside a circle to me. Print it, Joanna."

Near the rear of the crowd, Kim caught a glimpse of a third young man, much shorter hair, similar shirt but without an emblem. He wasn't yelling, and he did not have a fist raised. The frozen frame showed his head turned away from the camera and looking downward.

"Please back it up one frame," Kim said to Joanna.

Still looking away on the previous frame.

"Back one more, please."

He was nowhere in the field of view.

"Back to the first frame we froze." Kim stared intently at the screen where the subject was turned away. "Next frame." Still looking away. "One more."

He was out of view.

"He knew he was on camera," Kim said to Stransky. Then, to Joanna, "Please give me screenshots on all three frames he's in view."

"But you can't see his face," Lyons said. "What's the use?"

"Joanna, the prints, please?"

"Got 'em. Anything else?"

Kim thought a moment. "Yes. Do you remember which roadway the protesters took over the bridge?"

"Sure. The Manhattan-bound side after blocking traffic on the Brooklyn side. The side gate of City Hall Park facing Centre Street was closed, so they marched around to the gate at Park Row and Broadway."

***

"Exactly what am I supposed to be seeing?" Bostwick stared at all five prints in turn. "If it wasn't for the hair, I'd swear I was looking at the same guy in all of them. You can't make out their faces, and, other than the middle guy, you can't even say for sure the shirts are camo."

Kim was already pounding away at her laptop. "That we're on the right track."

She logged into the department's Real Time Crime Center—RTCC for short—the huge database at One-PP where video evidence from the various NYPD cameras around the city was stored. "According to Joanna, these guys came off the bridge on the inbound side at the merge of Park Row and Centre Street and entered the park from the south gate, which means they passed two NYPD cameras, one at Centre Street and one at Spruce Street."

Stransky broke into a grin. "That's only a block apart, so the relative positions of the three guys won't have changed much."

"But," Bostwick said, "they might have changed significantly when they arrived at the park."

"Only the third one, and he's the one I'm most interested in." Kim remained focused on the screen as she searched for Monday's data.

"Why him?" Bostwick asked.

"He was the sole protester who avoided the camera and who wasn't shouting."

# CHAPTER TWENTY-EIGHT

"It's harder because you've broken your sobriety more than once," the shrink said. Dr. Gloria Richards. She wasn't young and sweet, like Brynn, the counselor at the EAU. She was fortyish, with short blonde hair turning gray, and her manner was firm and clinical. "With each failure, you become more convinced that it's too hard, that you might as well surrender to it."

"Would going into a program help?"

She glanced at the form he'd completed. "You've been to two programs, one twenty-three years ago, and one eight years ago. We can explore the reasons you resumed drinking each time, as a program would do. I'm not sure how much you'd get out of a third, because a lot of it would be familiar to you, and you might simply tune it out."

"You mean I have to do it on my own?"

For the first time, she allowed a sympathetic smile. "You never have to do anything alone. But you told me that you couldn't resist drinking even after your session with the counselor at your department, even after resolving not to. That's not a very helpful beginning."

"It was stupid."

"No, Bob, it was self-destructive. Drinking is self-destructive. You knew it when you got drunk Wednesday night, and you knew it when you got drunk last night after resolving not to. You know all this, and yet you don't heed your own warnings. You're an intelligent man."

"You're saying I know why I'm doing this? That it's my own fault?"

The sympathetic smile faded. "Yes. And for some reason, you don't want to admit it, even to yourself. Until you do, all the programs and therapies in the world won't change you."

Now she was pissing him off. "Hey, I do want to change. It's why I went to the EAU, and it's why I came here today. Tell me what I need to do to start. That's what's scaring me this time—I can't even get started."

"Will you take my advice?"

He nodded.

"All right. I'll see you tomorrow at 1:00. I don't normally see patients on the weekend, but I'll make an exception." She plucked a business card from a holder on her desk. "If you need to talk to me before tomorrow's session, call me. You know the drill, Bob. One day at a time. Today is Day One. Get through today and early tomorrow sober, and we can talk about next steps."

***

Kim had the data from the camera on Park Row and Centre Street, with Stansky and Brogan by her side. "Okay, there's Prinz leading the charge. In the ITN video, the first guy was near the front of the crowd."

"These cameras don't give the same quality as ITN's," Stransky said. "They're fixed-focus."

Kim agreed. "The crowd is walking almost directly under them and… there!" She froze the image. The same guy with shoulder-length black hair.

"Definitely a camo shirt," Stransky said.

"The circled star on the left side," Brogan added.

Kim downloaded the screen shot to her laptop. "Calling him 'Subject One'. The second guy followed soon after."

"But that was in City Hall Park," Stransky said. "Here, they're not as spread out, side to side."

"But they're moving." Kim's gaze remained glued to the screen. And then she froze it. "There's Subject Two, neck-length hair."

"And that's definitely the same shirt," Stransky said.

Kim downloaded that one, too. "On to Subject Three." But as the remainder of the marchers passed, she didn't see him. "Shit." She rewound and ran it again. "No sign of him."

She switched to the camera at Spruce Street. They saw the same subjects, but not the third, despite getting a clear view. "There's only one explanation. He met them in the park, coming in from another direction."

Bostwick, who'd been watching the whole time, spoke up. "Now, what?"

He came in from a different direction. Which way? How did he get there? "Okay, guys, we need to dig in, here. He didn't arrive with the marchers, so, he probably came by subway. The most obvious stops would be Brooklyn Bridge on the Four, Five or Six; City Hall on the R; or Chambers Street on the J or Z."

"We also can't rule out Fulton Street on the A and C," Bostwick added, "or Park Place on the Two and Three. That's five major subway stations, each with multiple cameras. And the captain wants us upstairs for a status meeting with Driscoll, Kim."

Another time-suck, although she got it. Brandt had put Colangelo in charge. "Lieutenant, can we get Rydell to help us out?"

"Let's see who Driscoll can provide, first."

***

As they walked into the conference room next to Colangelo's office, the wide-screen TV was on and Driscoll was waiting.

Wonderful. Driscoll wasn't even here.

Colangelo got them started. "Lieutenant Driscoll, thanks for joining us. I thought video would do for now." He turned to Kim. "I hope you folks agree."

"For now," Kim said. "Lieutenant Driscoll, how's your manpower issue?"

"Better. My two flu-stricken detectives return on Monday. Meanwhile, we received Ballistics' analysis of the slugs recovered from the Red Hook patrolmen. They were nine-millimeter cartridges fired from a SIG Sauer P210A."

Matching neither shell type found at the Park shooting.

"Anything further on what the two patrolmen were doing there?" the captain asked.

"No, sir. No one seems to know." Driscoll paused. "Or if they do, they ain't saying."

"Do we need more pressure?" Colangelo asked.

"I'd rather not do that, Captain. Might lead to unnecessary tensions around here."

"What do you think, Kim?" Colangelo asked.

She'd worked damned hard to establish a partnership with Driscoll. She wasn't about to throw it away so early in the game. "I agree, Captain. At this point, we have no reason to suspect any unlawful activity on their part." She updated Colangelo and Driscoll on what the video had revealed.

Colangelo came half out of his seat. "So, you're saying these shootings are the work of Prinz and his group?"

"No, although I find it odd that his group's had nothing to say since Monday. Perhaps there are other reasons for that. All I'm saying is that three men wearing what appear to be similar shirts to the one worn by one of the Park shooters have been caught on video, and that warrants additional investigation. I'm hoping Lieutenant Driscoll's people will be able to assist with that?"

"Absolutely. I'll check if they can come in before Monday."

Excellent. "Thank you. Whenever they return, could they report here?"

"Is it absolutely necessary?" Driscoll asked.

"Not absolutely, but it would make it easier if everyone working with the RTCC is here. We have a large conference room that we can dedicate to this investigation, and everyone can share information and post key findings on the board."

On screen, Driscoll appeared to be thinking it over.

"Lieutenant," Kim added, "if it's important to you, we can come to you."

"No," Driscoll said at last, "Considering that this task force is under Captain Colangelo's command, going there makes more sense. But I do have one question for you: in light of the ballistics report on the waterfront shooting, do you still think it's linked to the park attack?"

"Yes. If the men in the City Hall video are wearing the same shirt as the Prospect Park shooter, we must assume we're dealing with a larger group."

"In other words," Colangelo said, "a well-organized group."

"Exactly. What's more, the P210A is another pistol favored by target shooters, like the Glock 34. Different weapon, same desire for accuracy."

Kim's cell vibrated with a text from Ken Taylor. *Need to meet.*

# CHAPTER TWENTY-NINE

"Are you sure this is a group you're dealing with?" Taylor asked as Kim entered his office.

"I wasn't until this morning." She laid the printouts of the screenshots on his desk.

He examined each one in detail before commenting. "They don't really show much. The resolution is lousy, and they're wearing shades."

"But the ones from the RTCC show the insignia." She also told him about the ballistics from the latest shooting.

"Two more black cops. I guess that helps the white ultranationalist theory."

"Which I've decided is helpful."

He considered it. "It certainly is viable. Does that mean you're accepting it?"

"Just the opposite. Even though you can't see their faces, you can tell they're not white guys."

"You can't really tell."

She laughed. "Are you busting my chops, or are you just not looking?"

"I could ask you if you're just suffering from confirmation bias."

"You know me better than that. Look at their faces."

He shuffled through the images once again. "I can't see most of their faces."

"You can see their cheekbones."

He took a closer look. "Damn, Kim, you're right. High cheekbones, not a typical Caucasian feature, although not completely unknown."

"In one guy, perhaps. But three, all wearing the same shirt?"

He stared at them a little longer. "Okay, you sold me."

"Great. So, why did you summon me? Couldn't you just tell me over the phone?"

"Zero luck on a group using this insignia. I wanted to talk to you to get more information, but you've already given me some."

"You mean you were stuck on the ultranationalist thing?"

He shrugged. "It seemed the most likely option." He returned to the images. "There are only seven. Shouldn't there be two more?"

"See? I knew that brain of yours would kick in sooner or later. Can you guess who's missing?"

More shuffling. "The one with the shortest hair. Not in the march, but he was caught on camera in City Hall Park looking away from the camera. Which means he's careful to avoid being photographed."

"I think it means more than that. Perhaps he's the leader of this little cabal. The guys are reviewing RTCC video from the surrounding subway stations as we speak, and if we come up with something, you'll be the first to know. But if you have the slightest inkling regarding the identity of these guys…"

"I don't. You know I wouldn't hold back on you if I did."

"Good," she said. "Because the emergence of a third gun, and therefore most likely a third shooter, tells me we could be heading for major shit. For what it's worth, I think we're looking for guys with either a military or law-enforcement background."

***

Get through today and early tomorrow sober. Dr. Richards had said it like she expected him to fail. Just as he was expecting to fail.

Dr. Richards was a bitch.

But at least she'd agreed to see him on Saturday. And since she fully expected him to fuck up once again, he was going to make sure he didn't.

Just to regain a measure of self-respect.

He entered the Castle expecting baleful stares, but only Marshal Dhillon greeted him. "Morning, Detective. Detective Brady is in the conference room with Lieutenant Driscoll and the others. She said to tell you to join them if you come in."

He found Kim, Brogan and Stransky pounding away at their laptops in the conference room. They all greeted him cheerfully enough.

Kim brought him up to speed on the visit to ITN. "They don't show a whole lot, but Taylor agrees it's enough to say they're not white guys."

Bob examined the photos. "I can't put my finger on why, but I agree with you."

Kim explained where they were with the search. "Tim, Martin, and I are checking subway videos in the stations near City Hall. Why don't you join us? You can start with the NYPD cameras on Broadway. There's a set at Murray Street and another at Warren."

It felt great to be asked. Trying not to look too eager, he pulled his laptop from his desk.

Before he could join them in the conference room, Kim stopped him. "Hey. Are you okay?"

"Honestly? I haven't been okay in a while. But I'm hanging in."

"Good. I need your best on this case, whatever that is. Based on ballistics, it appears there's a third shooter involved."

***

It was slow going. Shortly before three, Bob broke the silence that had become oppressive. "Kim, I think I got something."

Kim hated the interruption, because she thought she'd picked up something at the Park Place station, but she rolled her chair over to Bob. Brogan and Stransky stood behind them watching while Bob rewound and replayed what he'd found.

One look told Kim it was their guy, crossing Warren Street, north to south, on the opposite side of Broadway from City Hall. He was too far away to see his face, or to discern any camo pattern on his shirt, but the hair and sunglasses were a perfect match. "So, he didn't emerge from any of the City Hall area stations."

"Unless he did and then doubled back," Brogan said.

"Highly unlikely. He's working hard to avoid detection, but that doesn't mean he's planning that far ahead."

"Maybe he's a good chess player," Bob said.

It pulled her up short, reminding her of Lodemay. She looked more closely at the screen. "Definitely not Caucasian. What do you think, Bob?"

"Latino or Middle Eastern."

"Bob, check the cameras at Murray Street, same time frame. He would have wanted to cross by then."

He saved the screenshot and then backed out, going to the Murray Street camera. Following an extensive search, he said, "Possible hit."

Kim returned to check.

"It's the view looking South," Bob said. "Check at the very edge."

"Yes, that's him crossing. Nearly at Park Row." Kim slid back to her place and initiated a new search. "I'm checking the Chambers Street station for the A and C. Somebody check the One, Two, and Three. Bob, are there any cameras in City Hall Park?"

"Only near the roof of City Hall itself."

"Holy shit," Brogan said, "one of the most popular protest sites in the city, and there's no video?"

"Welcome to New York," Bob replied.

"I'm on the other Chambers Street Station," Stransky said.

Come on, you fucker. You didn't walk down from midtown, or wherever the fuck you're from. Like Brooklyn. The A, Two, and Three lines enter Manhattan from Brooklyn. She tried to calculate how long it would have taken him to climb out of the station, then walk the one block up Church Street to Chambers, then another block over to Broadway, and then down to Warren. She allowed some extra time, then clicked on the video surveillance.

Nothing.

"Got him," Stransky called out. "You can see him putting his shades on as he's getting off the Two train."

"Uptown or Downtown side?" Kim asked.

"Uptown."

Brooklyn guy. But while the video showed him settling the sunglasses in place, his face was already partially obscured by the glasses. She couldn't be certain what he looked like. "Print a screenshot of that, Martin." Because she knew someone who might. "Come on, Bob. We're going to One-PP to see Sheila Gregg."

# CHAPTER THIRTY

In Kim's opinion, Sheila Gregg was the very best sketch artist in the NYPD, and they'd been working together for years.

But Sheila did a double-take seeing Kim and Bob in person. Kim almost always dealt with her by phone unless she was babysitting a witness. "What's up?"

"I need you to do one of your speculation specials. We caught this guy on a subway station video. We need your best estimate of what his face looks like without the shades." She laid both the Chambers Street screenshot and the Warren Street screenshot on her desk.

"I'm not a magician, Kim. I can't conjure up a portrait for you. Not from this."

"You've done pretty well in the past."

"Working with a full profile view. You have anything else I can use? I can't even see his nose in these shots."

Kim gave her the shot she'd gotten from ITN.

Sheila groaned. "Oh, yeah, that helps a lot."

"Well, you can see his nose. Besides, aren't you always telling me that suspect sketches are all about impressions?"

"Yeah, that witnesses get from seeing firsthand and repeat to me."

Kim turned serious. "I'm kind of desperate on this one. This is about the cop shootings."

"Aw shit. Great. Pile on the guilt." She stared at the three shots. "All right, Kim. Give me some time and I'll see what I can do. But promise me now that you won't ever ask me to stand up in court and swear to it."

Relief. "I won't even ask you to sign your name to it."

"Yeah, like that will make a difference. I'll e-mail you if I come up with something."

***

"Since we're already in Manhattan, how about another stop?" Kim didn't wait for an answer.

Once they boarded an uptown J train, Bob made a guess at the destination. "Essex Street?"

"Give the man a cigar."

"Prinz?"

"Two for two."

"You going to ask him about the guys in the camo shirts and shades?"

"What? And tip our hand? If he's working with them, he'll deny knowing anything about them, and if he isn't, he'll still deny knowing anything about them because this is playing right into his hands. Or, at least it should be."

"Meaning what?"

"If he really believes this is some white ultranationalist plot, he should be screaming to high heaven that the police aren't protecting nonwhite citizens. But he isn't."

"So what do you hope to accomplish?"

"I want to squeeze him a bit and see how much shit spills out."

The condo Prinz had inherited from Sabrina Dunn was only a block from the Essex Street station. "Bob, I'll press the button and you do your Con Ed thing."

She buzzed.

"Yeah?" Prinz sounded groggy.

"Con Ed," Bob said. "We got a complaint of a gas leak."

The door lock clicked, and they entered the lobby. "I'll bet any amount he's stoned."

When Prinz answered, he took a moment to focus. "Aw, shit, you again?"

"I'm like the proverbial bad penny, Felipe. I'm sure you remember my partner, Detective Nolan. May we come in?"

"I ain't done nothing."

"We're not claiming otherwise. We just want to chat."

He waved them inside. Kim was taken aback because the apartment didn't reek of cannabis smoke. "Are you okay, Felipe?"

"Fine. What's up, oh tough police lady?"

A hookah stood on a corner table. Perhaps he'd cleared the air in the apartment. Or he might be using something else. "Did you hear about two more police officers being killed in Brooklyn early this morning?"

"Wasn't me. I haven't been anywhere near Brooklyn since Monday."

She chuckled. "No, Felipe, we don't suspect you. But you were vocal on Monday about a possible white ultranationalist conspiracy. Since the two police officers killed this morning were black, I thought you'd be outspoken about it."

"Yeah, like you'd do anything about it."

She leaned forward. "You know me, Felipe. I nailed those bankers two years ago for Sabrina's murder. You may not like me or what I do, but you can't accuse me of protecting white criminals."

"Whatever."

"Here's what's bothering me. If white ultranationalists are responsible for these shootings, why haven't you persisted in demanding justice?"

"I thought you didn't want me interfering with your investigation?"

"Since when do you pay attention to anything I ask? No, Felipe, you're up to something."

"Maybe I've changed my mind about the ultranationalist plot. How about that?"

"I'd be interested to hear your thinking."

For a moment, he appeared utterly confused. "Nothin'. I've got nothin' to say."

She turned to Bob. "A rare moment."

The needle sank home. "Hey, bitch, whaddaya want from me?"

"Your thoughts, Felipe. If you can express them coherently."

"You think I'm involved in this?"

She looked him in the eye. "Should I?"

He stood. "I think you should get the fuck out of my apartment."

Kim paused at the door. "You mean Sabrina's apartment, don't you?"

Once outside, Bob said, "What was the point of pissing him off? Especially the shot as we were leaving."

She heaved a sigh. "Yeah, I don't know. I'm not proud of that. Sometimes he just irritates me." As they started down the subway stairs, she added, "At least I shook him up a little, got him out of his comfort zone. I need sleep. See you in the morning."

Once on the platform, as a train approached the station, her phone vibrated with a text from Ken Taylor. *I may have something. Call me in the morning.*

# CHAPTER THIRTY-ONE

*Saturday, April 26, 5:56 a.m.*

Bob hadn't slept well. Too much coffee had left him tossing and turning. He'd read for an hour, which had helped a little.

He'd now showered and dressed. There wasn't much in the apartment for breakfast, so he nuked last night's leftover coffee and headed for the Castle. He'd grab breakfast at the Firehouse Deli.

The roads were empty. He cruised over the Verrazano, chuckling to himself about having to pay a toll to get off Staten Island but not to get on, and continued up the Brooklyn-Queens Expressway. The cool morning air filling the car in a rush was refreshing, and he opted to stay on the highway rather than wending his way through Brooklyn's parquet-pattern streets and endless traffic lights. From the exit at Flushing Avenue, it was a straight shot to Wilson and then to the Castle. And he arrived early enough to find a spot in the tiny parking lot in the back.

"Good morning, Detective Bob."

"Morning, Marshal. Early for you, isn't it?"

"Sergeant Tolbert went home sick. He called and asked if I would finish his shift. My oldest is starting to think about college, so I make extra money where I can. It is early for you, also, is it not?"

"I have an appointment at one, so I'll be signing out early."

"I shall make the change to the Duty Roster this instant. Nothing serious, I hope."

A matter of life and death. "No, just a consultation. Thanks, Marshal."

He finished his bacon-and-egg sandwich and moved into the conference room, where he nearly had a heart attack. "Cord! What the fuck are you doing here?"

Washington turned away from the marker board and grinned. "I love you, too, Bob. I'm just tidying up the case profile a bit. Kim's usually better at this than I am, but, by the looks of it, she's been rather busy. I'll bet she hasn't even been keeping up with her running."

"Aren't you supposed to be home recuperating?"

Cord laughed. "After that hospital, I was ready to do a little shootin' myself. They said no work for another month. Ain't no way I was gonna survive that."

"No way you'll survive this, either. Kim will flip out when she finds out."

A voice from behind. "Brilliant American Lady Detective will have to get in line."

Bob turned. "Hello, Vera. Good to see you."

"Never mind sweet talk." She pointed at Cord. "He already break his promise."

"What promise?" Cord asked.

She put her hands on her hips. "You promise to stay off feet. You promise to take easy."

"I can't write on the marker board sitting down."

Vera's reaction to Cord's logic made it impossible for Bob not to laugh. "You two ought to get married."

"He promised that, too."

Cord turned serious. "As soon as I fully recover. That one, I'll keep. I also promised that I'd take a rest if you thought I needed one."

"Good. Take rest now."

He sat at the table. "Your wish is my command."

She bit her lip. "*Spasibo.*"

"That means 'thank you'," Cord said.

"Now," Vera said to Bob, "I can help, yes?"

***

Following a good night's sleep, Kim finally got a run in. As always, she began with an easy jog down to Joralemon Street, past the Seven-Six, and on to Brooklyn Bridge Park. Passing the Seven-Six reminded her of all the work she needed to do. The case board needed a lot of updating, and she needed to talk to other officers in the precinct. Curiosity about what the two patrolmen had been doing in their car before they were shot continued to gnaw at her.

But as she entered the park and ran along the greenway, kicking her pace up close to racing speed, all of that melted away. Two loops around the park and then back to the house on Monroe Place made it five miles, an excellent back-to-the-road run.

As she wound down to a cool-down jog at Monroe and Pierrepont Street, thoughts of work returned, and she began to plan her day. But as she approached the house, she spotted an all-too-familiar figure sitting on her front steps.

"Glad seeing you back running," Justin called out to her. "I imagine you haven't been able to run much since Sunday."

"And to what do I owe a morning visit from the mayor's top aide?" Although she was glad to see him. Over the years, they'd become good friends.

"Ricky sent me with a message from Bryce Mitchell."

"The Brooklyn District Attorney has a message for me, that he entrusted to Rick who entrusted it to you? What have I done, now?" Mr. Mitchell had not always approved of Kim's actions.

Justin raised both hands. "It is one of peace, and it originated from that fine American jurist, Judge Ronald C. Vickers."

That got her attention. "I'm listening."

"The New York Bar Association is giving a dinner tonight honoring his honor for his twenty years of dedicated service on the bench. The judge saw the guest list last night and immediately contacted Mr. Mitchell to inform him that he wanted you and your husband invited."

"That's insane. Why would he want me?"

"He didn't say."

She turned serious. "Give it your best shot, please."

"He respects you. Even when you've disagreed, you've always done so in a professional and polite manner. I suspect solving the Sabrina Dunn murder may also be a factor." He laughed. "Relax. You'll be at the same table as Ricky and me. Bryce Mitchell, too. Cocktails at six-thirty, dinner at eight. It's at the Marriott, Brooklyn Bridge. Walking distance for you."

"Not when I'm wearing heels."

***

Felipe Prinz didn't like being summoned. In fact, he didn't like a lot about the direction his life was taking. Before Sabrina's death, he'd envisioned himself as a Latino Al Sharpton, a man he'd admired since his college years, who'd based his entire career as a spokesman for his race on a fiction. And yet, here he was today, a regular on cable news, sought for comments on all things political.

He'd left his Philip King identity behind, and even had done time, giving him street cred. And the wealthy white ruling class had provided him with a juicy issue—gentrification. He'd founded

Come Home Ernesto, now universally referred to as CHE, in honor of his hero.

But the solving of Sabrina's murder had thrown him. A billionaire had been convicted of accessory, and the masterminds of the murder had been killed. The city had celebrated, and Felipe had suddenly found himself without an issue. Now, here he was in a small park in Greenpoint overlooking the East River.

"You're late."

Felipe gestured across the river. "Lovely view of the Con Ed plant."

"Urban decay, anathema to the bourgeoisie."

"What is important enough for you to drag me here? Shit, I had to take the M, L, and fucking G trains."

"You had visitors last evening."

"How did you know that?"

Franco shrugged. "It's my business to know. What did they want?"

Good question. He hadn't been at his best. "They never made it clear."

"They didn't make it clear, or you were too out of it to understand? I'm surprised you don't get it. They legalized it as a way of holding power."

"People wanted it legalized."

Franco snarled. "Don't be stupid. Didn't you ever read *Brave New World*? Huxley knew. He, in effect, predicted that rulers would at some point legalize a drug that allowed people to escape. 'Soma', he called it, and people who spent extensive amounts of time under its influence were said to be on 'Soma Holiday'. And the rulers did this because when people choose to escape, they become impotent to stop the rulers from crushing them."

This was ridiculous. "For years, we fought for legalization."

"As an element of the counterculture. But it risked the power structure eventually legalizing it. And now, they have. Anyway, are you able to recall anything from last night's encounter with the law?"

It came into focus. "She couldn't understand why the protests had stopped, why I'd stopped claiming the Park shooting was the work of white ultranationalists."

"That makes two of us."

"The news outlets have picked it up and run with it. There's no reason…"

"There is every reason. You are conspicuous by your absence. You need visibility. And stop smoking that shit, or eating it, or whatever you're doing."

# CHAPTER THIRTY-FIVE

Kim thought about heading into Manhattan first, to see Ken Taylor, but decided against it. She wanted to see how Bob was doing, and she needed time to pull everything together. The case board was a mess.

Marshal Dhillon greeted her, but her response was cut short by a glimpse of Vera Koshkin going into the conference room. When she saw Cord, she understood. "You have no business being here."

"Ah," Vera said. "Brilliant American Lady Detective puts it perfectly. Tell him, Kim."

Cord stood and embraced her, and all Kim could say was, "I'm glad you're still with us." She then saw the reorganized case board. "And you've been busy. Thank you. I was planning on taking care of this today." She recapped their meeting with Prinz the night before.

"Something about him wasn't right," Bob said.

"I still think he was stoned," Kim replied. "I'm just not sure on what. There was no odor."

"He might've eaten some hashish," Cord said. "That lasts for hours."

Kim, Bob, and Vera all glared at them.

Cord held up his arms. "So they tell me."

After setting up her laptop, Kim opened an e-mail from Sheila Gregg. It had a JPEG file attached, the sketch she'd done. She linked her laptop to the big-screen monitor on the wall and opened the file.

"You were right," Bob said. "He looks Latino."

"He's a mix," Cord said. "Look at his nose. Definitely some African blood. You think he might be one of the shooters?"

"I only know he was part of the protest at City Hall on Monday, and he and two other participants were wearing shirts like the one that one of the shooters wore on Sunday." She forwarded the e-mail to Ken Taylor, explaining who it was.

Taylor responded by text. *How did you get this?*

Kim replied. *Artist's best guess based on photos.*

A couple of minutes later, his response came in. *We're drawing a blank on the insignia. Looks like it's the classic circled star of the army. I've sent requests to both army intelligence and Homeland Security.*

"Bob," she said, "two of the weapons we've identified are pistols favored by target shooters. There are two shooting ranges in Brooklyn. Let's take this sketch and see if it rings any bells. We can stop at that deli/grocery in Red Hook. Then we'll return to the Seven-Six and try to discover what those two patrolmen were doing Friday morning."

Bob gestured for Kim to follow him out. "I'll do whatever you need this morning, but I need to sign out by noon."

"Are you okay?"

"Yeah, and I'm trying to stay that way. I have an appointment... with a shrink."

She squeezed his arm. "I'm glad. Sure, whatever you need. Tell you what, you take care of the shooting ranges, and I'll take care of the Seven-Six."

"Don't go alone."

"I'll take Tim or Martin with me."

***

Before they left, Kim printed out the ID photos of both officers. Stransky was first in, so she took him along.

"I'm amazed at Cord," Stransky said once they were in an unmarked Toyota Camry Hybrid.

"I just hope he doesn't overdo it. Although I doubt Vera will let him."

"Which reminds me, Marisa wants to know if there's anything she can do to help. I think she misses undercover work."

"Not surprising, since she was good at it. You guys have anything in mind?"

"I saw your note on the board about Prinz. You think he might be involved?"

"I doubt it. He's been acting weird, but not guilty weird. Why?"

"Marisa wondered if you'd like her to try to infiltrate his group."

Kim drove the rest of the way to Red Hook deep in thought. She found the deli/grocery on Clinton Street and parked. "We're not set up for that kind of operation. We'd need to monitor her and be ready if things went south. Let's see how our investigation progresses, then we can discuss it with the captain if necessary."

Her first thought entering the store was wondering how they stayed in business. A young woman, heavyset and wearing a long, floral print shift, was behind the counter. "You want somet'ing?"

Kim and Martin showed their badges.

"We ain't done nothin' wrong."

Kim smiled at the Jamaican accent, thick enough to cut with a knife. "Do you ever work nights?"

"All de time. Usually, nine to nine. No rest for de weary."

Kim laid the two photos on the counter. "You ever see these men in here?"

"Dey de two who got shot Thursday night. Yeah, dey come in all de time. Like pretty much every night."

"Any idea why?"

"Maybe 'cause we de only place open all night. Dey always comin' in for coffee and something to eat."

"Did they ever mention why they were in this neighborhood?" When the woman looked wary, Kim added, "It's okay. Where they've gone, they won't hear a thing."

"Got a couple bars by de water. Sometimes customers come out real late, get mugged going to dere cars."

Kim exchanged a glance with Stransky. No one had mentioned anything about that. "Okay, thanks."

Once outside, she suggested they check the bars near the river to see if anyone there recognized the officers.

***

Bob's search had turned up five shooting ranges in Brooklyn and Queens, so Bob decided to start with the three in Queens and work his way down to Bay Ridge. By then it would be noon and he could head home for his appointment with Dr. Richards. The first was the Stuyvesant Rod and Gun Club in Middle Village. He nearly missed the single door tucked among a cluster of storefronts with a small sign on the door. He had to be buzzed in.

Bob displayed his badge and identified himself. "Not easy to spot this place."

"This is a conservative neighborhood, but shooting ranges attract all sorts of crazies. What brings you here?"

"Do you get any army vets in here for target shooting?"

The manager only glared at him.

"Let me narrow it down a little," Bob added. "I'm looking for someone who likes to wear camo shirts with an army star right here." He touched the left side of his chest.

The glare continued. "This is about all those cops getting shot, isn't it? And you came here because it's a white neighborhood, and of course if a black cop got shot, a white guy musta done it."

"You're correct, this is about the police officers who were shot. One of them, the guy who survived Sunday's attack, is a partner of mine. The guy who shot him used a Glock 34 with nine-millimeter +P ammo. We think this guy…" he laid the copy of the sketch on the counter. "…is connected. Now, I don't know what you think, but he don't look white to me."

The manager studied the sketch and nodded. "Sorry. Folks around here are pissed at all the anti-white shit."

"You've got plenty of company there, Mac. We have two other surveillance photos. They don't show much, but maybe you've seen one of them." He laid the photos from City Hall Park on the counter.

"I don't think they're white, either." He studied them for over a minute. "I wish I could help you, Detective, but this is a private club, and I know all the members."

"Do any of your members like to target shoot with a Glock 34 and that ammo?"

"Glock 34s, yes. But most of them use standard nine-millimeter shells. +Ps are expensive for target practice. And most of our guys are only in it for target shooting."

Bob laid his card on the counter. "Please call me if you see anything."

# CHAPTER THIRTY-SIX

Most of the places near the water closed at eleven, and Kim was starting to think they were wasting their time. "Looks like Sunny's is our last shot."

Outside, it didn't look like much. "Looks like your standard-issue neighborhood dive bar."

"Marisa and I have been here several times. It's her concession to my bluegrass obsession."

"You like bluegrass?"

"Love it, and they have live performers here." He held the door for her.

Once inside, she could see it was the kind of place that could develop a cult following. From the neon anchor in the front window to the upright bass standing in the corner and the spinet that looked like it dated from Scott Joplin's time, it struck her as a place with a rich history.

"We're not open yet," a gray-haired man with a pot belly said from the bar.

Kim showed her badge. "NYPD detectives. We'd like to ask you a few questions."

He dropped his voice to a whisper. "Is this about the policemen murdered the other night?" When Kim nodded, he called out, "Jackie, would you please go into the office and check those bills? I'd like to send them out today."

The girl disappeared.

"I didn't want her to get upset," he said. "What would you like to know?"

"Why would she get upset?" Kim asked.

"Because she was seeing one of the officers. Joey Hughes. Nice kid. His partner, Bensen, was a good guy, too."

"That's why they were in the neighborhood? To see Jackie?"

"Joey always worried about her going home so late. A lotta dirtbags still hang around here, so when they were on the graveyard shift, they'd pick her up and drive her home. She don't live that far—Bay Ridge—but she'd need to take the B61 up to Court Street and then the R train down to Bay Ridge. And late at night, the bus doesn't run that often. So, he's been driving her ever since they started dating." He shook his head. "What a nice guy. What a fucking shame."

"So, he drove her home every night he was on duty?" Kim asked.

"Hey, you're not going to fuck with whatever his family gets, will ya?"

She patted his arm. "No, of course not. It's just that he was on rotating shifts, so that he'd only be working the graveyard shift two weeks out of every six. What did he do…"

"He'd come and hang out, then take her home. I'm telling you, Detective, those kids were serious."

She only had one more question. "So, I checked online and saw you close on Thursday nights at one in the morning. The shooting occurred shortly after two, and they were three blocks away."

He gave a sad smile. "We close at one, but it kinda varies, you know? People don't leave exactly on the dot. Once we close, there's cleaning up to do and Jackie helps with that. Two o'clock is average for her to leave. When Joey first started coming around while on duty, it freaked my customers out seeing a police car out front. They thought they were looking to bag 'em for drunk driving. They started parking where they were the other night, first to keep outta sight, but then also because we've had a few muggings and car thefts while customers were here. By hanging out on Ferris, they kept it safe for everyone who parked their cars down that way."

"Did they always wait in the same spot?" Kim asked.

"Yep. Jackie would call or text 'em when she was ready to go. A couple of times she had to wait because Joey saw a customer come out, none too steady, and he wouldn't let them drive. He'd call a cab and wait until the customer got in before leaving. I'm telling you, Detective, not takin' anything away from anyone else on the force, but we lost two damned good men."

***

The Second Queens shooting range, located in Woodhaven, was a repeat of Bob's experience at the first, but the first thing he noticed about the Ridgewood Range was that it was open to the public. The second was that they were open six days a week from nine in the morning to nine at night. Again, he was faced with hostility and suspicion until the person who greeted him realized why he was there. Bob repeated his pitch.

"Yeah," the guy said as he checked the photos. "I seen some guys in here with these kinda shirts. But I never seen the guy in the sketch."

"That's okay. Can you tell me if any of them shoot with a Glock 34?"

He thought it over. "Glock 34, that's a nice piece."

Bob grinned at him. "Is that a yes?"

"Not sure. You know what ammo he uses?"

"The guy I'm looking for uses nine-millimeter +P."

A humorless laugh. "Whoa, that's fucking serious. We don't sell 'em here, so if anyone's using them, they bring 'em in from the outside."

"What about a SIG Sauer P210A? With nine-millimeter ammo?"

"I've definitely seen a few of those, but I don't recall what they were wearing. Are you saying those two pieces were used in the cop shootings?"

"Yes, as well as an AR-15."

"Don't get many AR-15s for target shooting. But I'll keep an eye out."

"I'd appreciate it." Bob handed over a card with his cell number hand-written. "If you see anyone using any of the three pieces I've told you, please call me immediately. If I can't come over, one of my partners will."

Bob checked his watch. 11:05. Plenty of time to get to the shooting ranges in Brooklyn and still make it to Dr. Richards' by one o'clock.

# CHAPTER THIRTY-SEVEN

"This is Rita Henshaw with breaking news here on *City News*. A group of protesters have gathered to block traffic on the Verrazano-Narrows Bridge and police are urging travelers to take other routes onto Staten Island. The group, CHE, is demanding swift action on the investigation of what CHE leader Felipe Prinz calls 'the white war against nonwhites'. The police commissioner has not commented on the situation."

***

The mayor took a deep breath before picking up the phone. "Get me the police commissioner."

A moment later, the commissioner was on the line. "Yes, Mr. Mayor."

"What the hell is happening on the Verrazano Bridge?"

"We're investigating now, sir. A bunch…"

"It's Prinz, God damn it, and how is it that *City News* knows more about it than you do, and already has people on site?"

"It's only an opinion, sir, but I suspect it may have something to do with Prinz having given them advance notice. They're getting nice close-ups."

"Too damn nice. Have you deployed the SRG?"

"I don't think this calls for the Strategic Resource Group, sir. This isn't a riot, and there have been no violent acts. But we will continue to monitor the situation, and we will clear it as soon as we can."

***

Both Brooklyn ranges were private clubs. The one on President Street was only opened three days a week, Saturday not being one of them, and the Bay Ridge Gun Range on Fort Hamilton Parkway was only open on Saturdays for law enforcement training classes. Although he couldn't see the BQE when he parked the car, he knew it was only a short distance away.

He found the manager of the range immediately, although talking over the sound of gunfire was difficult.

"Sorry," the manager said. "I'd remember a guy with a Glock 34 and that ammo. That's a honey of a weapon. What do you carry?"

"Glock 19."

"Use it much?"

"Only to keep my qualification." Bob snuck a peek at his watch. 12:04. He needed to wrap this up, so he left a card with his cell number and thanked the manager.

Once back in the car, he drove down Fort Hamilton Parkway, confident he'd get to Richards' office with plenty of time to spare. Traffic continued to move as he passed McKinley Park.

He'd made it to Saturday afternoon. He'd gotten through the first twenty-four hours. Richards would know he was serious. He'd stopped feeling like he was sliding into an abyss.

He reached 78th Street, where Fort Hamilton Parkway veers to the right and crosses the BQE.

And then he saw it: the traffic slowing to a crawl.

Must be an accident on the bridge. It'll be slow, but I'll make it.

But when he pulled onto the Gowanus Expressway, everyone ground to a halt.

Three lanes of vehicles stood still.

***

Kim and Stransky stopped at Brooklyn South to bring Driscoll up to date. "But I just don't understand why no one in the Seven-Six would tell us what Hughes and Benson were doing there. It's not like they had anything to hide."

"They were probably afraid you'd make an issue of Hughes driving his girlfriend home," Driscoll replied. "There's no way they would have been doing that without their supervising officer knowing, and maybe even the precinct commander. And, let's face it, if you were the commanding officer, what would you have done about it?"

"Which is one reason I will never be anyone's supervising officer. But, since you asked, I'd have looked at it as an interesting take on community policing."

Driscoll snickered. "They'd never expect a former IAB detective to believe that."

"People need to get past that."

She paused to check the text she'd received from Bob while driving. *Checked three shooting ranges in Queens and two in Brooklyn. Got one "maybe" on the SIG Sauer. Promises from all to keep a sharp eye for all three pieces.*

She texted back. *Nice work, Bob. On your way home?*

"Where does this leave you with the investigation of Thursday's shooting?" Driscoll asked.

"We know what they were doing there, we know they were there every night they were on the graveyard shift, and we can assume that the shooter figured out the pattern, which explains how he knew where to wait. They parked at the same intersection every night, so the shooter didn't need to follow them in, he was already there when they pulled in."

Kim's cell pinged. Another text from Bob. *The BQE is a parking lot! WTF!*

Kim and Driscoll exchanged glances. Driscoll returned to the squad room, where a TV was on. A moment later he returned. "CHE has shut down traffic on the Verrazano."

Kim texted the information to Bob. *Get off the highway and take the ferry back to Staten Island.*

It was less than a minute when she got his response. *I'm locked in! I can't move!*

Oh, shit. *Leave the car. Text me the location.*

# CHAPTER THIRTY-EIGHT

Bob called Dr. Richards, but it rang and then went to voicemail. Right. She didn't have office hours on Saturday, so she wasn't near her phone, which was in her office. He tried checking for her number on the online directories, but all he could find was her office number.

He texted Kim and asked her to use police resources to get the number.

After a half hour, she replied that she had come up empty.

Even if he abandoned his car, which he was considering, he wasn't going to make it.

Movement to his right. Not much, but something.

Space in the right lane. He moved into it. If they didn't clear the blockage on the bridge, he'd be forced into a desperate move.

The car moving on the right stopped. Bob was stuck between lanes. He checked his watch. 12:45.

He waved to the driver he'd just cut off, gesturing to back up. The driver spread his hands. Helpless. Bob held up his hand showing thumb and forefinger barely apart.

The other driver, nodding, backed up but not enough. Bob held up his thumb and forefinger again, and the driver, with a look of exasperation, again backed up, this time drawing a long horn blast from the car behind him. He held up both hands.

Bob gave him a thumbs-up. He had space to cut across the lane, but possibly not enough to turn once he got to the shoulder. What was worse, he'd be pulling onto an embankment.

Deep breath.

He inched his way between the two cars and rocked with the bump of the curb of the shoulder. After stopping to cut the wheel as hard to the left as possible, he again inched forward, desperate not to hit either car as he turned.

The right side of the front bumper hit the guard rail between the shoulder of the highway and Gatling Place, which ran alongside. He stopped and cut the wheel hard to the right and shifted into reverse. But the moment he moved, the driver behind him leaned on the horn.

Okay, okay, give me a break.

He cut the wheel back to the left. The car that had been in front of him inched forward just a bit. He moved forward. He might just have enough…

His bumper ran against the guard rail with a loud screech. But he was clear of the other car, so he pulled up on the embankment, shut off the engine, locked the car and climbed over the guard rail and onto Gatling Place, crossing to the right-hand side and walking as quickly as he could up to 84th Street. He was four blocks from the 86th Street R train station, fifteen stops from Whitehall Street, from which he'd walk to the Staten Island ferry.

A glance at his watch. 1:10.

***

Kim invited Driscoll to join her and Stansky back at Brooklyn North for the update of Colangelo, and he accepted. She also wanted to get the latest from Vitello on the Red Hook crime scene.

But as they entered the Castle, Marshal Dhillon called out to her. "Detective Kim, Captain Colangelo is looking for you. Very upset."

"Thanks, Marshal. And if you see Phil Vitello, please send him in." They found the captain, Bostwick, and the team in the conference room.

"Kim," Colangelo said, "where have you been? We've been trying to raise you on the radio for almost an hour."

She and Stransky exchanged looks. "We never heard anything, Captain. I'll refer the car to the motor pool to check the radio…"

Bostwick took over. "Never mind that. Where the hell is Bob? No one's seen him since early this morning."

"That's right. He came in early and signed in. Marshal Dhillon can vouch for him. He went to check on several shooting ranges to see if he could drum up any leads on our three shooters."

"How long could that take?" Bostwick asked. "There are two shooting ranges in Brooklyn."

"There are also three in Queens; he checked those too. He asked me to sign out for him, which I intended to do when I got back. He said something about an appointment. I didn't expect to be this late getting back."

"What kind of appointment?" Colangelo this time.

"I didn't ask, and I wouldn't try to guess. He wanted me to sign him out at noon, and I will. Now, what's all the commotion about?"

"Prinz and his pals have shut down the Verrazano," Colangelo said. "It's all over the news stations, he's yelling about a 'white war'."

"I know that, I heard about it at Brooklyn South while I was briefing Lieutenant Driscoll. I'm sorry about that, especially since it's going to play hell with Bob making his appointment, but since we're not SRG, I don't see how it concerns us."

Vitello joined them. "I heard you were looking for me, Kim. We got information on the prints we took yesterday morning. Tires first. Heavy tread, most likely from an SUV, and the wear pattern suggests that the owner has done a fair amount of off-road driving."

"Can we narrow down the type of SUV?" Kim asked.

"Not from the tracks alone. That takes us to the footprint. Or, should I say, boot print? Heavy boot, definitely military."

"Could the vehicle be a Hummer?" Stransky asked.

"Not likely," Kim said. "That would stick out like a sore thumb in the Red Hook waterfront. I'm thinking a bit smaller, and maybe more rugged looking, like a Jeep Cherokee or Liberty."

"What about a Range Rover?" Brogan asked.

"Their compact is the Evoque," Vitello said. "And it looks like something a suburban soccer mom would drive."

"We're looking for something bursting with testosterone," Kim said, making Vera giggle.

"No," Vitello said. "Kim is right. Ford came out with a version of its Bronco a few years ago, called Badlands. And the tire print would fit that."

"So, what are you saying?" Colangelo asked. "We need to do a search on all Jeep Cherokees and Ford Broncos registered in the city?"

Kim laughed. "No, Captain. This is useful information, to which we need to keep adding. At some point, someone will tell us, 'It's a black Jeep Cherokee' or 'a flat gray Bronco Badlands' and then we can start searching databases." She turned back to Vitello. "Any other juicy tidbits to file away for later?"

"Just that the boot print we found is from the wearer's left foot and shows extremely heavy pronation."

It rang a bell. "Which means he has flat feet, and so he either was never in the army, or he may have suffered an injury that got him discharged."

"How do you know that?" Driscoll asked.

It was Cord who answered. "She's a runner. And it sounds like we've got the beginning of a profile."

Marshal Dhillon burst in. "You need to see this, I think."

Everyone in the squad room was crowded around the wide screen TV.

"We repeat, the New York City Police Department has deployed the controversial Strategic Resource Group to crush the peaceful demonstration by CHE on the Verrazano-Narrows Bridge. *City News* special reporter Rita Henshaw is on the scene."

The reporter appeared, decked out in protective gear.

"Nice touch," Bostwick said.

"Are we live? Thank you. This is Rita Henshaw reporting from the Brooklyn side of the Verrazano-Narrows Bridge, where moments ago an NYPD riot squad waded into peaceful protesters armed with clubs and tasers and forcibly removed them and placed them all, including their leader, Felipe Prinz, under arrest. According to our early reports, several protesters, none of whom were armed, were seriously injured. Speaker Lawrence Barnett has said he will convene a session of the City Council to consider legislation to defund the police department."

# CHAPTER THIRTY-NINE

By the time Bob arrived at Dr. Richards' house, it was nearly three. He'd run every chance he got, including up the steep hill from the ferry to Dr. Richards' house in St. George. It took another ten minutes for her to answer the door. "You're two hours late, and you look like you spent it at a tavern."

He was still gasping. "No."

"Then what's your excuse? Your dog ate my card?" She started to close the door.

He slammed his hand against it to stop her. "It was not my fault that some son of a bitch shut down the Verrazano Bridge, and it was not possible to foresee that event. If you bother to check your office voicemail, you will see that I left several messages."

She rolled her eyes. "Right."

"Check. I'll wait. Go ahead. I didn't know what had happened on the bridge when I got on the Gowanus in Bay Ridge, but when I found out, I left my car and came here by public transportation, including running up that fucking hill. Now, you check those messages, and if there are none, I'll go quietly."

"It's all right. I…"

"No. Check them. You can't trust me. I'm a drunk."

She called voicemail while he waited at her door.

After she listened, he asked. "How many messages did I leave?"

"Five. Detective Nolan, I apologize. But…"

"I know. You couldn't trust me. I wouldn't have, either."

"Please come in. Would you like some coffee? Something to eat?"

***

Jake was already dressed in his best suit when she walked into the apartment. "Will we make it?"

It was 5:25. "Yes, but we'll be fashionably late. Anyway, I'm not sure I can stomach a ninety-minute cocktail hour."

Forty-five minutes later, she emerged wearing a black cocktail dress she'd bought for Jake's parents' fiftieth anniversary, black suede pumps, and a pearl choker with matching earrings. She'd also spent more time applying makeup than in the past month, combined.

Jake popped out of his chair. "Wow! The hell with the judge. Let's eat in."

She kissed his cheek, careful not to leave any lipstick. "You know we can't."

Despite the proximity of the Marriott, they took a cab over.

"You're going to get a lot of comments, you know." Jake cast a sidelong glance at her. "You'd better hope Brandt isn't there."

Her heart sank. He'd said it as a joke, but she could hear the tension underneath. "It wouldn't matter if he was. You know that."

But as they alighted from the cab, she spied Justin Cates at the main entrance.

Justin waited as they approached. "Good evening. Kim, you are a vision. Jake, great to see you." As they started inside, Justin lowered his voice and added, "No, he's not coming tonight. He was invited but declined."

"So, you're here as his eyes and ears?" She shot him a conspiratorial grin.

"I'm here with Ricky."

"Going public at last?"

"Most people already know, anyway. You two are at our table." He stepped aside and allowed her and Jake to get on the elevator, first. As soon as the door closed, he turned serious. "We're at Bryce Mitchell's table."

Her inner alarm sounded. "Whose idea was that?"

"Mitchell's. He wasn't happy that the judge wanted you there, and I suspect he wants to keep an eye on you."

She was already regretting coming. "For God's sake, we're supposed to be on the same side. What other surprises await me? Best to give it to me all at once."

"The police commissioner and the Brooklyn North borough commander are the only others from the department. The rest are other judges, lawyers, and a few media types."

She was sure Joanna wouldn't be among them.

"The lobby outside the ballroom is where the cocktail hour is taking place," he added as the elevator door opened.

Kim did a quick scan to satisfy her concern that she was neither under- nor over-dressed. Rick Conti, standing with Judge Vickers, waved them over. "Your honor, I'm sure you remember Detective Brady."

He took her hand. "So glad you could come."

"Thank you, your honor. And this is my husband, Jake Dudek."

He shook Jake's hand. "Director of Analytics for my favorite basketball team. An honor, Mr. Dudek."

"The honor is mine," Jake replied.

The judge introduced Jake to his clerk. "An even bigger fan than I am."

The clerk grabbed Jake's hand. "This is great…" and steered him away.

The judge turned back to Kim. "I've always thought you were attractive, but tonight… You are a beautiful woman."

She refused to give herself over to a flood of flattery. "Thank you, but I'm curious—why are you so glad I came?"

He turned serious. "Because I have an abiding respect for you. We have crossed paths several times in the past few years…"

"You could say we've crossed swords." She wondered if he'd chuckle.

He did. "I could, but I didn't. When we've disagreed, you've always remained reasonable and professional. So much so that I've often wondered why you didn't go to law school."

"My dad wanted me to, but I preferred to join the force."

"Like your father and your grandfather. And you do them both proud. Despite my reputation to the contrary, I have great respect for the police and the work they do. But, as you know, probably better than most, given your experience in Internal Affairs, not all police respect the law or those of us who struggle to maintain a balance between public safety and individual rights. But you do."

She accepted a glass of white wine from a passing server. "Thank you."

"This case you're on now has the whole city concerned. Do you think the speculation about ultranationalists is correct?"

So, that was it. "Your honor, you know I can't discuss an ongoing investigation, especially to speculate on a possible outcome to you."

He took a sip of his own drink, which appeared to be his preferred Jack Daniels on the rocks. "You will probably need to tell me sooner or later, and I prefer to avoid surprises." His manner remained sociable, but the tenor had shifted a bit.

She turned serious. "I may very well need a warrant or a subpoena at some point, you are correct. I may need to testify at trial with your honor presiding. If and when I do, I'd prefer to come before you with no preconceived notions."

"I should have known."

She allowed herself a small smirk. "Indeed. I'll just say this—I try never to jump to conclusions until the evidence is in."

"Fair enough. Enjoy the evening, Detective. I hope we get to chat a little more later."

# CHAPTER FORTY

Dr. Richards apologized and agreed to take Bob on as a patient. She would see him twice each week, and he'd agreed to attend weekly AA meetings without fail.

His ground-floor apartment felt desolate, but there was nothing to tempt him. He took out a burger from the refrigerator and tossed it into a skillet, suddenly hungry.

He pulled his cell from his shirt pocket, remembering he'd silenced the ringer when he'd arrived at Dr. Richards' house. It had buzzed a couple of times, but he'd ignored it, then forgotten it.

There were texts from Kim, asking if he was all right and telling him she'd be at some dinner for Let 'em Run Ron. Now, that was funny.

He texted her he was fine and would see her in the morning. Then, he turned the ringer back on.

It rang just as he teams flipping the burger. "Detective Nolan? Manny, the manager of the Ridgewood Range from this morning. A guy was in here target shooting with a Glock 34 who looks like he could be one of the guys in the pictures you showed me. Not the sketch guy; one of the others. He bought a box of nine-millimeter +P ammo."

Bob checked his watch. Almost 7:00. And his car was still sitting on the shoulder of the BQE. "You're open until nine, right?"

"Yes, sir."

"Okay, I'll try to make it tonight. If not, I'll see you Monday morning. And thanks."

He tossed the burger into the garbage and filled the skillet with water and detergent while he tried to figure his best option. He could take a Lyft to where he'd left the car in Bay Ridge, but the Traffic Division would have almost certainly towed it by now. That meant it would likely be at the Brooklyn Navy Yard.

At least he'd had the good sense to leave his laptop locked in his desk at the Castle.

The doorbell rang.

It was Martin Stransky. "Hey, nice to see you haven't fallen off the face of the Earth."

"Thanks. What brings you here?"

"I brought your car, which I rescued from the BQE before the tow trucks could get to it. Then, thanks to the SRG, the mess on the bridge was cleared this afternoon, so I was able to deliver it without too much fuss."

Bob shook his hand. "Thanks very much. I'll drive you home if you don't mind making a stop first."

***

"You're Kim Brady, aren't you? Rita Henshaw, *City News*."

Kim showed no sign of recognition. "Nice to meet you."

"May I ask you something off the record?"

Kim flashed a humorless smile. "It's been my experience that off-the-record comments have a nasty habit of becoming on-the-record with no notice."

"I assure you; this is solely for my own personal knowledge. Is it true that you are here at the specific invitation of the judge?"

She couldn't think of any harm it would do, and it was true. "Yes, why?"

"I'm just curious. Judge Vickers isn't known for his friendships with law enforcement."

"I respect his position, and I believe he respects mine." Also true, and harmless, but this was moving a little closer to the edge.

"Interesting, especially as you seem to have a similar relationship with the current mayor."

Uh huh. "What's your point?"

Henshaw feigned innocence. "No point, just asking. I'm told the mayor admires you greatly."

"You should discuss that with him. I'm just a cop on the job."

"Thanks, I'll keep that in mind. You've got a tough one now, though, with these ultranationalist shootings."

Kim gave her a wide-eyed look of surprise. "You know this? Do you have further information I can use?"

"No, not information, exactly, but it seems obvious that…"

"Relying on one's own preconceived notions is not a useful investigative technique. Tell you what, Ms. Henshaw, you stick to your job, and I'll stick to mine. And if you want to know about an ongoing investigation, please contact DCPI."

***

Once outside, Martin told Bob he had company—his wife, Marisa. She would follow them to Queens and then drive Martin home.

"After we've stopped somewhere for something to eat," Bob had said.

As they entered the building, completely devoid of signage, Bob noted something he hadn't seen that morning—a video camera. When Manny greeted them, the first thing Bob said after introducing Marisa and Martin was, "Did you get video of him?"

"I haven't checked, yet." He gestured behind him. "But I'm sure we got him." Behind the counter were two cameras. "You were right, the pics you got don't show much about his face. But when you see him, it's obvious he's a pretty good match. He wasn't wearing the shirt with the star, just a khaki tee and camo cargo pants."

"Do you require any ID?"

"Yep. A driver's license or other state ID." He pulled out a photocopy. "We scan every one of 'em." He returned to his station behind the counter and tapped several buttons on a keyboard. A printer on the shelf behind him sprang to life, and a moment later, he handed Bob a copy.

Bob studied it. "Did his face match the photo?"

"Sure did. A twenty-second check."

"Had you ever seen him before?" Bob asked.

"I don't recall it, but according to our system's records, he's been here several times." The manager clicked a few more buttons, and the printer spit out another sheet. "This is what the video cameras caught.

Bob did his own twenty second check, then handed the copy of the driver's license to Stransky. "Let's check this out on the DMV database. I'd be surprised if the license is really his."

"If it ain't," Stransky replied, "it's a damned good phony."

"Thank you." Bob shook the manager's hand. "This is a huge help. If he comes in again, please call me right away."

***

Kim wasn't surprised when she was waylaid by the commissioner. "Good evening, sir. I'm surprised to see you here."

Not even a hint of a smile. "As I am to see you. I'm afraid this does little to help your claim of wishing to avoid politics, but I must say you look very… attractive tonight."

"Thank you. My husband likes to say I 'fix up good'. As for politics, I would hope you've realized by now that they find me, I don't seek them."

He showed a glimmer of good humor. "So it seems. I couldn't help noticing you chatting with that reporter from *City News*."

Kim recounted the conversation.

The commissioner paused to digest it. "I think you handled it perfectly. But I need to know: whom do you think is behind these shootings?"

"Are you asking me if it's possible that Felipe Prinz could be right?" When he nodded, she said, "I can only say that it's highly unlikely. I've asked Agent Taylor of the FBI for any information he might have on ultranationalist groups, but I think…"

The commissioner held up a hand and pulled out his cell. "Yes?... When?... Where?... Are you sure?... All right, thank you."

Kim's internal alarm was already screaming. "That sounded serious."

He held up a finger to ask her to wait and pulled up another number on his cell. "Captain Colangelo?... Yes, it's me. I'm at the dinner for Vickers with Detective Brady. I've just been informed of another police shooting near the 74th Street and Roosevelt Avenue subway station in Jackson Heights… yes, that's the One-Fifteen. Two officers, Juanita Lopez and Aroldis Figueroa. I am personally assigning this shooting to your task force. Hold a moment." He turned to Kim. "How quickly can you get over there?"

"I can call the other members of my team and get them moving right away. I'll need to change into something more appropriate."

He looked her up and down, smirking. "You don't have the time."

She recalled another time when she'd been dressed up for an evening out and had been summoned to a crime scene. She'd gone wearing heels and had regretted it. "I'll just change my shoes, then."

"Thank you." He turned back to the phone. "Kim is leaving now. Please get Sergeant Vitello there, too." He ended the call. "Get your husband as quietly as you can. Not a word to anyone. I'll explain to the judge."

# CHAPTER FORTY-ONE

The head of the NYPD security detail at the hotel arranged for a squad car to drive Kim and Jake home. While on the way, she called Bob, and was glad to hear that Martin and Marisa were with him. Then she called Tim Brogan.

"Are you really not going to change?" Jake asked as they entered the apartment.

"Shoes only." She pulled on an old pair of running shoes that were too worn to be used for running. She also checked to be sure she had her badge and took her Chief's Special from the safe.

"How will you carry that?" Jake asked.

Good question. She put it back and took her Glock 21 and its shoulder holster and slipped it on over the cocktail dress.

"Very ladylike." Jake suppressed a chuckle. "Want me to drive you?"

"No, that's okay. I'll check in with you every hour or so by text. I doubt I'll have time to chat."

Driving up the BQE, she reflected on what Bob had said. "We got a photo on a suspect." She hadn't had time to digest anything else, but that was intriguing. She activated Bluetooth in their car and called Colangelo.

He was chuckling when he answered. "I can't wait to see you when you get here."

"I didn't have time to change."

"That's what I mean. Tim is already here, and the others are en route. The guys from the Queens ME office just arrived, so we may have more information for you when you get here. So, please don't be reckless."

***

Bob's first thought as he followed Martin and Marisa up 69th Street in Maspeth was to be thankful Marisa had suggested eating at Rosa's Pizza, which had not only been as good as she'd claimed but had made the run up to Jackson Heights a lot easier. Because whoever had laid out the street plan for Southern Queens must have wanted to make driving pure hell. At least the lights were with them. They only ran a few reds.

Martin turned right onto Woodside Avenue and then left on 75th Street. They parked at Broadway, where local police already had the area blocked off.

Bob immediately spotted Vitello. "What do we know?"

***

Kim got off the BQE at the Broadway/Roosevelt Avenue exit, which put her on Broadway heading southeast. She got as close as she could and parked in front of a restaurant called Kababish. She ran toward the barricades the One-Fifteen had set up and held out her badge.

"You Brady?" a sergeant asked.

"That's me."

He gave her the once-over. "The commissioner told us to expect you, but…"

No time for this. "What do you have so far?"

"Two dead cops. Damned good ones."

"Do you know how it happened?"

"They were stationed at the subway stop, posted in the area outside the turnstiles."

"Were they shot inside the station?"

"No, they came outside on break. They were walking up Broadway, heading for that Kababish place for something to eat. It's a favorite for a lot of our guys."

"What time was that?"

"About 7:15, maybe a little earlier. They were on the four-to-twelve."

"Where were they shot?"

The sergeant pointed to a spot she'd passed walking down. "See that construction site beyond the group of stores? Right there. Two slugs each in the back. Sorry, Detective, that's all I know." His eyes lingered on her bust line.

"Thanks, Sergeant. I see my captain." Maybe she should have chosen a dress that showed a little less cleavage.

Colangelo appeared like he wanted to make an inappropriate comment but changed his mind. "Aren't you chilly?"

"Not yet." She should have brought a sweater.

Bob, Martin, Tim, and Marisa all ran up and began speaking at once.

"We have a lead on the shooter."

"Bob rescued his car."

"Vitello's here and has…"

"You look lovely, but those shoes clash with that dress."

Kim acknowledged the last comment first. "Thank you, Marisa. I once raced to a crime scene in heels and swore I'd never do that again. Okay, one at a time. Bob first. Tell me about the shooter."

Bob recounted what they'd learned at the shooting range. "I'm sure the license is doctored, but the photo on it matches the screenshot from the security video. What's more, the timing fits.

He left the range at 5:45, which gave him plenty of time to be here and positioned to shoot by 7:00."

Kim studied the photocopy of the license and the printout from the video. It wasn't the guy in the sketch, but it was the first one she'd spotted in the photos from the Park Row cameras. Definitely Latino. "This is a break, no question. What else do we have?"

Brogan was next. "Vitello's guys recovered four shells. And the ME confirms both victims suffered two gunshot wounds in the back."

Kim was staring at the spot where the two slain officers lay. Vitello was chatting with someone, probably a technician from the ME office. "I need a closer look."

Marisa walked next to Kim. "I spoke to several people on the street, but the most helpful was the guy at the food cart on the corner of 73rd Street. When he heard the shots, he immediately looked over. A moment later, he saw a black Jeep pull out and drive up Broadway toward the BQE."

"Did he say what kind of Jeep?"

"No, just a Jeep. He'd seen it a little earlier because it passed him on the corner, turning onto Broadway, and it nearly hit a pedestrian."

Kim took out her cell, opened her Notes App, and made an entry.

"Ah, the lovely Kim," Vitello called out. "Glad to see you ditched the heels before dropping by." He obviously remembered the last time.

"Talk to me, Phil. Martin said you recovered shells."

"Yes, nine-millimeter +P shells, to be precise. Ballistics should be able to tell us if they match the ones from the Park shooting."

She thought of Cord. "I guess this time he wasn't taking any chances."

"Jumping to conclusions, Kim? That's not like you."

"Not jumping, just allowing for the possibility." Her voice trailed off as she surveyed the crime scene. "Any exit wounds on the victims?"

"One on one victim, none on the other. What are you thinking?"

She approached the victims, turning to face the curbside dining shed of the restaurant at the end of the chain of stores. "That shed is the furthest point from which to shoot. But he was probably closer to here. He'd have wanted to shoot as soon as they passed his vehicle."

"And as far from the shed as possible," Bob said. "Those shots would have sounded like cannon fire."

"Phil, what's the closest he could have been to get off a shot, assuming he was right-handed?" Kim asked.

Vitello walked several feet. "Here, assuming he leaned out the window."

Kim stood in the spot and leaned to her right, pointing an imaginary weapon. "And what if he was left-handed?"

"He could have shot as soon as they passed him."

She approached the technician. "I know we'll need to wait until the autopsy for a definite answer, but can you tell me if the slugs entered the officers' bodies at an angle?"

The technician glanced down at the bodies. "Judging by the one exit wound, I'd say there was little or no angle between entry and exit. Straight through."

She made another note. "Guys, we now can assume our shooter is left-handed."

Colangelo gathered them together. "I want to thank all of you for responding as quickly as you did, and for the thorough job you did once you arrived. We'll get the group together tomorrow at the Castle for a full briefing, but I'll give Lieutenant Bostwick the skinny tonight, as well as the commissioner."

"I'll call Driscoll once I'm back in my car." Kim shivered slightly against the encroaching chill. She scanned the block. "I can't believe there aren't any security cameras in sight. An area this busy, so close to a major transit hub…"

"I see one of ours." Stransky pointed to the light pole on the corner of 73rd Street.

Kim followed it. "I'll be damned, right next to the food cart. Okay, Martin, first thing in the morning, check the RTCC. Also, check the camera map for any others in the area. We need to know how he came here and how he escaped. No guesswork."

# CHAPTER FORTY-TWO

Kim got back in her car, started the engine, and turned on the heater. She was freezing.

And she hadn't checked in with Jake since she'd arrived.

She had five texts from Jake and two missed calls, plus she had another text from a number she didn't recognize.

She called Jake first and assured him she was all right and was on her way home.

The text from the strange number was next. *I must reach out to you, oh noble sister of the knighthood. For I have a sense of great foreboding for our order.* Lodemay. The message had been received at 8:05, while she was speeding to the crime scene. Nothing had been said to the press. In fact, she'd seen no press vans at all at the scene. *I've not had a sense of such impending doom since our horrific loss of Jerusalem to Saladin in 1187. I beg you to be most careful, oh fair lady, and take no risks to defeat the infidel.*

She debated calling him but decided against it. He was obviously agitated, and she didn't want to make it worse.

But how had he known?

***

Justin was talking to Rick and Judge Vickers as the dinner was winding down and people were leaving. The commissioner had left right after Kim, along with the Brooklyn borough commander.

"The commissioner requested I not say anything about the shooting," Vickers said, "so I didn't. If anyone asks, all I knew was that he left on urgent police business."

"Word must have gotten out, somehow," Justin said. "Around 8:30, I saw Rita Henshaw rush out. Kim said nothing other than it was an emergency, but I guessed right away."

"Has she mentioned who she thinks might be responsible?" the judge asked.

Sorry, Judge, you're not getting it out of me. "If she had, I'm sure she would have sworn me to secrecy."

***

Kim finally stopped shivering and decided to answer Lodemay's text. *I'm always careful, John, but thank you for thinking of me. We'll talk soon.* Like tomorrow. Because something had triggered his fear.

Sudden tapping on the driver's side window made her jump.

Joanna Dunbar. "Got a minute?"

Kim lowered the window, irritated at the prospect of letting cold air in. "You know I can't talk about it."

"Two more nonwhite victims."

As much as she wanted to snap at Joanna, she knew she needed the white ultranationalist theory to stay in the mainstream. "True. Have you gotten anything like a manifesto?" It was worth a shot.

"If I had, you'd be the first to know. Any idea why they chose here? A block away from Diversity Plaza?"

"Nope." But she knew why. It kept the notion of white ultranationalists alive. She also knew that fairy tale was about to be shattered, regardless of what she wanted. "I'm sorry, Joanna, I really can't go into it. You must trust me."

***

"It's all over the news."

Kim loved it when Jake hit her with something like that the moment she walked in.

"I've been bouncing between *City News* and ITN. Henshaw and Dunbar. Henshaw seems pissed that you guys aren't admitting this the work of an ultranationalist cabal."

"She was at the event tonight. I had to tell her off. I guess it didn't take. Another fan I won't have."

He took her in his arms. "You okay? You must have been freezing out there."

"I'm fine." Her cell rang. She glanced at the screen. It was the mayor. "Oh, God damn it!" She considered ignoring the call, but that would only make things worse. "Yes, Mr. Mayor."

"What the hell happened?"

"This is totally improper, sir. You should be asking the commissioner."

"He doesn't know anything, yet, but you must."

Either Colangelo hadn't yet reported up the chain, or the commissioner was playing hard to get. Better if it was the former. "I just got home."

"Then you can talk."

She told him everything they'd learned.

"So, you know they're not white."

Just what she'd known he'd say. "Yes, but we can't allow that to be known, nor can we say we know what the shooter looks like or even that we have a lead."

"The city needs assurances the police are on this. Barnett wants to defund the department and spend it all on social programs."

"Mr. Barnett is your problem, Mr. Mayor, not mine. The minute we let it be known for certain that these guys aren't white, the minute we kill that theory, these killers will change tactics. They'll probably kill tonight's shooter as a bad security risk, which he very likely is. We know there are at least two shooters, possibly three. There may be more."

"So, you agree it's a conspiracy of some kind."

"Yes. Now, you've had your briefing, Mr. Mayor, so please allow me time with my husband."

His voice grew softer. "Thank you, Kim."

"I've told you before, Detective Brady, please." The minute she said it, she knew it had been a mistake.

# CHAPTER FORTY-THREE

*Sunday, April 27, 7:45 a.m.*

Kim had been exhausted and skipped her morning run, but she was out the door before Jake was up. She made a mental note to check in with him during the day.

Marshal Dhillon was coming on duty, and PBBN was at its normal level of activity.

Kim called Driscoll and asked him to come in for a status conference at nine. "And please bring anyone you can with you."

As soon as Colangelo came in, she followed him upstairs and told him about her call from the mayor the night before. "It was after eleven."

Colangelo dropped into his chair. "I called the commissioner from my car on the way home."

"Which means the commissioner was holding back."

"That would be my guess. I suspect the mayor's effort to promote you via holy writ still rankles. Before our meeting, I'll call him and get his side of it. This is no time for internecine squabbling."

When she returned to the squad room, Cord was at his desk. "Vera's here, too. She wouldn't let me come unless she could keep an eye on me. She's over at the deli getting some coffees."

He looked better today. "Good. We need everyone we can get." She gave him the latest.

"Ah!" Vera called as she returned balancing two trays of coffees, one on top of the other. "Is Brilliant American Lady Detective."

"And good morning to you, Beautiful Émigré IT Genius."

"If we can adjourn the mutual admiration society," Cord said, "what can I do to assist?"

"We need to track last night's shooter. Cord, I need you to get into the RTCC and access the data from the police camera at Broadway and 73rd Street in Jackson Heights." She drew a crude map of the area. "Here's the corner—it's a sharp right onto Broadway—and here are the storefronts, ending with this restaurant… with this curbside shed… followed by a stretch with plywood walls for a construction project… followed by more stores… to the corner of 72nd Street." She marked an X where the two officers were shot. "We're looking for a black Jeep that turned that corner sometime between 6:30 and 7:15 and then parked somewhere between here…" She made a dot next to the shed. "… and here." She made another one next to the X.

Cord studied the map. "Got it."

"Not done, yet. With luck, the shooting was caught by the camera, as well as the direction he went afterward. I need however much as you can. Print out as many screenshots as possible. If he turned onto 72nd Street, we need to know that, and we need to track him, whatever he did. So, I'll need information on the location of every NYPD camera in that neighborhood, and along whatever route he took."

"Is that all? I mean, before lunch, that is."

"I'm hoping to have some extra pairs of hands to help you before long." She told him about the 9:00 meeting.

Cord reached over and took Vera's hand. "I've already got one."

"Is true. I am at your service."

"She's even a bigger whiz at the RTCC than I am," Cord said. And that was saying a lot.

"Thanks, guys." She laid a copy of the shooter's driver's license on the desk. "Vera, I need you to track this license. It's almost certainly someone else's with this photo pasted on, but see what you can find out."

***

Justin had given the mayor a minute-by-minute description of the dinner for Judge Vickers last night, including the chat he'd seen but not heard between the judge and Kim and the lengthy speech given by Speaker Barnett outlining his plan for new policing legislation. The mayor was now recounting it all for his top contributor, Kyle Emory, omitting the part about Kim.

How stunning she must have looked.

"So," Emory said, "Mr. Barnett is going on the attack. I can't say I'm surprised. He seems to be getting a boost with these shootings and all the talk about white ultranationalists. I take it your star detective hasn't gathered any information with which to fight that canard."

"How do you know it's a canard?"

"Isn't it?"

He didn't like lying to Emory, but Kim had had a point. "That's what the police are trying to determine. This has shocked the city, and…"

"It certainly has. And, according to the news reports this morning, Mr. Barnett would like to put the police out of business. You need to fight fire with fire."

"I think the neighborhoods will help. They know they need a strong police force."

"Raymond, remember the neighborhoods have little to say about who runs this city. The elites hold power, through contributions and activism, and these days they hold the keys to most of the media outlets in this city." He stood to leave. "By the way, the impression I'm getting is that you and your police commissioner don't seem to get on too well. If you want to be a law-and-order mayor, you need to repair that."

***

Whenever Kim ended a call, her cell rang again. But this one saved her from making a call of her own.

"I thought you might need to hear a friendly voice this morning." It was Ken Taylor.

"I've heard several so far." Although Jake's had not been among them. Another call she needed to make before the 9:00 meeting. "I'm e-mailing a scan of a driver's license we're certain belongs to last night's shooter. I've already sent a copy to our Face Recognition Unit, but I'd like you to let me know if it rings a bell."

"Sure thing. But is it legit?"

"The license probably isn't, but the photo is the key."

"Send it. I'll get back to you."

Next, she called Jake's cell. It went right to voicemail. He must be talking with someone else. She shot him a text. *Tried to call but I guess you're busy. I have a meeting in ten minutes, so if you can call me before then, I'd love to hear from you. Otherwise, I'll call you after the meeting. Love you.*

"Kim?" Cord waved her over. "You need to see this."

On his screen was a paused video from the camera on Broadway. The clock in the corner indicated 18:42—6:42 p.m. in military time. The image showed the food cart, several pedestrians, and a black Jeep Wrangler. "I've scanned from 18:15 to 19:30. This is the only SUV to turn that corner. Now…" He hit play and then paused it.

The Wrangler had moved a short distance but was under the streetlight and beyond the food cart.

"There's no one in the passenger's seat," Kim said. Then, she saw it. "Those tires are huge."

"That's why she's the best." Vitello had joined them. "Those are Cooper Evolution M/T tires. Made for heavy off-road use." He handed her the lab report. "That's the report on the impressions we took in Red Hook."

"Cooper Evolution M/T tires." She turned back to Cord. "Roll it."

On the screen, the Wrangler made the sharp right, passed the restaurant, and pulled over several yards beyond the shed.

"Close to where the bodies were found," Kim said. "Our shooter is a left-handed shot."

"Which explains why the shot that hit me in the park entered at an angle. A right-handed shooter would've had a more direct line of fire." Cord's tone was detached and analytical. He hit play.

Nothing changed until the two officers approached, passed the Wrangler, and, a moment later, both collapsed on the sidewalk.

The Wrangler pulled away from the curb and drove at a normal speed up Broadway.

"He didn't turn," Kim said.

"Doesn't surprise me." Bob had joined them just as Cord had begun the video. "Less chance that he'd pass someone closely enough for them to ID him. Easier to drive up Broadway and get lost in the traffic."

"Now for bad news," Vera said. "Is no other police camera on Broadway anywhere. And, more bad news, I checked DMV database. This license number does not exist."

# CHAPTER FORTY-FOUR

Colangelo called the meeting to order and then promptly turned everything over to Kim.

Martin had brought Marisa along, and Driscoll had brought two detectives from his Brooklyn South Homicide Unit, Doug Cameron and Andy Costello. With Bostwick, Tim Brogan, and Phil Vitello, that brought their number to twelve. They'd rolled extra chairs into the crowded conference room.

Kim recapped everything they had, including the latest information on the Wrangler. "We couldn't get the plate number from the video. We also came up empty on the driver's license ID number."

"Can I see it?" Vitello studied the printout. "Anyone have a magnifying glass?"

Kim was about to chuckle when Bostwick produced one.

Vitello studied the image more closely. "The number's been altered." He waved Kim over. "See? The last six digits are slightly mis-aligned with the first three. He managed to find a number that hasn't been used yet. Which means he's either very lucky or very smart."

"Or he knows someone at the DMV." Kim moved on. "Okay. He made the turn off 73rd Street, a one-way street going south. He then proceeded north on Broadway."

"Going back the way he came?" Bob asked.

"Or trying to throw us off." It was Andy Costello's first comment since the introductions.

"He's already been sloppy," Kim said, "so I'm leaning toward the former. We need to see if we can track his approach and his route out."

Colangelo handed Kim a slip of notepaper. "I've discussed this with the precinct commander at the One-Fifteen. He's placed their detective squad at our disposal. He's expecting your call."

"Great. They can check private security cameras along the way and see if we can find a pattern for his approach. Doug and Andy, you guys can help, too. Bob, take them to the shooting location and work your way up Broadway. Check in during the day to keep Lieutenant Bostwick informed of your progress. Get flash drives of any videos you find that include the Wrangler. And if you get a shot with his plate number, let us know immediately." She turned back to Phil. "On the license, has the name has been altered?"

"Doesn't look like it," he replied.

"I did search on name," Vera said. "Is not in system, either. Not for registrations, either."

Kim checked the address on the license. "35-21 71st Street, East Elmhurst. Let's have the guys from the One-Fifteen check that one out, too."

Bob spoke up. "That's not East Elmhurst. That's Jackson Heights. What's the zip code?"

Kim checked. "11372."

"That's Jackson Heights, too." Bob shook his head. "It can't be that easy."

"We'll wait for the word from the One-Fifteen guys. In the meantime, Martin and Tim, I want you guys to work with Cord on the RTCC. I'm interested in anything to the northwest of the shooting."

Bostwick spoke up. "Isn't that putting all your eggs in one basket? Besides, both previous attacks were in Brooklyn, which suggests they may be based there. He might have gone north on Broadway only to the entrance to the BQE.

"Definitely a possibility," Kim said. "If either of our two teams come up with anything from private video to suggest a different direction, we'll adjust. Until then, let's try to get a leg up on these bastards. The name on the license is Henry Salcedo. Let's do a search on his name."

Cord glanced at the license. "He don't look like a Henry to me."

"Let's see what we find. Marisa, I'd like you to start checking social media for anything on this guy, or anything related to these shootings. Also, see if there's anything interesting on Prinz and CHE."

"And where will you be while we're all being busy bees?" Cord asked.

"Federal Plaza to see Ken Taylor."

***

Kim was walking toward the subway on Myrtle Avenue when her cell pinged. It was a text from Jake. *Meeting over yet?*

She answered immediately. *Just now.* A little fib, but she didn't want him to think she'd forgotten. Which she had. *I missed you this morning.*

She walked a half block, and no response. *Hey, you okay?*

She stopped, waiting for a response and ready to call if she didn't get one.

*Fine.*

She called, but he didn't answer. Back to texting. *Come on, Jake, I know you're there. Please pick up.* She called again.

"Yeah?" His voice was flat.

"What's the matter? Why won't you talk to me?"

"They fired me. The GM called me a little while ago. 'Going in a different direction,' he said."

"Oh, God, Jake I'm so sorry. But you'll find a better situation. I know you will."

"Hope so. But how will you feel about it?"

"I'll be thrilled, of course. Why wouldn't I be?"

"Even if it means moving to another city?"

She hadn't considered that. She hadn't even believed they would fire him. "We'll work out whatever comes. You know that." She glanced at her watch.

"Yeah." Clearly, he didn't believe that.

# CHAPTER FORTY-FIVE

Kim's head was still swimming when she took a seat in Ken Taylor's office.

"Thanks for stopping by, Kim. You must be totally swamped with this case. I forwarded the photo you sent me to our own Face Recognition Unit. We're linked in with Homeland Security, the CIA, and Army Intelligence."

That pulled her back. "Are any of those relevant?"

"It's possible. I'm hoping to hear back sometime today." He picked up a copy of the license she'd sent. "You see that extremely faint image of his photo? This is one of those Real ID licenses. It's impossible to pull the old trick of pasting a new photo over someone else's document. I'd thought it was equally impossible to alter the information on it, but he, or someone helping him, has clearly done that. So, this is his license."

Kim mentioned the number being changed as well. "This one doesn't exist."

"Another good reason to bring in the other agencies I mentioned. Altering this license took a lot of skill. You said you got this from a shooting range?"

"Yes, they'd scanned it."

"Scanned it or read the magnetic strip?"

"I don't know. I wasn't there. Bob Nolan was. Why?"

"See if you can find out. If they just scanned into a PC, that's one thing. But if they read the magnetic strip and got this, that means the information on the strip was altered, too, and that's something else we thought was impossible."

"I'll ask Bob to check it out." There was something else, but she couldn't remember.

"Hey, you okay?"

"My husband lost his job this morning. He's a basketball analytics guy and getting a new job may mean moving to a new city."

"Gee, Kim, sorry to hear that. I can't imagine the Department without you."

"And I can't imagine myself without the Department." Refocus. What was it? Right, Prinz. "I don't get what's going on with Prinz and CHE. Right after the shooting, he takes to the streets, then crickets. Then, yesterday, immediately following the attack in Red Hook, he shuts down the Verrazano. But this morning, more crickets."

Taylor sat back and spread his arms. "So, what are you thinking?"

She held up the copy of the license. "This, plus the other photos we got from the City Hall protest, convince me we're not dealing with white ultranationalists. Yes, the victims were black, but that was a device to feed the assumption, and the media swallowed it whole. But all the targets were police officers, and easily identified as such."

"Then why shoot the four teens in the park?"

It had just occurred to her. "They were closest to the second shooter." She brandished the license again. "This guy. He very likely feared they'd seen him."

"And so...?"

"It's a group, all right, and a violent one. We've been working very hard not to correct the media's take on it because we're afraid when the information we have gets out, the group will kick it up to the next level, which could mean widespread mayhem."

"A reasonable assumption. And you think Prinz is involved?"

"He's connected in some way. I just can't figure out what." She mentioned Marisa's idea of trying to infiltrate CHE. "She's over thirty but can still pass for 17 or 18."

Taylor stared at his desk. "Is she trained for undercover work?"

"She trained in it at the Academy and worked extensively in it in her early years in the Department."

"It's not a bad idea, but I need to get more up-to-date information on Mr. Prinz and his cohorts. Based on what we've seen in the past, I don't think he's behind these attacks, but I agree with you that he may be involved with whoever is. Give me a few days to hear from the other agencies on the photo and sketch."

***

After showing the two guys from Brooklyn South the site of the shooting, Bob had led them north on Broadway. Most video cameras were trained on the approach from the sidewalk. But they spotted one mounted on a house, now a medical office, that captured part of the street and pointed north.

"I must live right," Bob said.

The waiting room was crowded with patients, all of whom appeared to be from the Indian Subcontinent. The receptionist was cool to Bob until he explained why they were there. Soon, Bob, Andy, and Doug were crowded around the receptionist's desktop reviewing footage from the night before and watching the clock in the lower right-hand corner advance. At 7:15, Andy slowed the video to normal speed.

7:17. "There." Andy froze the image.

"Definitely a black Wrangler with off-road tires," Bob said. "Advance it one frame."

The Wrangler jumped a few feet forward.

Bob squinted, trying to get the plate number. "I can only read the last four digits. 8891."

Andy and Doug agreed.

"Print the image, Andy, then resume the video frame by frame."

Andy advanced the images. "There he goes… approaching the big pain-in-the-ass intersection… past 37th Avenue… we're gonna lose him in a minute… gone."

"Looks like he continued up Broadway," Doug said.

Andy agreed. "If he'd gotten onto the BQE, he'd have veered to the right after crossing 37th. And if he'd wanted to go south on the BQE, he'd have gotten into the left lane, which he didn't."

Bob asked the receptionist for the entire video on a flash drive. "Let's search for a camera closer to the intersection. In the meantime, I'll text Kim what we just found."

***

Kim was standing on the platform at the Fulton Street station, waiting for a J or Z train back to Brooklyn, when she got the text from Bob. *Wrangler appears to have headed north on Broadway, past the BQE. Got last 4 digits of plate: 8891.*

Just as a J train rolled in, her cell pinged with another text, this time from one of the detectives from the One-Fifteen. *At a Western Union on 35th Avenue and 73rd Street in Jackson Heights. Video caught subject Wrangler at 18:40 southbound on 73rd. Plate number VQX-8891.*

Kim let the train go. *Please get it on a flash drive. Fantastic work. Please work your way north, as we discussed.*

The response came two minutes later. *One other thing, There is no 35-21 71st Street, because 71st ends at 35th Avenue.*

Kim then texted Vera with the plate number. *Search DMV records and let me know what you find.*

***

The mayor stared across the desk that had once been Fiorello LaGuardia's at the police commissioner. "I don't think you're hearing me. Where are the police on these shootings? This is turning the city into a shooting gallery. I can't believe you don't know more than you're telling me."

"Mr. Mayor, you have already dealt this investigation a setback by trying to end-run departmental procedures. I appreciate you have political concerns, but they cannot justify subverting a difficult investigation."

"When have I…?

The commissioner met the mayor's glare. "Don't force me to embarrass you."

He had a point. Trying to force them to promote Kim to captain had been a major blunder, no matter how much she might have deserved it, which she did.

The commissioner continued. "I told you when you appointed me that I wouldn't hold still for City Hall micromanaging police operations, and it still goes. If you want to help the investigation, kill Barnett's defunding bill."

# CHAPTER FORTY-SIX

The view from a camera at an apartment building on the corner of Broadway and 65th Street showed the black Wrangler continuing north on Broadway at 7:20. A camera on the adjacent building at Broadway and 64th showed it turning right on 64th Street, and revealed the first three letters of the plate number, which Bob immediately texted to Kim.

No one had been home at the house on the corner of 64th Street and 35th Avenue, so they couldn't tell whether the Wrangler had turned onto 35th Avenue or continued north. An automotive repair shop further up the block had a video camera with a good angle on the street, but there was no sign of the black Wrangler.

"He must have turned right onto 35th Avenue," Andy said.

Great. A residential area. Maybe he really did live in Jackson Heights.

***

Justin shifted in his seat under the mayor's questioning. "I already told you, sir, I had very little chance to talk to Kim last night. She wasn't there very long when she got news of the shooting, and the time she was there was spent with Judge Vickers, then with Rita Henshaw, and finally the commissioner."

"Henshaw? What the hell was she doing talking with her?"

"Henshaw approached Kim. And, from my reading of it, Kim gave her a very cool reception. Mr. Mayor, I know you can't say anything about the investigation, but you need to jump on this defunding bill with both feet."

"You're right. I'm scheduling a press conference at noon. Have you heard from Kim this morning?"

Geez, did this guy ever give up? Time for a bucket of cold water. "Yeah. Her husband just lost his job."

***

There'd been nothing from anyone since Bob's text about the Wrangler having most likely turned into Jackson Heights. At the last moment, she'd changed her mind about the J train and switched to the Two Train instead. Jake would be home, and he needed her.

He was sitting at the desktop when she walked in, staring at the screen.

It was heartbreaking to see. How to even approach him? "Hi."

He started. "Oh. Hi. I didn't hear you come in." He'd been staring at his e-mails.

She nodded toward the screen. "Anything, yet?"

"Mostly condolences from friends of mine in the field. But a couple of feelers."

"Great. Who from?"

"Philly and Sacramento. I can't see myself in either, although Sacramento was the more positive." He snorted. "Guess that would finally tell us what's what."

She knew what he meant. This needed to come out, now. "Please come sit with me, and let's talk about this eye to eye."

After a moment's hesitation, he joined her on the couch.

She took his hands in hers. "I love you. When you proposed to me, I was afraid. But I accepted because I realized we were perfect for each other. You convinced me that we would be fine. And we have been."

"Until…"

"No 'until'. We've never not been fine."

"What about, 'Detective Brady, please'?"

"You picked up on Brandt's interest in me even before I did, and the truth is I'm no happier about it than you are. But unless he makes an overt move, there isn't much I can do about it except to discourage it."

"He tried to promote you…"

"And I threatened to resign from the department if he went through with it. I can't believe you would think I'd ever be interested in any other man, but especially him."

"He's helped you before. Put you back on the Dunn murder case after the brass pulled you off."

"He did that to save himself and to assert his own authority. And you'll recall I was ready to resign then, too." Damn, the tension had crept back into her voice. This was not what she wanted. "What are you really afraid of?"

"That Sacramento may be the only offer I get."

***

A camera on an apartment building at 35th Avenue and Leverich Street had caught the black Wrangler heading east. But another, on a building one block further east, showed nothing.

So, the shooter had turned north on 72nd Street. At the corner of Northern Boulevard, the video system had caught the black Wrangler turning west on Northern.

"What now?" Cameron asked as Bob gathered them outside.

The BQE was three blocks away. There were no video cameras within three blocks in either direction of the overpass. When they found a business with video surveillance, there was no sign of the black Wrangler.

Bob stared back at the overpass. "He got on that fucking highway, and we don't have a fucking clue which way he went." He texted the bad news to Kim and then turned back to BQE, heading back to Wilson Street.

# CHAPTER FORTY-SEVEN

"Whatever the best job is for you, all things considered, you should take. There are police departments everywhere, so I'll be fine."

Those were the words Kim had left him with, as her cell had been silently hailing an onslaught of text messages to which she had yet to respond. And she'd been sincere. But now, sitting on the B38 bus heading back to the Castle, she knew she should be reading and replying to the texts, but the conversation with Jake kept replaying in her mind.

Could she really leave New York? Leave the Department? Twice in recent years she'd been on the verge of quitting, but both times the reasons had faded. Jake had wooed her with persistence, and she'd never regretted marrying him. When a series of miscarriages had plunged her into depression, he'd whisked her off to Bermuda for a dream vacation during which she'd rediscovered her love of running. And when she'd been summoned back to the city to solve a political assassination, he hadn't batted an eye.

Financially, they were fine and could weather Jake being out of work indefinitely, even permanently. His father had died a year earlier, leaving the Monroe Place brownstone in which they lived to Jake. The perk of living there rent-free had suddenly morphed into sizable monthly rental income from four tenants.

The rationalizations were piling up quickly.

But Jake was already grinding his teeth at the idea of extended idleness.

Maybe Sacramento wouldn't materialize, and she wouldn't need to choose.

She turned back to her cell. A string of several texts from Bob ended, *we're certain the bastard got on the BQE, but we have no clue which direction.*

From Vera: *Traced the license number provided by 115 guys. Belongs to a 2003 Silver Toyota Camry, reported stolen in June 2020, registered to Juan Riccardo of Astoria.*

Great, another dead end.

From the detectives of the One-Fifteen: *Traced video up 73rd Street to Northern Boulevard and west as far as the BQE. Lost him after that.*

From Justin: *Are you okay? I told him he owes you more than he can ever repay, and his behavior is making that debt worse. Hope you don't mind, but he's pissing me off.*

She had no doubt who "he" was. She replied to Justin first. *Thanks, Justin. No worries.*

Then she texted everyone on the team. *ETA at the Castle is 30 minutes. We'll convene then. Good work, everybody. Don't despair.* Then, she added: *See what else we can find out about that 2003 Camry. If it was reported stolen, there must be details.*

*****

Everyone in the squad room was clustered around the big TV. The mayor was giving a press conference at City Hall, and by the hushed atmosphere in the room, it was a stemwinder.

"…am forced to ask, 'Have we learned nothing in the past five years?' We have a police commissioner who has successfully brought us back to the Community Policing model that most of us agree is essential to maintaining law and order in this city. Our training programs are the best in the country, morale in the department has been rebuilt from its historic low of just a few years ago, and yet we are faced now with a bill put forward by my opponent in the upcoming election that would rob the department of the funds it needs to keep that training program going, to keep salaries at a level sufficient to compete with the departments of our northern and eastern suburbs, and ultimately to keep our streets safe."

Cheers went up in the squad room.

The mayor continued, "The record proves that attacking law enforcement provides an open invitation to criminals. They tried it in Minneapolis. They tried it in Portland. They tried it in Seattle. And those police departments are scrambling, desperate to find recruits to restock their ranks. Now, Mr. Barnett wants to bring this chaos to New York, and he wants the people of this good city to elect him mayor so he can perpetrate even more damage. Well, I'm here this afternoon to assure the people of New York that I will fight this evil measure to my last breath. And I ask every citizen in every district in every borough to contact their Council members and let them know you oppose this bill as much as I do, and that you will remember how they vote in November when it's your turn to vote."

Marshal Dhillon sidled up to Kim. "Wow."

"I'll take a few questions," the mayor said. "Ms. Henshaw."

"He wants to stay on the attack," Kim said.

"Mr. Mayor, do you deny that poorly funded schools and social programs contribute to high levels of street crime, and that improving education and programs for the disadvantaged can have a positive effect on reducing crime?"

"Certainly not," he replied, sounding reasonable. "But there are numerous other factors that contribute to learned criminal behavior, most of which are beyond governmental control. And it's because of these factors that we need effective law enforcement." He pointed in the opposite direction. "Ms. Dunbar?"

"Mr. Mayor, do you think the fact that this has been proposed in the middle of an unsolved case that has seen several police officers killed will affect the bill's final outcome?"

"I don't see how it can't affect it. We are seeing, in an exceedingly graphic way, the dangers police officers continually face. This bill is an affront to every officer. Next?"

"Mr. Mayor," Rita Henshaw called out. "A follow-up?"

"Yes, alright."

"If the police can't or won't solve a series of shootings targeting people of color, including their own officers…."

"Ms. Henshaw, do you have any proof that the department can't or won't solve these shootings? You know something about this investigation that I don't? Because if you do, I'd love to hear it and so would your fellow citizens."

"It's obvious that nothing is being done, and the conclusion that this must be the work of white ultranationalists is painfully obvious." Her smug expression was impossible to miss.

"Don't you dare," Kim muttered under her breath.

"Your first 'obvious' point is completely wrong. The police have good reasons not to conduct this investigation in the press, and I'm sorry if that's inconvenient for you. As for the second, that is simply your guess. The police will follow the evidence wherever it leads. My only hope is that when the killers are caught, the ridiculously restrictive rules of evidence that the prior administration put in place with the help of the City Council, won't prevent the killers from being convicted."

"I take it you'll want those new rules repealed?" Henshaw again.

"And twice on Sunday. Thank you, all." And the mayor stormed off.

"He didn't," Dhillon said with a smile.

Kim got her group together. "Conference room, now."

# CHAPTER FORTY-EIGHT

Captain Colangelo joined them just as they were starting. "Go ahead, Kim. I'll have something to say when you're finished."

She reviewed everything they had so far.

"On the Camry," Cord said, "there was a police report filed. The car was reported stolen from a spot across the street from Mr. Riccardo's residence, a second-floor apartment over a laundromat on 34th Avenue in Astoria. The car was never recovered, and after a lengthy investigation, the insurance paid forty-three hundred bucks on his claim."

Kim made a note on the board. "So, they suspected a scam." Cord had already hung a detailed map of Queens alongside the map of Brooklyn already up. She stared at the northwest corner of it.

"What?" Bostwick asked.

She didn't answer. She shifted her attention to the center of the map. "The One-Fifteen guys said the address on the driver's license is a phony, that 71st Street ends before 35th Avenue. And it does, right here." She pointed to the spot on the map.

"What's you point, Kim?" Bob asked.

"How did he pick that address? It's clear he chose to use it as a decoy, but why that one?"

"He needed an address that didn't exist," Bob replied. "That's not hard."

But there was more to it, and it had been bothering her since she'd learned of the shooting at the dinner. "Why Jackson Heights? Two shootings in Brooklyn, then suddenly one in Queens, in the same neighborhood he'd already picked as a phony residence."

Colangelo spoke up. "I'm baffled, Kim. Why don't you just spill it?"

"The phony residence was established long before there was a shooting anywhere." She turned to Cord. "You and Vera, check if his Wrangler is insured and when and where it was purchased. My gut is telling me around June 2020, which would have been a perfect time because we were neck-deep in Covid, and everyone was operating on a shoestring."

"Okay," Cord replied.

"*Da*," Vera added. "Now, please, you were saying?"

"He picked the address because he needed someplace different from where he lived." She turned to Vitello. "Did it appear the entire address had been altered?"

"It showed no marks of being altered at all."

Now, she was rolling. "Which means he probably altered very little about it. How many streets in Queens ending in '1' have a 35-21 address?" Before anyone could answer, she muttered, "Shit." She turned back to the map. "It's staring us right in the fucking face. Astoria. If he got the plates from Riccardo, who lives in Astoria, that's our starting point."

"Um, okay," Bostwick said.

And then another piece fell into place. "Wait a minute." She pulled up her Notes App. She'd replaced her cell twice since that case in the Meat Packing District, but she was sure she'd carried over every note with each change.

And there it was. "He's on 21st Street. The Ravenswood Houses." She turned to Colangelo. "You may remember the case."

He laughed. "I do, indeed. Let's get a team over there."

Bostwick spoke up. "Since that's NYCHA Housing, we should already have feeds in the RTCC. We'll start taking shifts on the 35-21 building. Okay, Kim?"

"Thanks, Lieu. I also think we need to pick Riccardo up for questioning. Let's…" Her cell vibrated with a text. She snuck a peak. Ken Taylor.

"Give me a minute." She pulled up the text.

*I need to meet you and Captain Colangelo in my office at 8:00 tomorrow morning. You two, but no one else. Do you copy?*

She read it aloud.

"Fine," Colangelo said. "I'll meet you there and then I'll drive you here."

"I have a question," Driscoll said. "If we pick Riccardo up, won't that tip this other guy off that we're on to him?"

"I think we're at the point where we can take the risk," Kim replied.

Colangelo agreed. "Grab him first thing tomorrow morning. Find out what the FBI has learned before we question him."

Another idea. Kim answered Taylor. *We will both be there. In the meantime, can you tell me anything about a Juan Riccardo? Currently residing in Astoria?*

"I think that's enough for one day," Colangelo said.

# CHAPTER FORTY-NINE

*Monday, April 28, 8:05 a.m.*

Kim's first shock of the day was that the Commissioner was at Federal Plaza with Colangelo when she arrived. Her first thought was to wonder if he would be as cordial as he'd been at the dinner two nights earlier.

"Good morning, Detective," he said. "Nice to see you again. I hope you don't mind if I asked Agent Taylor not to disclose that I would be here."

"Good to see you, sir. And, no, not at all." But she was now on full alert. Taylor's people had obviously found something.

Taylor led them upstairs to a spacious conference room with a 77-inch TV monitor mounted on the wall. Three other men she'd never seen were already at the table.

Ken introduced the Commissioner, Colangelo, and Kim. "And these gentlemen, from left to right are Josh Lewin from Homeland Security, Colonel David Spiers from Army Intelligence, and my boss, Leonard Cavendish. Let's sit and see what we have. First, Detective Brady, do you have anything new to report since last evening?"

His formality made sense, given the others in the room. She decided to respond in a similar fashion. "No, Agent Taylor, I don't. You know as much as we do."

Colonel Spiers spoke up. "We've done some digging on the person pictured on the driver's license you sent. His real name is Enrique Cruz, a Colombian immigrant who joined the army in 2011 and did a tour in Afghanistan. In December 2013, he was part of a squad clearing a building of Taliban supporters when one of his squad members triggered an Individual Explosive Device killing two soldiers. Up until that time, he had been an exemplary soldier, but after the incident, he became increasingly insubordinate and bordering on incorrigible. He was discharged in early 2014."

"A dishonorable discharge?" Kim asked.

"No, a medical discharge. His commanding officer believed his behavior was an aftermath of the IED explosion and he prevailed."

"But it wasn't unanimous?" the commissioner asked.

"No. We had already begun receiving reports on him wandering off at odd times, and we suspected he was meeting with members of the Taliban. We kept tabs on him when he returned home."

Mr. Lewin spoke up. "That's when we got involved. Beginning in late 2018, we became aware of groups possibly working with the drug cartels to recruit dissidents from various ethnic groups."

"To deal drugs?" Colangelo asked.

"No," Lewin replied, "to create general instability. Agent Taylor had been keeping us apprised of the group called Come Home Ernesto, and we investigated them, but they appeared to be only a local group. However, considering recent events, we think that may have changed."

Ken took the floor. "Detective Brady, your observations about Prinz got our attention. As you suspected, his protests appear to have been solely to serve keeping a false narrative in the media and to throw off you folks in your investigation. Mr. Lewin also found the sketch you sent us to be of value."

"His name is Yasiel Coravos, also Colombian, also a veteran of Afghanistan, with a history of revolutionary activities. At present we don't know where he is or what name he is using, but in the aftermath of the first shooting, we believe he is based in Brooklyn. In early 2019, he was actively recruiting dissident US Army veterans, which explains his connection to Mr. Cruz. Mr. Riccardo is another story. It appears he's a longtime friend of Cruz, but nothing more."

"Does Coravos' group have a name?" Kim asked.

"None that we know," Taylor replied. "We think they've infiltrated CHE and are using their identity."

"Sounds rather parasitic." Kim said it more to herself.

But Mr. Cavendish, speaking for the first time, picked up on it. "That's the perfect term for these folks. They are most definitely parasites. It's a way for them to hide in plain sight." He held up one of the Park Row photos. "As these clearly confirm."

"Members of our team are picking up Mr. Riccardo as we speak," Kim said.

"You're arresting him?" Taylor again. "On what charge?"

"We're bringing him in for questioning," she replied, aware that what was coming next would be new to Colangelo, but they hadn't had a chance to talk it through. "If he gives us enough to go on, we'll hold him as a material witness. If not, we can threaten him with a conspiracy charge."

All eyes slid to Colangelo, who shrugged. "It's the best we've got at the moment."

Relief. "Also, if he says he has a lawyer, I'll let Agent Taylor know his name and that can provide any other leads. But the key is finding Coravos." One more thing. "We have someone who's volunteering to go undercover to infiltrate CHE."

"Who?" the commissioner asked.

"Marisa Fuentes, currently of the Brooklyn SVU."

The commissioner shook his head. "A lot of red tape. Bryce Mitchell would need to sign off."

"A lengthy process," Colangelo said.

"And," Kim added, "it would alert people to the operation."

The commissioner considered that. "If you decide to proceed, have her take a leave of absence for personal reasons. The department will compensate her for her time as a consultant."

"Detective Brady and I will coordinate," Taylor said.

But Kim had more questions. "Colonel, you said that up until the IED incident, Cruz had an exemplary record. In what way?"

Colonel Spiers consulted his notes. "Private Cruz qualified at the marksman level for the pistol in his first attempt and later qualified at the sharpshooter level. That's…"

"Twenty-one out of thirty." Kim had recently qualified at the sharpshooter level on the Glock 21, earning herself a new ribbon for her badge holder. "What about Coravos?"

Spiers again checked his notes. "Expert on the rifle, and on the automatic rifle."

Kim was making notes. Coravos may have been the AR-15 shooter in the park. "Were they in the same unit?"

"Same brigade, different companies. Coravos was honorably discharged shortly after his unit returned from Afghanistan in 2014."

"Our first indications of possible revolutionary activities occurred the following year," Lewin said.

Same brigade at the same time with badges for marksmanship excellence. "Colonel, is it possible to get additional information on that brigade?"

"Such as?"

"Immigrant soldiers with expertise in marksmanship."

***

"Thanks for covering for me on the material witness thing," Kim said to Colangelo once they picked up his car over at One-PP. "I'd have discussed it with you first if we'd had the chance."

"I assumed you were improvising, but it was solid. Just don't go too far afield."

"The clock is ticking, Captain. We need to squeeze Riccardo effectively, or the next dead body may belong to Enrique Cruz."

Her cell buzzed. A text from Bob. *Have Riccardo in custody, heading for the Castle.*

Kim responded: *Is he talking?*

Bob's reply: *We haven't asked him anything yet.*

Colangelo liked it. "Playing it close to the vest."

# CHAPTER FIFTY

"This is Joanna Dunbar for ITN. Mayor Brandt yesterday stated he was opposed to Speaker Barnett's proposal to reduce funding for policing to provide more funding for education and various as yet unnamed social programs. The mayor denounced the bill as dangerous and called upon all New Yorkers to contact their City Council representatives to express their outrage. Overnight polls suggest that New Yorkers have been doing exactly that, with those stating their opposition to the bill making up 72% of all calls. Polls also show the mayor leading Council Speaker Barnett in the race for the mayoralty by a margin of 65% to 30%, with 5% undecided."

***

"Detective Bob is already in Interrogation Room One," Marshal Dhillon said as Kim and Colangelo walked in. Kim stopped by the conference room while Colangelo headed up to his office.

"We haven't seen Cruz yet," Cord said. "But the lieu put an APB out on his plate number."

"As soon as we see him, let me know. We'll need to go mobile." She proceeded to Room One.

Riccardo was sitting on one side of the long table, Bob and Martin on the other, with an empty chair in the middle, directly across from Riccardo.

Kim took it. "Well, Mr. Riccardo, any idea why we wanted to speak with you?"

"These guys ain't told me nothin'. And I ain't done nothin'."

She flashed a disarming smile. "I'm sure you haven't. We brought you in because we need some information."

His eyes narrowed. "I ain't in no trouble?"

"You just said you haven't done anything. You had a car stolen in 2020, correct?" He nodded. "According to the Department of Motor Vehicles, the license plates were never recovered, suggesting the car was never found. Is that right?"

He showed signs of relaxing. "Yeah, that's right. The insurance company waited a long time before they paid off on my claim."

For the first time, Kim made a show of consulting her notes. "And that was for just over $4,000?"

"Yeah, it was."

She placed her cell on the table. "We've located the plates."

"Huh?"

"The license plates from your Camry, plate number VQX-8891, were recently seen on another vehicle."

"I guess the DMV issued the number to someone else."

"See?" she asked Bob. "Isn't that just what I said?"

"It is," Bob replied.

Riccardo again relaxed.

Kim's smile vanished. "Except we checked yesterday, and DMV's records still show that number as belonging to your Camry, although the registration expired."

"I don't understand," Riccardo said.

"Someone took the plates from your old Camry and put them on his vehicle." She picked up her cell again and reopened the Notes app. "A black 2019 Jeep Wrangler belonging to someone you may know, Enrique Cruz, also known as Henry Salcedo."

Riccardo paled before he could recover. "I… I don't know anyone by that name. Either name."

"Oh, I think you do, Mr. Riccardo. He lives near you, over on 21st Street in the Ravenswood Houses. I think you knew at the time of the theft of your car that it was Mr. Cruz who took it; whatever the insurance paid would be more than it was worth. You never bought another car, did you?"

"Um… no."

"So that four grand was pure profit. If I'm right about this, we have a term for that: insurance fraud. If the fraud is between $3,000 and $50,000, which this is, that's a Class D felony, which carries a prison term of up to seven years."

"I didn't… I mean…"

Kim dropped her friendly manner. "Those old plates of yours are currently on a 2019 black Jeep Wrangler. 2019. Does that year ring a bell? What's more, that vehicle was used in the murders of two police officers two nights ago." She rose from her seat. "So, don't fuck with me or you'll be grabbing your ankles at Attica before I'm through with you."

Riccardo shrank back in his seat. "Oh, shit… he never said… oh, shit…"

Kim sat and resumed her friendly manner. "Now, I don't believe that you were involved with any shootings. And it's entirely plausible that you had no idea why Cruz wanted your car's plates. I can also see that the thought of seven years of painful humiliation behind bars is repugnant to you. So, here's what we'll do. Assuming that you are telling the truth, and that the car scheme was Cruz's idea, you're going to give us a statement that Cruz took your Camry without your permission. If he threatened you if you didn't cooperate, mention that as well."

He gave them the statement. "You gotta protect me, though."

"Consider it done."

Once outside Room One, Bob took Kim aside. "I gotta hand it to you. I've seen the good cop/bad cop routine many times in my career, but I've never seen both roles played by the same person in the same interview."

"Thanks, Bob. The minute we get a call on that plate number..."

Cord called out, "Kim. Got him on the RTCC leaving his building."

Kim rushed into Bostwick's office with Bob right behind and gave him the word.

"Okay, Kim. Take Martin with you and cruise the BQE. Bob, you and Tim take another car and cruise the Grand Central. Take unmarked radio cars. I'll put out an alert and I'll have the captain get us a chopper airborne. I'll also call Driscoll and have him get his guys mobile as well."

"Please also call Rick Conti for an arrest warrant for Cruz," Kim said. "I don't want any judicial screwups."

# CHAPTER FIFTY-ONE

Felipe Prinz looked away from his companion and stared across the river from the little park in Greenpoint, not sure he'd heard correctly.

"That's not quite the reaction I was looking for," his companion said.

"I wasn't expecting a demand like that," Prinz replied. "In case you haven't noticed, CHE is an advocacy group, not a paramilitary unit."

"And in case you haven't noticed, we are now in a shooting war. Everyone needs to do their part. You didn't mind when your advocates set two buildings ablaze five years ago in the cause of justice, and you didn't bat an eye when one of them killed a firefighter. You even did time for that. It's a badge you should wear with pride."

He didn't need to be reminded. "That guy was stupid…"

"But you knew he had the gun, and you tried to protect him." His companion broke into a nasty sneer. "You were perfectly willing for the shooting to happen if you weren't the one pulling the trigger. I'll even bet you've never even held a firearm, let alone shot one."

Again, he averted his eyes.

"Of course not. You've raised an army, but you're not a general. You're not a leader at all. You're just a mouthpiece, a front man. You idolize Che Guevara without having the first idea of who he really was. Why do you think his image on the T-shirts of white kids from the suburbs continues to freak out the establishment? Why do they wear his image and not, say, Fidel's? A better question: why did Fidel, as brilliant as he was, need Che Guevara?"

"I never claimed to be Che."

"No, you just played on his name. But now, I'm bringing his true meaning to the organization that bears his name, and I will see to it that we do that name justice. You will continue to be the organization's public face, its mouthpiece. But you will speak the words I tell you to speak."

He had no choice. "All right."

"Good. We need to be recognized as attacking. This bill the City Council is considering about defunding the police. That would be a huge help to us."

"You want me to organize a demonstration supporting the bill?"

"No, Felipe. We should oppose it as not going far enough, a halfway measure that will continue to leave our people underserved." He smirked at Felipe's shock. "Look at it on the bright side—it will get you on TV, possibly even an interview. You love being on TV, don't you, Phil?"

Felipe hated when he called him Phil.

His companion's cell rang. "Yeah?... When?... They arrested him?... I agree, they must know a lot more than they've let on. Fuck. Okay, you know what you need to do." He ended the call.

"What was that all about?" Felipe asked.

"None of your concern. You have your job to do, I have mine."

***

The radio squawked. "Subject just passed camera on the corner of 21st Street and 41st Avenue, heading south."

Kim picked up the mic. "Car One, roger that. Can we get eyes on him?"

Cord's voice. "Lieu says at least twenty minutes before we can get a bird up. Highway units have been alerted and will come online shortly. What's the plan?"

She turned to Martin. "How the hell can we have a plan when we don't know where he's going?" But he was heading south on 21st Street, while Martin was just making the left from Wilson onto Flushing Avenue with Bob and Tim close behind. She hit the mic again. "Okay, Cord, the Lieu should ask Highway Patrol to cruise the Grand Central and the Long Island Expressway. But our focus is Queens into Brooklyn."

"Base to Car One, roger that."

"Car One to Car Two. Bob you guys continue to the BQE." She turned to Martin. "Right turn on Graham." Keyed the mic again. "Cover the BQE from Newtown Creek south. We'll head north on Graham to possibly catch him coming south on McGuinness."

"Car Two, got it, Kim."

"Car One to base, who else we got?"

"Base to Car One. Doug and Andy are in Car Three."

Great. Another set of eyes. "Car One to Car Three."

"Car Three here. Hey, Kim."

"What's your location, Car Three?"

"Currently northbound on the Gowanus. What's your pleasure, Kim?"

"Car One to Car Three, appropriate radio protocol, please. Continue north on the BQE as far as McGuinness Boulevard exit, then turn south. Repeat cycle. Car Two will be heading in the opposite direction."

"Roger that."

"Car Two, this is Car One, Change of plan. Proceed south on the BQE to the Verrazano, then back north. You cruise one direction while Car Three cruises the other."

"South on BQE. Roger that."

"Car One out."

"Putting all our eggs in one basket, aren't we, Kim?" Martin asked.

"Once I knew he was heading south, it made sense. We have the highway units covering the less likely avenues. I just wish we had that chopper up. It will be a lot harder to spot Cruz from the air if they need to search a wide area."

Martin made the turn onto Graham Avenue. "Did the captain tell you? The commissioner approved Marisa's undercover idea."

# CHAPTER FIFTY-TWO

It had been difficult getting it organized on such short notice, but Felipe had to admit they'd managed to put a good crowd together. The evening rush was well underway when they formed a human chain across the Brooklyn-bound side of the Brooklyn Bridge. Angry motorists sent up a cacophony that nearly drowned out the cries of the protesters.

What a beautiful noise.

But another noise sounded from behind, the wail of sirens heralding the arrival of police. He turned to assess the situation and large police vans.

The Brooklyn SRG was deploying behind his group of protesters, using the traffic jam only a few feet in front of him, which he'd created, as a wall that few could penetrate.

"Felipe, over here."

She was hot, and no older than a college freshman, with long hair framing her face and skin-tight leggings and a low-cut top that hinted at further delights. And she was urging him to escape past the jammed-up cars to the Manhattan side.

If he went with her, he'd be abandoning his people, something he'd never done before.

If he stayed, he could play the tormented but brilliant leader, a role he'd embraced ever since getting kicked out of law school. Nothing stoked the media like a celebrity advocate being silenced by the police, and he had lots of experience.

But this was different from the other times. He now had a rap sheet with a felony conviction on it. And his organization was no longer his own. Even this protest hadn't been his idea; he'd been ordered by a force he had not understood when it first invaded his group, but whose purpose was now becoming clear.

"Felipe, hurry!"

He'd never seen her before, but she sounded like she really cared.

How much did he owe these new leaders of his movement? How much of their mayhem would be hung around his neck?

"Felipe!" She sounded like she was starting to cry.

There was a narrow space between two cars in front of him. The cops were already compressing his group, an adaptation of the hated "kettle" tactic. The news vans couldn't get a good closeup of him being arrested.

Fuck it.

***

"Face it, Kim, he slipped away."

She had to admit Martin was right. They'd driven up and down the McGuinness/Graham corridor several times, then branched out into different areas of Brooklyn. Cars Two and Three had patrolled the BQE and then the Belt Parkway well into the afternoon, and the Highway units had seen nothing on the Long Island Expressway or the Grand Central.

It was nearly six.

Colangelo was waiting for them when they returned to the Castle.

She didn't wait for him to say it. "I know, I bet the ranch on a hunch."

He put his hand on her shoulder. "It was a good hunch, Kim. If we'd gotten a chopper in the air sooner, we might have gotten him. We put his plate number and a description of the vehicle out on the radio several times during the day, but no one reported anything."

"I take it he never showed up anywhere on the RTCC?"

"No. We've been watching the cameras on the approaches to all the bridges and tunnels. No sign of him. We've placed Riccardo in protective custody."

She'd been thinking of questioning him further but decided it was pointless. "I'm going home."

"Good idea."

But she didn't move.

"Something wrong?" he asked.

"Plenty. We should remain alert for anything breaking tonight."

"Like what?"

"We put that plate number out in an APB as soon as we got it." She looked him in the eye. "Bad guys use police scanners."

"Yes, I thought of that, too." He pointed to the TV mounted on the wall showing scenes of mayhem on the Brooklyn Bridge. "Mr. Prinz has been busy today."

Something else she didn't like. "His protests certainly have been oddly timed these days."

"Marisa's part of the operation has begun."

***

The Manhattan end of the Bridge was bedlam and, holding hands, they were kids caught in the midst of pandemonium. No one paid any attention to them, and Felipe tried to block the cries and screams of the protesters he'd left behind as he kept his head down so no one would recognize him.

It was every-man-for-himself time.

"Let's go down to the subway and get away from here," she said

He pointed to the entrance to the Brooklyn Bridge/Chambers Street station. "This way."

"Where are we going?"

"We'll grab the first uptown train and go someplace we can talk. What's your name?"

"Maria Santos. I've watched you on TV. You're amazing. I wanted to be part of it."

An uptown Z train pulled into the station. He drank her in with his eyes one more time.

Every man for himself.

***

Jake was upbeat when she arrived home, giving her a huge hug and a long kiss. "You look like you've had a bad day."

"Not good. I hope yours was better."

"I did get a call from Sacramento, asking me if I'd consider relocating. I told them it would depend on several things, and I'd need to think things over very carefully, including discussing them with my lovely wife, before I could make that kind of commitment."

At least he hadn't jumped at the idea. She kissed his cheek. "Thanks."

"There was also an opinion column in the *New York Post* saying the Nets were crazy to get rid of me. It won't help my current situation much, but it was nice to read."

"It publicizes your availability. I'd call that helpful." The TV was on with the sound off, and it caught her attention. The camera had zoomed in on the protesters being compressed against the blocked cars.

"Using the 'kettle' again." Jake's voice dripped with disapproval.

But that's not what attracted her attention. "Where's Prinz?"

"I don't know. They've talked about him, but I haven't seen him. That's odd. Doesn't he usually mug for the cameras at these things?"

He certainly does.

# CHAPTER FIFTY-THREE

It hadn't taken much to convince the lovely Maria Santos, a sophomore at Hostos Community College in the Bronx, to come back to his place with him. Of course, she'd insisted that he promise not to hit on her, and, of course, he'd promised.

"Wow, this is amazing!"

Good, she was suitably impressed. He pulled out a blunt, figuring to let things take their natural course.

"Oh, please don't," she said, her voice plaintive.

"You're not that kind of girl?" It was hard to believe, given the way she looked.

"I'm seriously allergic. I get asthma." She pulled an inhaler out of her bag to show him. "I can't be anywhere near it."

He couldn't argue with that.

"Besides," she said with a disarming smile, "I really want to talk to you. I'd like to be part of your organization."

"Why?"

"I remember when you were fighting gentrification in Brooklyn a few years ago. My grandparents lived in Williamsburg, and they lost their home because they couldn't afford the rising rents. They moved into city housing in Brownsville, and they would have lost that if you and Sabrina Dunn hadn't fought that horrible project."

"You knew about Sabrina and me?"

"Only what they said on TV. I was heartbroken when she died."

That touched him. She was a nice kid, if a little naïve. "So was I. We were… a couple. This was her place. She left it to me."

Maria giggled. "So, you're, like, rich?"

"Not rich, but I use what I have for important causes."

She sat on the sofa. "I'd love to hear about the causes you support. I'd like to be a part of it."

He sat next to her. "Tell me more about yourself, first."

She looked hurt. "You don't trust me?"

"I can't afford to completely trust anyone, but I want to know I can trust you."

The hurt vanished. "Oh, okay. Both sets of grandparents moved here from Puerto Rico, but my mother insisted we only speak English at home."

"Which explains why you sound like an Anglo."

"*Si.* But I still have cousins just outside of San Juan and I've been back a few times. I wrote for my high school newspaper and I'm a good student. After Hostos, I want to go to one of the CUNY schools, and I was hoping to go to law school so I could really help people…"

"You mean, working within the system."

"Yes, but now I'm beginning to read a lot more and I'm realizing that the system may never work for our people. I'm thinking I need a better way."

"And you sought me out this particular day because…"

"I've been trying to find out where and how to reach you, but CHE doesn't have a website, and all I could find online were articles about it. So, when I heard that a protest had blocked traffic on the Brooklyn Bridge, I knew it had to be you, and I figured I'd have a good chance to see you." She broke into a dazzling smile. "And I did."

Maria was the first girl he'd looked at since he'd lost Sabrina. She had Sabrina's combination of commitment and naivete.

The touch of her hand on his cheek aroused him. "You're a good leader, Felipe. Please tell me how I can help."

The impulse to kiss her was too strong, and he was thrilled when she came to him willingly.

But she broke it off before it could become more. "Not yet, Felipe. First, the cause, then… we'll see."

***

Just before eleven, Kim's cell signaled a text. It was from Ken Taylor. *Marisa got some interesting stuff from Prinz. We have it on tape. Meet us at Federal Plaza tomorrow morning.*

She had just acknowledged the text when she got a call from Bostwick. "Sorry to bother you at this late hour, Kim, but I need everybody to come in as soon as possible."

"What is it?"

"Officers of the One-Oh-Eight found Cruz in his Wrangler on Railroad Avenue next to Newtown Creek in Long Island City, dead by gunshot. The best route is up Greenpoint Avenue, cross the bridge and make a right on Review Avenue. About a quarter mile down, with the cemetery on your left, you'll see an access road on your right, with a sign that says 'asphalt'. Make the right if CSU doesn't already have it blocked off and follow it to the tracks. Otherwise, you'll have to walk it. It's not far."

The One-Oh-Eight was Queens North. "Does Queens North…?"

"They know it's ours, Kim. Someone recognized the plate number and notified us. Vitello's guys are already on their way."

She kissed Jake goodbye and was surprised when he held her longer than usual.

"Be careful out there, Kim. You're getting into very deep shit, here."

***

Queens North CSU had the access road blocked off, so Kim had to park on Review Avenue. The narrow two-lane access road and the surrounding buildings were lit up with flashing blue and red lights from a dozen emergency vehicles. When she reached the two-track rail line, Cruz's black Wrangler was parked on the other side, pulled up on the grass off the narrow strip of pavement the city called Railroad Avenue.

Phil Vitello was waiting. "Single gunshot in the mouth with his own weapon, the Glock 34."

"Please tell me you found prints other than his on the weapon."

"We don't know whose prints they are, yet. But it looks like there's only one set."

"Goddamn it." Deep breath. Wait. "Phil, why would someone lead us on a wild goose chase from Queens into Brooklyn, then come back and kill himself here?"

"Good question."

She thought a little more. "Where did they find the gun?"

"In his right hand, resting in his lap."

Alarm bells. "So, he shot himself in the mouth, then, after he was dead, made sure he didn't drop the gun on the floor?"

"An even better question."

And then it hit her. "Phil, Cruz was left-handed."

"You are three for three."

Bob joined them and Kim recapped for him. "So, we know someone else killed him. The thing is, he wouldn't have sat still while someone shoved his own gun in his mouth and pulled the trigger. We'll need the autopsy report as soon as they have it."

"You don't think the shot in the mouth killed him?" Bob asked.

She walked over to the Wrangler. Cruz's body was still in the driver's seat. She studied his head for signs of bruising. "It might, but it certainly wasn't the first attack. Phil, please make sure we impound the vehicle and do a complete study on it—scan for prints, for blood, for any DNA."

"You think he might have been killed someplace else and left here?"

She glanced around. "No, this is where he was killed. No witnesses to hear the shot, and a major pain for us to reach." She spotted a sergeant from the 108th. "How did you guys learn about this?"

"Someone called in a tip about a vehicle on the tracks."

Bob studied the surrounding industrial buildings and parking lots. "Must have been one of the neighbors."

"Can you get me the number?" Kim asked.

"Sure, but it'll probably be a burner."

# CHAPTER FIFTY-FOUR

*Tuesday, April 29, 8:31 a.m.*

"Good morning. The police commissioner announced this morning that the department now has a lead on the shootings that have plagued the city over the past nine days. A ninth victim was claimed last night in Long Island City, but the police will not release the name or whether the victim was a member of the department. They do confirm, however, that he is connected to the other killings. The commissioner was emphatic that the group behind these shootings is not a white ultranationalist group, but he would go no further. This is Joanna Dunbar reporting for ITN."

***

Again, Kim's workday began at 26 Federal Plaza. Mr. Lewin and Colonel Spiers were present, along with Colangelo.

Colonel Spiers slid a printout over to Kim. "We found three other names in the same brigade as Coravos and Cruz who fit your criteria. I've included their last-known addresses."

"I have a copy," Lewin added. "And I'd ask you to keep me informed of any additional information you find on these guys."

Kim studied the list. "All three are Latinos."

"Wasn't that what you were checking?" Spiers asked.

"I thought we said any immigrants."

"But the photos you showed us were all of Latino men." Spiers turned sour. "Or is this a reflection of New York's paranoia about 'racial profiling'?"

She remained serious. "Colonel, I pay very little attention to such things. We are talking about a group committed to inciting mayhem and killing police officers, with a leader who sought out non-citizen marksmen for the task. It is not beyond the realm of possibility that he might have attracted a member or two who was non-Latino but easily radicalized."

"Very well, Detective, I'll tell my people to search again."

Ken Taylor played the recording of Marisa's encounter with Prinz.

"She was wearing a wire?" Colangelo asked.

"That was the point," Taylor replied. "It was a tiny transmitter in a small broach on her top."

Kim listened as they entered Prinz's apartment. "Figures, two minutes after he gets her inside, he's trying to get her stoned."

"She's good," Taylor said. "Just a hint of flirting with a dash of hero-worship."

At the kiss, Colangelo said, "Better not let Martin hear."

"She probably told him as soon as she got home."

Between bouts of flirting followed by, "not yet", Prinz told Marisa more about himself and CHE.

"So." Marisa's voice. "You must be happy seeing the group moving forward to more than mere protesting."

"It's a fine line," Prinz replied. "I want to threaten enough to attract attention, but not enough to alienate our people. These new guys don't understand that. But you don't want to hear about that..."

Sounds of rustling, like she was sliding away from him. "Oh, but I do, Felipe. Maybe I can help you. You sound like you need support, someone who understands you and cares for you."

"She's good," Taylor said.

Felipe's voice, "Okay, what do you want to know?"

"Anything that troubles you. Great leaders are always troubled by something. What troubles you?"

A pause. "I really like you."

"I like you, too, Felipe."

Another silence. Rustling. Another kiss, longer this time.

Kim shook her head. Marisa's playing with fire. Careful, girl.

"Later, Felipe. We need to talk. You mentioned the new guys who don't understand. What did you mean by that?"

A loud sigh, followed by a cell phone ringtone. "Shit, I gotta get this… Yeah?… I know, I planned it that way… No, getting arrested was not part of my plan… the others can afford it, they don't have a felony conviction on their sheet… That's too bad, Yasiel, because I'm sick of doing this shit to decoy the cops for you and your guys, and I sure as hell am not going to get arrested if I can avoid it… Well, maybe it's best if you guys hook up with someone else, and CHE can get back to what we do best… No… not saying that… no, I get it."

The next sound was a clattering.

Marisa's voice. "Are you okay?"

"No. Yeah, no, I'm fine. Look, I'm sorry, but I just don't feel like talking anymore."

"Okay. I understand. Here's my cell number. Call me when you feel better."

Taylor hit a button. "That was it. She left."

"She gave him her cell number?" Kim asked.

"Yes," Taylor replied. "A burner phone we supplied. If he calls her, we'll see what we want to do."

"I'm not wild about sending her back in," Colangelo said.

Kim considered it. "We may not need to. He mentioned Yasiel and 'the new guys' who he clearly does not like taking over CHE. That's enough to give us probable cause to bring him in for questioning, even to hold him as a material witness."

Colangelo shook his head. "I want to debrief Marisa, first, in case there's anything we didn't hear on the tape that we need to know."

But as Kim dwelled on it, the greater she felt the urgency to act immediately. "They've already killed one of their own—Cruz. They won't hesitate to kill Prinz if they feel he's no longer useful, and his side of that conversation certainly sounded like they're leaning that way."

"I agree with Detective Brady," Lewin said. "Suppose all three men on the colonel's list are active in Coravos' group. Plus Coravos…"

"Plus the third shooter, the one who gunned down the two officers in Red Hook," Kim said.

The colonel nodded. "Exactly. That's five trained gunmen. And there may be others. It could be deadly if we delay."

"I understand," Colangelo replied. "But the moment we pull Prinz in, we lose any link to Coravos. I just want to make sure we have a full understanding before we move forward." He turned to Kim. "You're still awaiting forensic analysis on the evidence from last night's shooting. Let's discuss this with the team back at the Castle."

"Is that okay with you, Ken?" she asked.

He spread his arms. "This is your show, guys. But you can call on us if you need logistical support."

# CHAPTER FIFTY-FIVE

Kim and Colangelo were walking up DeKalb Avenue from the Central Avenue subway stop when they heard the brief toot of a car horn a half block from the Castle.

It was Bob. He stopped and lowered the passenger side window. "Want a lift?"

Kim laughed. "No thanks, Bob. We'll see you there."

He drove off.

"I'm worried about all of you," Colangelo said. "When we convene in a few minutes, I'm ordering all of you to wear vests when on duty."

"Isn't that a little extreme?"

"You tell me."

She thought about it. "We all take risks every shift we work. We manage those risks as best we can, but we can never eliminate them. Take our present dilemma of either bringing Prinz in or leaving him on the street a while longer. Each has a risk."

"Yes, but one risks his life and the other risks the lives of fellow cops. Right now, I'm leaning more on protecting our people than him."

"But he's a key piece," Kim said. "And, to our knowledge, there's no hierarchy in CHE. It's all him." They reached the corner of DeKalb and Wilson. "It's always been all about him."

They started across Wilson as Bob turned into the parking lot behind the Castle.

They crossed the street and turned toward the main door.

Two shots in rapid succession.

Kim and Colangelo crouched against the brick wall.

Kim pulled her Glock and scooted back toward DeKalb while Colangelo covered her.

Screech of tires.

A small car sped through the intersection toward Myrtle Avenue.

Kim strained to catch the plate number.

"Anything on the vehicle?"

"Looked like a Camry, silver. Didn't get the plate." Then she realized. "Oh, God, Captain, he was shooting at Bob."

"Go! I'll get help inside."

She ran around to the back. Bob was lying on his back. She checked his pulse.

Weak, but still there.

Two abdominal wounds.

Bleeding out.

Kim pulled her cell and called 9-1-1. Then she cried out, "Officer down!"

Bostwick was already out the back door.

***

Speaker Barnett appeared distinctly uncomfortable as he sat across the LaGuardia desk from the mayor. It wasn't difficult to see why. The man had to be desperate.

And the mayor would take full advantage. "I'm surprised to see you here, Larry. I would have thought you'd be out soapboxing for your defunding bill. But then I guess you're seeing the same numbers I'm seeing. The phone calls have been running increasingly against you."

Barnett shifted again in his seat. "I have noticed, and I'm thinking that perhaps there might be some middle ground we could find."

The intercom buzzed. He'd told his assistant he wanted no interruptions. "What middle ground? Where is the halfway point between cutting police funding and not cutting? Cutting a little? Not cutting but micromanaging how their budget is spent?"

Barnett jumped at the opening. "I prefer to call it 'targeted spending'. We came to an agreement over the construction bill a couple of years ago. I thought we might reprise our success."

The mayor spread his hands apart. "I held good cards, then, so I was positioned to offer a compromise. I hold even better cards now, so you are only positioned to beg for a compromise. I…"

The door burst open. It was Justin Cates. "I'm sorry to interrupt, Mr. Mayor, but this is urgent. Another police officer has been shot. Detective Nolan of Brooklyn North Homicide."

Speaker Barnett faded to insignificance. "When and where?"

"The parking lot of the Castle about thirty minutes ago. No one else was hurt."

"Is he…?"

"Still alive, sir. An ambulance got to him within minutes. They're taking him to Wyckoff Heights."

He stood. "Barnett, get out. C'mon Justin."

***

The ambulance had just left. Kim Brady was riding to the hospital with Bob. Colangelo gathered everyone in the unit. "Okay, people. First, I want Felipe Prinz in custody this morning."

"On what charge?" Stransky asked.

"No charge. We're placing him in protective custody as a material witness. If there is a reason to change his status, we'll deal with it. Stransky and Brogan, you go and take Marisa. I'll send Cole Rydell as backup. Cord?"

"Here, Captain."

"Check the number Kim got from the sergeant in the 108th. Check its call history, both outgoing and incoming. Then check on every number it connected with. I want names, addresses, and tower pings."

"Vera's better at that, Captain. I can handle anything you need on the RTCC."

"Vera's not a member of this unit." But as soon as he said it, he knew the answer.

"She's available for anything we need."

"Very well. Search for the Wrangler on the RTCC from last night, including any indication of who might've been following him. And have Sergeant Vitello stay on top of the Queens ME and the crime lab. I want to know what we're dealing with."

"Captain," Bostwick said, "Kim's on her own at the hospital. I'm going to head over there since I suspect you want to stay here and keep in contact with everyone."

"Yes, okay. I also need to update the commissioner."

# CHAPTER FIFTY-SIX

The television in the waiting area was already blaring the first headlines of this latest obscenity. Kim tried to block it out.

Why did hospitals insist on televisions in their waiting areas? And if they must, why did they keep them on news stations?

She'd almost been sorry she'd ridden in the ambulance with Bob, because for the entire trip, she felt like she was in the way.

They got plasma running right away, as they had when she'd been shot all those years ago. Had she looked as deathly pale as Bob?

He'd been gray.

Almost lifeless, except for his chest rising and falling above his blood-stained abdomen.

She'd taken his hand.

Ice cold.

No, Bob, you can't leave us. Can't leave me.

He was the only remaining connection to Dad, with whom he'd worked, and whom he'd defended and tried to protect. She'd wrongly accused him of obstruction once, but then interceded during an Internal Affairs investigation, stepping as close as she'd dared to the line on coaching a witness, and she'd saved his career.

Now, he was fighting for his life, two years after she'd watched another good friend fight for his.

"Detective Brady?" A doctor in surgical scrubs, his mask off.

"Yes?" The hope in her voice died when she met his eyes.

"I'm very sorry. Detective Nolan died on the operating table a short while ago. We did everything…"

It faded to white noise.

What if she'd accepted the quick lift to the Castle?

The timing would have changed.

Maybe she would have seen something.

If only…

***

Felipe had just taken a few hits from his hookah when the phone rang. He wasn't in any mood to talk, and if it was Yasiel, it could mean the end was near. Better to just mellow out.

But a quick glance at his cell changed his mind.

Maria.

Last night wasn't for nothing. She certainly had seemed interested even if she was a major-league tease. "Hey, baby."

She giggled. "Sounds like you're in a better mood this morning."

"It's the sound of your voice that did it."

"Aww, that's sweet. I'm in the neighborhood. Would it be okay if I dropped by?"

"Sure thing, baby. We'll pick up where we left off."

"That's what I thought," she said in a sing-song voice. "Ten minutes?"

"I'll be ready and waiting."

He extinguished the hookah and opened the windows, letting lots of fresh spring air into the room.

***

"Kim?"

Colangelo's voice.

She couldn't find hers.

"Kim, I just heard. I'm so sorry."

"We should have taken his ride."

He touched her chin and made her meet his gaze. "Do you honestly think that would have changed anything? Either one of us might've been hit, too."

It didn't matter. Nothing mattered. She'd lost three unborn children to miscarriages, and none of them had cut as much as this did. Bob was a good friend and partner.

But one thought pounded hardest out of the mob of them hammering her brain. "He never had a chance to prove he'd beaten it."

"Beaten what, Kim?"

No. Letting Colangelo know Bob had fallen off the wagon would help no one. "Nothing." But the random thoughts kept pounding at her, and she couldn't keep another one from slipping out. "Maybe Sacramento will be better."

"I won't pretend I don't understand. I hope it doesn't come to that, but…"

There was another commotion. The mayor had arrived.

She turned to Colangelo. "I was hoping it wouldn't, too, Captain. But everyone has a breaking point. Sacramento can't be this bad. If Jake needs to relocate there, I'll join him."

"It might not be better once you settle…" He stopped.

Mayor Brandt was standing over them. "Captain Colangelo. Detective Brady." He paused.

Had he heard? She didn't care.

"You are two of the very best cops we have. Anything you need, you'll have."

Bob Nolan had no family. Who would arrange things? She could only think of one person. "Mike Resnick, my partner from my days at Manhattan South, was Bob Nolan's partner back in Narcotics. He might be the best person to handle the arrangements."

"No need, Detective," the mayor replied. "The department will handle it."

Colangelo waited for the mayor to walk away, readying his statement to the press. "Kim, do you want me to take you home?"

"Bring in Prinz."

"We are. As a material witness, remember?"

She stood and wiped the tears from her eyes. "Good. I need to be there. It's time to talk turkey to that asshole."

***

Felipe still had a buzz on when he answered the door. "Hey, Maria, come on in." But something was different about her. She looked… corporate. Tailored blouse and slacks, a light jacket, black flats. He opened his arms for her, but she side-stepped him.

Two men in jackets and ties followed her.

"Who are these guys, Maria?"

She pulled out a folder with a gold shield. "Detective Marisa Fuentes to you. This is Detective Brogan and my husband, Detective Stransky. We are taking you into protective custody as a material witness."

Husband? She's married?

And she's a cop?

"Whoa, hold on. I'm not…"

"Please, Mr. Prinz, don't make us cuff you." Then she flashed the same sweet smile she had the night before.

The bitch.

The one she'd called her husband spoke next. "Let's move it along, Prinz. We have reason to believe your life is endangered."

His head was clearing. "Wait, what's all this about a material witness?"

Maria—or, rather, Marisa—spoke up. "A member of our unit was murdered this morning, and we think the guy you told me about last night, Coravos, is responsible. Pack a bag, because you'll be living someplace else for a while."

"I had nothing to do with that. I didn't even know about it. I don't think I can…"

Her sweetness vanished. "Don't fuck with us, Prinz. This is for your own protection. Now pack the fucking bag."

# CHAPTER FIFTY-SEVEN

As soon as Kim got out of the car at the Castle, she stepped aside and called Jake to let him know she was okay. So good to hear his voice.

Sacramento wouldn't be so bad.

She wasn't prepared to see a familiar face before she went inside.

"Hello, Detective," Lodemay said. "Please excuse my coming here, but my sister told me you visited her."

I am *so* not in the mood for this. Nevertheless, he'd provided her with important information that had gotten her investigation off to a good start. "Yes, I did."

"Did you think I was crazy?" His voice was soft, almost plaintive.

"I wasn't sure. I needed to know more about you."

"It's okay. Did she tell you about…?"

"The tumor?" He stiffened but said nothing, only nodding. "Yes, she did."

"And you want to convince me I should return to the doctor."

It was what she'd promised to do. "John, a few years ago, I suffered a series of three miscarriages. I underwent a lot of tests to try to determine the cause. But when the doctor called and asked me to set up an appointment to go over all the results, I kept putting it off."

"Because you were afraid?"

"Yes. But after a while, I realized that not knowing was worse than whatever they might tell me, because the worst thing they could tell me was only one of several possibilities."

"You think I'm afraid." When she said nothing, he continued, "I'm not afraid. A Templar faces dangers and accepts risks."

"So, what is it?"

He stared at the ground. "You are a sister knight of the highest status, facing death and danger every day and never flinching. And so, I will tell you what I've never told anyone else, not even my great ancestor, Jacques de Molay. It is not fear that grips me, it's… humiliation."

She was stunned. "Why on Earth would you feel humiliation?"

He finally met her eyes. "No Templar ever had a… tumor. They died on the battlefield or in their beds."

She touched his arm. "John, they had no idea what went on inside their bodies, inside their skulls. Some may have had brain tumors, or any illness we know nowadays. They called it 'God's will' and let it go at that."

Marshal Dhillon poked his head outside the door. "Detective Kim, they are waiting for you."

"In a minute."

"I'm sorry," Lodemay said. "I've detained you, and you've suffered a grievous loss, a fellow knight. May he rest in peace. We'll talk again soon."

He turned and walked away.

Dhillon was waiting as she entered. "Detective Kim, are you okay?"

Suddenly, she was back on track. "I'll be fine, thank you. Where is everyone?"

"Mostly in Room One. They just brought Prinz in a few minutes ago for questioning."

Bostwick came out of his office. "Glad to see you're okay."

"Who says I'm okay? Bob was the only partner both my dad and I ever had."

"Maybe you should sit this one out."

They had Prinz in custody, and there was no way anyone was going to keep her from interrogating him. "Thanks, Lieu. I appreciate your concern, but there's too much to do." He walked with her to Room One. Just before they entered, she said, "Whatever I do, I need you to back my play, okay?"

His eyes narrowed. "What do you have in mind?"

"Not sure. I'll play it by ear. Will you?"

"Okay, but watch it."

Prinz resembled a schoolyard bully who'd just been put in his place.

Martin and Marisa were already at the table with him, and Bostwick joined them. Cole Rydell stood at the door, a very threatening presence with his linebacker build.

Kim took her favorite seat, directly across from Prinz, whose eyes kept shifting to Marisa. "She conned you, didn't she? How old did you think she was? Eighteen? Nineteen?"

"Nineteen." He spat the word.

"She's one of the most effective undercovers I've ever seen. The first time I worked with her was eight years ago, and she was passing for sixteen then." Kim shook her head and chuckled. "You thought you were going to have her, didn't you? A nice, young piece of ass. But instead… here you are. Have they told you why?"

"Yeah. Material witness."

"That's right. Good boy. A buddy of yours, one Yasiel Coravos, has been merrily gunning down New York City cops for a week and a half. This morning, the senior member of this squad was his latest victim. Last night, one of his shooters, one Enrique Cruz, turned up dead in Long Island City."

"I can't tell you anything."

Marisa spoke up. "They already know everything you told me last night."

Kim broke into a cold grin. "That's right, Prinz. We have every word recorded."

"Recorded? How?"

Marisa leaned forward. "You remember the little rose pin I was wearing here?" She pointed to a spot between her breasts. "You should, you were staring at it long enough."

"Maybe it wasn't the pin he was staring at," Kim said.

Prinz dropped his head into his hands. "Shit."

Kim continued in a business-like tone. "Yes, but enough about you. The point is that Coravos is part of your organization. Which means you bear some responsibility for his actions. It also means you could have alerted us to his activities as early as a week ago, and six lives might have been saved. But you chose to cover for him. That's called obstruction, and it's a crime."

Bostwick spoke up. "You can help yourself out, here, by telling us where we can find Coravos, who the other members of his cabal are, where they live and where they hang out, any information to help us tighten the net."

Prinz looked helpless. "I can't."

"We'll place you in protective custody, so that Coravos can't get at you," Bostwick said.

But Prinz just sat, shaking his head.

Enough of this shit. "Lieutenant, let him go."

"Kim," Bostwick replied, "we should talk about this."

"No."

Prinz jumped from his seat. "You can't do that. Coravos has people watching me. He'll think I talked."

"Don't worry," Kim replied. "We'll have DCPI release a statement to the media saying we have a witness who has been most helpful."

Prinz wheeled on Marisa. "You said you'd protect me!"

"She also said she was nineteen and wanted to join your group." Kim turned to Bostwick. "Please release him, Lieutenant.

"Wait a minute." Prinz was growing frantic.

"Sorry, Mr. Prinz," Bostwick said. "We offered you protective custody on the condition that you would give us the information we need."

"It's very simple, Prinz," Kim added. "You give us information—correct, useful information that holds up at trial—and we protect your sorry ass. No information, no protection. In fact, I'll arrange right now to have a patrol car drop you off in front of your building on Norfolk Street."

"That's very thoughtful, Kim," Martin said.

# CHAPTER FIFTY-EIGHT

"Ladies and Gentlemen of the press, I have a short statement to make, and then I will take a few questions relating to this incident, but nothing else.

"This morning, a veteran detective was gunned down in cold blood in the Bushwick section of Brooklyn. We have every reason to believe that this atrocity was committed by the same group that has committed a rash of other police killings over the past ten days. Police have leads, now, thanks to some very fine investigative work. Once this case is solved, I'll speak more freely but rest assured that those responsible will be brought to justice."

"Mr. Mayor," Rita Henshaw called out, "are you prepared to identify the group responsible?

"Only to say, categorically, that it is not a white ultranationalist group, as so many have been speculating."

"Mr. Mayor," Joanna Dunbar called out, "to your knowledge, has the police department received assistance from any other law enforcement agency?"

"I'm sorry, Ms. Dunbar, but I can't comment on that. I can only say that the department will get whatever support it needs from me, and whatever resources are required. Bar none."

"Is that a shot at the Council Speaker?" Henshaw called out.

The mayor broke into a grin. "If you like."

"Mr. Mayor," another reporter said, "what is your reaction to the story reported by *City News* this morning that Council Speaker Barnett intends to bring a bill to the floor revoking the generous tax abatement that Madison Square Garden currently enjoys?"

"Thank you, all, this press conference is over."

***

Prinz didn't know Coravos' exact address, but he knew it was somewhere in Greenpoint. He gave Kim his cell number. It was a burner phone, but he rarely switched phones.

Kim showed Prinz the list of names she'd gotten from Colonel Spiers, but he didn't recognize any of them. Prinz described how Coravos had first approached him several months earlier, offering to infuse CHE with new energy and urging Prinz to become more militant in his advocacy.

"How many supporters does he have within your organization?" Bostwick asked.

"He says he has fifteen, but I don't think it's nearly that many."

Kim showed the photos from the City Hall protest. "Are these among them?"

He studied the first two. "Yeah. The first one is Enrique Cruz."

"Now deceased," Kim said.

"I heard. The second one is Ibraham Aziz. He lives somewhere in East New York." Prinz provided his cell number, too.

"Did Coravos ever discuss his violent plans with you?" Kim asked.

"Nothing specific, but he talked a lot about how we needed to stop talking and start shooting. I never took him seriously until the day after the Prospect Park shooting. He came to me and said we needed to organize a demonstration—the City Hall thing—saying it had to be white ultranationalists. But his expression made it obvious that he didn't believe it."

A facial expression wasn't probable cause. "Did he ever say anything to you suggesting he was responsible?"

"Nothing directly, but he talked about how the cops got what they deserved, and the shootings were a step toward bringing about change."

Still not enough. "Did you know he and Mr. Cruz were crack shots?"

"Yeah. He bragged about that, about having gotten high marks in the army. Cruz and Aziz, too. And he talked a lot about how we'd soon have guns on our side of the politics, including AR-15s."

"Did he mention any other weapons by name?"

"Just the AR-15." Prinz thought for a moment. "He once mentioned that they all kept their shooting skills sharp."

Kim's ears perked up. "Did he say where?"

"He said he liked some public shooting range in New Jersey."

***

"This morning, following the shooting death of yet another New York City cop, Mayor Brandt announced that police had a lead in the string of shootings. He also said that police had categorically eliminated the possibility that white ultranationalists were behind it all. He pledged to give the department all the resources it needed to bring the killers to justice, an apparent slap in the face to Council Speaker Barnett, whose proposal to defund the police department in favor of social programs the mayor continued to denounce. Joanna Dunbar, ITN."

***

"At his press conference this morning, the mayor alternatively took shots at Council Speaker Barnett and this reporter as he stated that police had finally come up with a lead—but, apparently, no suspects—in the recent spree of shootings that has plagued people of color in this city. He dismissed out of hand the suggestion by many responsible sources that the shootings might be the work of some white ultranationalist group, but he declined to mention whom the police might suspect. Rita Henshaw, *City News.*"

***

Before they charged across the Hudson, Kim called Colonel Spiers and asked if one of the names he'd left off his list of potential suspects might have been Ibrahim Aziz. After a much shorter wait than she'd expected, he came back on the line and said it was.

"Could you please e-mail photos of all the men on the list, plus Aziz?" she asked.

He agreed, and five minutes later, she was printing them out.

# CHAPTER FIFTY-NINE

It was late afternoon, and Kim was glad she'd let Martin drive. He was certainly less drained than she was.

And he had more patience for heavy traffic. "I hate driving to Jersey, especially at this time of day and especially from Brooklyn. You pick your poison."

She looked up from the photos she'd been studying. "So which poison did you pick?"

"Our destination is a straight shot from the Lincoln Tunnel, so…"

"Choice made." Her cell pinged. A text from Jake, whom she'd already told she'd be late again. *I know you're pushing hard on this one, and I understand why. I'm so sorry about Bob, but I also worry about you. Please come home after this stop, whether you get what you're after or not. Love you.*

That was Jake all the way. *Thank you. Yes, this my last task tonight. We're getting close. How about you? Any leads on the job front?*

A moment later, she got his response. *Feelers from Sacramento, New Orleans, and Phoenix.*

With progress being made on the case, running away suddenly appealed less to her. But a promise was a promise. *Tell me about them tonight. Love you, too.*

A moment later, another ping. But this one wasn't from Jake, and she didn't recognize the number. *Nf3.*

She didn't recognize the message, either.

***

The sun was already setting when they pulled into the parking lot of the shooting range.

"That was fun," Kim said with a groan.

Martin stretched and locked the car. "Buckets of fun."

Kim pointed to two video cameras covering the parking lot and the entrance. "There's a plus."

Once inside, they flashed their badges at the guy behind the counter and asked to see the manager. They were escorted immediately into a small office.

"What's this all about?" the manager asked after checking their IDs and checking out Kim.

Kim informed him of their investigation.

"I read the papers," the manager said. "How do you think I can help?"

"We have reason to believe that at least one and possibly two of the shooters have used this range for target practice. One uses an AR-15, and the other uses a SIG Sauer P210A. I'm going to show you a series of photographs and ask you if you've seen any of these men in here."

One by one, he examined the photos, taking his time. The third photo in, he stopped. "This guy. He's the one with the AR-15, a real nice piece and he keeps it in perfect condition. A crack shot, too."

It was Yasiel Coravos.

He continued to examine the photos, and with each shuffling of a page and shaking of his head, Kim's heart sank a little.

Last page. "Yeah, this middle eastern guy. He uses a pistol, but I can't say which one. Real good shot. Tell you the truth, he makes me a little nervous every time he comes in." A shrug of the shoulders. "Yeah, I know, racial profiling, but what can I say? I was here on 9/11; I stood outside and watched the towers come down."

"I remember. I was thirteen at the time."

"I bet you were cute at thirteen."

She ignored the comment and Martin's smirk. "Did you ever see these men together or with others?"

"I don't recall, sorry."

"Do you keep track of the people who use this range?" Kim asked. "Are they required to show ID to get in?"

"Yeah. And we scan whatever they show us."

Now for the key question. "Are your records searchable by name?"

"Not by name. Only by date."

Shit.

"Now," the manager said with a groan, "why am I convinced your next request is to search our records, week by week, back to the Reagan Administration? Starting right now?"

She had to laugh. "Not quite that far, but yes." But the prospect of looking with him made her want to groan.

The manager pointed to a coffee pot on a side table. "Well, that's a fresh pot, so I guess we can get started."

Great, more caffeine. Her left eyelid was already twitching.

"Kim," Martin said. "This doesn't need two of us, and you've had it a lot rougher today than I have. Grab a cab home, and I'll take care of this. I'll see you at the Castle in the morning."

***

The mayor was just about to call it a day when Justin Cates entered his office. "Sorry for the interruption, sir, but I've been waiting all day to talk to you."

"Have a seat. What's on your mind?"

"At your press conference this morning, a reporter mentioned a bill to revoke Madison Square Garden's tax abatement."

The mayor remembered. "Yes, I've been meaning to ask you what that's all about."

"The Speaker is trying to use the proposal, which he assumes you'll oppose, to show you really don't want to spend more on social programs."

"So, it's really tied to his defunding bill."

"Yes, sir. And every Council person I've spoken to tells me their constituents are raising hell about that. None of them want to allow Barnett to bring it to the floor for a vote. The thing is, many of those constituents also don't like billionaire sports team owners getting huge tax breaks when the city clearly needs revenue."

The mayor considered it. "So, if I give in on the tax issue, I save myself the grief of being accused of gutting social programs, and he gets to say he got the additional funding for social programs without defunding the police."

"That's about the size of it, sir."

But tax issues weren't foremost on his mind. "Have you spoken with Kim Brady today?"

"Very briefly. She's pretty upset about Bob Nolan. She's become even more intense than usual about this case. Plus, her husband is out of a job."

"Any leads for him?"

"I don't know. She said something about Sacramento."

***

Sitting in the cab making its way through the Holland Tunnel, Kim sat back and closed her eyes, desperate to sleep and fearful it might come. After a few minutes, she shook herself to alertness.

She remembered the strange text. It remained, but there'd been nothing further.

*Nf3.*

Still no idea what it might mean. She replied. *I'm sorry, but who are you?*

The car emerged from the tunnel and made its way along Canal Street, passing close to the scene of another horrific crime eight years ago.

A reply. *Jacques de Molay.*

Lodemay. She should have known. *Sorry, I didn't recognize the number. Are you okay?*

His reply came in almost immediately. *I am quite well, dear sister of the knighthood. I've been worried about you.*

She tried not to dwell on what his attraction to her might mean. *I'm doing all right, thank you.*

The car turned from Canal onto the Bowery. *I've been thinking about our talk this morning. I thought I would honor you with the knight move.*

What knight move? She scanned back to the top of the group of texts. Nf3. It was a chess move—knight to king's bishop three. It brought a smile to her face. *The Reti Opening.*

His response came as the car turned onto Delancey Street, heading for the Williamsburg Bridge, which was near the scene of another case she'd solved, maybe the most important one to her family. *Chess is wonderful therapy when the world becomes too awful to bear. You mentioned that you play, so if you don't mind taking the black pieces, I've made my first move. We can play by text, each moving at our leisure.*

She hadn't played in a long time, but it struck her as an excellent idea. *Okay. In that case, 1... d5.*

For a moment she considered asking about his condition but decided against it. Why ruin one of the few pleasant moments she'd had all day?

# CHAPTER SIXTY

*Wednesday, April 30, 9:30 a.m.*

The pleasant moment had lasted longer than she'd expected. Jake had dinner waiting for her, including a glass of the most wonderful Montepulciano. They'd talked about Sacramento, New Orleans, and Phoenix, but Jake hadn't sounded enthusiastic about any of them.

After dinner, she'd dug out an old wooden chessboard and chess set, opened a snack table, and set up the position of her game with Lodemay.

Jake had approved. He'd also approved of her getting in a run this morning. Four miles wasn't much, but it was enough to get the adrenaline flowing. And she needed that.

The Castle was like a wake, an impression strengthened when she walked in and saw her old partner from Manhattan South Homicide, Mike Resnick, sitting at her desk.

"I came by to see edow you were doing," he said as they embraced.

"I'm okay, considering. How about you?"

"Dropping my papers at the end of the month. I thought I'd made it through my whole career without losing a partner." He stopped, looking sad. "I heard you were with him at the end."

"Not quite, but close enough."

Mike dropped his voice. "I also heard Bob was back on the sauce. I hope it's not true."

"He fell off the wagon and was struggling with it. That's one more awful thing about his death—I really believed he was going to make it. He and I talked about it—tough talk, you know?"

"I know. I'd had a few of those conversations with him, myself."

"I was convinced he would get back on track."

"He's at peace, Kim. Just like your dad. Anyway, I know he has no family, so I figured maybe you'd need some help with the arrangements."

"Thanks, but no, I don't. The department is handling that."

"Kim," Bostwick called to her, "we need to meet with the captain."

"Just a minute. Sorry, Mike…"

"Duty calls. They're probably going to throw me a shindig of some kind. I hope you'll come."

She kissed him on the cheek. "Wouldn't miss it for the world."

***

Martin led off. They'd found both Coravos and Aziz in the shooting range's system, both with assumed names and addresses that didn't exist.

"Clearly, Cruz hadn't dreamed it up on his own." Kim turned to Vera. "Any luck with the cell numbers?"

"*Da.* Find lots of tower pings all over city, but for Coravos, many clustered around tower in Greenpoint, and for Aziz, East New York."

Colangelo rolled his eyes. "Why do I know what's coming next?"

"Because we've been through this drill before," Kim replied. "We need Stingrays, and we need to deploy them ASAP. I'll call Rick Conti for a warrant. Anything on the Cruz murder?"

Vitello spoke up. "Two things. The Queens Medical Examiner discovered a second gunshot wound under his left armpit."

"The shot with the Glock was a ruse?" Martin asked. "Didn't they think we'd notice the second wound?"

"They probably figured it would be lost in the confusion," Kim said, "and in the short term it was. Phil, please tell me you got a take on the slug."

"Shell casing was found on the floor of Cruz's Wrangler, a nine-millimeter, and the ME recovered the slug from the body. Rifling on the slug matches a SIG Sauer P210A."

"Aziz," Martin said.

"Let's hope," Kim replied. "Phil, did the rifling match…"

"The slugs from the Red Hook shootings? That was next on my list. Yes, they did. I don't have anything, yet, on the slugs from Bob Nolan's murder, yet. But we found nine-millimeter shells in the street, so we're keeping our fingers crossed."

"I'll call Rick right now."

She received a text from Lodemay. *2. g6*

I don't have time, John. "Anything on the vehicle from yesterday?"

"Caught some local video. Silver Camry, can't tell the year. Got a partial on the plate number. Ended with -2832. I'm trying to search, but it would be easier if we had the first three letters."

"Keep me posted," Kim said.

***

The mayor was reading over the latest reports from ComStat, the NYPD's crime database. Homicides in the city had been trending toward a ten-year low until these recent shootings had started. The remaining numbers were uniformly good, if not spectacular.

Other than that, Mrs. Lincoln, how was the play?

His admin buzzed. "Mr. Mayor, the owner of Madison Square Garden called. He'd like to meet with you."

No doubt about the subject.

Which was why the course he'd discussed with Justin Cates wouldn't be as easy as it might have appeared. "Invite him to dinner at Gracie Mansion tonight."

***

After reviewing everything else they had and updating the case board, Kim texted Lodemay her move. *2... c6.*

His response was immediate. *Ah! Someone who knows her way around the Reti! 3. c4.*

Rick Conti was approaching; she hoped he had the requested warrant. She texted Lodemay, *Things are starting to get busy. You may not hear from me for a while.*

"Hi, Kim." Conti's tone of voice dashed her hopes. This wasn't good news. But he nodded to her cell. "Having fun?"

"I was, but I suspect that's done for now. You didn't get the warrant?"

"Not yet. Judge Vickers is the only one available. I need you to come with me in case he gets scratchy on probable cause."

***

Kim followed Rick into the judge's chambers.

"Oh, dear," the judge said as they sat before him. "Mr. Conti and Detective Brady. Looks like I'm in for a difficult afternoon."

"Not at all, your honor," Rick said. "This relates to the series of police shootings, so we want to make sure everything is understood up front."

"I understand the department has leads. What are we looking for?"

Rick handed him the affidavit that Kim had signed. "Warrants for electronic surveillance on two suspects, one living in Greenpoint, the other in East New York, but with specific addresses unknown. Mr. Coravos is a suspect in the Prospect Park shooting, while Mr. Aziz is a suspect in the Red Hook shooting, the murder of Detective Nolan, and the murder of Mr. Cruz, who was the other shooter in Prospect Park."

"Alleged shooter," Vickers said.

"No, your honor." Kim knew she should have waited for Rick's signal, but this was too important to sacrifice for protocol. "Mr. Cruz was found dead in his own car, shot with his own weapon, which ballistics matched to slugs recovered from five victims in Prospect Park. We also have an affidavit from the manager of a shooting range in Queens affirming that Mr. Cruz was seen with the same model weapon at the range, using the same ammunition."

"How do we know it was the same gun?" Vickers asked.

"We can infer it because the ammunition is rarely used for target shooting, which is a prime use of the Glock 34."

Vickers studied the affidavit.

Kim also explained the connection of the three.

"It's still circumstantial," Vickers said. "All of it."

"I believe that's why we call it 'probable cause'."

Rick glared at her, but Vickers broke into a small grin. "Touché, Detective." The grin vanished. "However, I must balance this against what we already know about this case and this investigation."

"Which is what, exactly?" Now, he was pissing her off. When he hesitated, she pressed on. "Everything else that's known by the public is not 'known' at all; it's speculation accepted as fact." She'd seen the stunned look on his face as he studied the photos of Coravos, Cruz, and Aziz. "I told you at your dinner I didn't accept the white ultranationalist theory. This was never about race. It's about revolutionaries."

The judge leaned forward. "I beg your pardon?"

Rick jumped in. "Your honor, Kim is right. If you read Felipe Prinz's affidavit, this group of Coravos' infiltrated CHE with the intention of turning it from an advocacy group to one of violent rebellion."

Kim explained that Prinz was now in protective custody, and that his affidavit was a repeat of everything they'd caught on Marisa's wire. "When," she added, "he had no way of knowing she was a detective."

"And the purpose of the Stingray surveillance is to locate the residences of the individuals in question?" Vickers asked.

Kim was about to respond when she felt Rick's knee against hers, so she decided she'd already said enough.

"That's correct, your honor," Rick replied, "at which time the police intend to place both individuals under arrest."

# CHAPTER SIXTY-ONE

When Kim returned to the Castle with the warrants in hand, two Stingray units were sitting on the table in the conference room, while Doug Cameron and Andy Costello from Brooklyn South were getting a refresher course in their use from Vera. Not surprisingly, the two students were distracted by their comely instructor. Tim Brogan and Cord looked on.

Cole Rydell sauntered in. "Lieutenant Bostwick said you needed some extra hands." His eyes quickly fell on Vera. "I'm glad to help in any way I can."

Cord spoke up from the end of the table. "She be okay, bro."

Rydell glared at him but said nothing.

Kim took charge. "Thank you, Vera. And thank you for spending your time and effort with us. Captain Colangelo is going to send a memo to your commander praising your efforts."

Vera bowed low. "Thank you."

"Okay," Kim said. "We have three crews of two. With Cord still on light duty, Martin and I have the most experience with Stingrays, so Martin will take one and I'll take the other. Tim will be my driver, and we'll cruise Greenpoint. Andy will be Martin's driver, and you guys cruise East New York. Cole and Doug, I want you two mobile and ready if either team locates their man."

***

Tim drove while Kim worked the Stingray. She was glad she'd caught some of Vera's refresher course, and it had all come back to her. "These things have gotten more sophisticated since the last time I used one."

"Technology usually does. How long ago was that?"

"Seven years, when we *were* looking for an ultranationalist group. One leader had a chop shop around here." She glanced around. "It's gotten nicer since then."

"Ah, the joys of gentrification."

"It was the first case I worked with Bob. He was at Brooklyn North, and I was with Internal Affairs."

*I should have accepted his offer of a ride.*

"Hey, you okay, Kim?"

She shook herself. "It just backs up on me sometimes." *Back to the scanner.*

The radio crackled. "Scanner Two to Scanner One." Martin's voice.

Kim picked up the mic. "Scanner One, go ahead Scanner Two."

"Nothing yet. We're scanning along Dumont Avenue. How sure was Vera of this location? Over."

"She said the tower was four blocks from the Livonia Train Yard, and that the calls could have come from anywhere from a quarter mile to a one-mile radius. Over."

"Should we be patrolling the same area?"

"Copy that, Scanner Two, but we can't risk catching one and alerting the other. Out."

"Roger that, Scanner One. Out."

Lodemay texted her. *In my delirium, I can think only of you, my queen. To you I pledge my honor and my life. If you could but grace me with your move, it would cheer me greatly. With warmest regards, your most loyal servant, Jacques de Molay.*

"Jake?" Tim asked.

"No, it's from Lodemay. We're playing a game of chess. Sort of."

He chuckled. "I don't know what that means."

She didn't answer. Lodemay's text was not just strange, it was troubling, as if he were deteriorating. She thought back on what his sister had told her and dialed her number.

"This is Susan."

"Ms. Garmin, Detective Brady. I wanted to let you know that I've received two texts today from your brother, and they're very troubling."

A pause. "Why are you texting my brother?"

"He asked me to play a game of chess with him, so we've been exchanging moves by text."

Ms. Garmin's tone immediately softened. "That's very thoughtful of you, Detective. Thank you."

"I've also encouraged him to call you. I take it he hasn't."

"No. What about the texts? What's wrong with them?"

"Both times, he's referred to himself as Jacques de Molay. Also, his language is… odd." She read the last text to her. "I thought you should know."

"Thank you, Detective. I'll look in on him this evening. Please continue the game as long as you can."

"Why wouldn't I?"

But the call had already dropped.

She texted the next move in the opening. *You're a good man. 3… Bg4.*

***

How does one appear welcoming for a person one dislikes intensely?

The mayor contemplated that question as the owner of Madison Square Garden made his long-winded request. In truth, the man had been a generous contributor and had been enthusiastic when the mayor announced he was running for re-election as an independent. Moreover, he'd made no demands on the mayor.

Until now.

Having gone on at great length about how both the Knicks and Rangers were at the heart of New York Sports, and the Knicks, especially, were so engrained in the city's history and sports culture, and how he had invested billions of dollars in a massive renovation and makeover of the building, he finally got down to the heart of it as the mayor was finishing his coffee.

"This tax abatement bill the Speaker is pushing would be disastrous for us, Mr. Mayor. We invested in those renovations without government assistance on the understanding that the abatement would remain in place. Remove the abatement, and our presence at that location becomes untenable. Consider the businesses in that location relying on people coming to events there for their income. Consider the riders on mass transit."

"I do understand the problem. But, if the governor pursues her plans for a new Penn Station, won't you be forced to find a new location, or to relocate temporarily while a new arena is built there?"

"You and I both know that future governors and future legislators might very well scrap that whole ridiculous plan. You've spoken on our behalf in other issues. I was hoping we could count on you for this one."

"Let's put all our cards on the table," the mayor said. "While the loss of the abatement would certainly hurt your bottom line, it would be nothing next to the cost of securing more debt to build yet another arena elsewhere, not to mention leasing space in other existing arenas for your sports teams or the loss of revenue from the non-sporting events you would need to forego while a new arena was being built."

"You're unwilling to act?"

Not yet. "I need to be mindful the potential revenue gain for the city if the abatement is revoked. It might mean a new gym for a high school in Woodside, or a day care center in Brownsville, or a self-help program in Manhattan. It might mean a hundred more police officers per year." He watched as his guest held his breath, waiting. "Of course, it's no secret that this proposal didn't just pop up out of nowhere, nor did it spring from a long-advocated grassroots effort. Let me consider it."

His guest exhaled. "If there's anything I can do to assuage your concerns…"

Now. "There might be. There just might be."

***

"Scanner One, this is Scanner Three." Rydell's voice. "How much longer we gonna keep this up? It's nearly midnight, for Christ's sake."

Kim keyed the mic. "Scanner Three, this is Scanner One. It's only 11:15. We'll continue to one, then call it a night. Over."

"You mind if I ask what the hell you expect to find in the next hour and three quarters that we haven't found already?"

"Scanner Three, this is Scanner One. I mind a whole lot when radio protocol isn't followed. And the last time I checked, killers don't usually punch a clock. Scanner One out."

Tim chuckled. "That's telling him, Kim. He's just annoyed because he didn't get to do any scanning."

But Kim wasn't laughing. There should have been something by now. She texted Vera. *Any new activity on the records of the two cell numbers we're tracking?*

It was several minutes before she got a response. *Nyet. Nothing since early this morning.*

She resisted the urge to hurl her cell out the window and snatched the radio mic instead. "Scanner One to Scanner Two and Three. Return to the Castle. Repeat, break off surveillance and return to the Castle. Out."

"What is it?" Brogan asked.

"They've ditched their burners. Prinz claimed he was being watched. They must have seen us take him into custody and figured he'd give up their cell numbers."

"So, what do we do, now?"

"That's a damned good question."

# CHAPTER SIXTY-TWO

*Thursday, May 1, 8:01 a.m.*

"We at *City News* have it on good authority that Felipe Prinz, head of CHE, is being held by police. He was seen being taken from his home on the Lower East Side yesterday and has been held *incommunicado* ever since. There can be no question that the police are seeking to silence an organization that has been openly critical of them and whom the police have often resorted to violence to quell. This is Rita Henshaw reporting."

***

Kim flopped into a chair in the conference room as Colangelo gathered them together.

"Okay, folks," he said. "First of all, forget the shit we heard this morning from *City News*. It has no bearing on our investigation, and DCPI will deal with it. Our main concern is how to proceed now that we can't use our Stingrays to track Coravos and Aziz. Any ideas?"

Kim walked to the board and picked up a marker. "I think we need to make sure we've got all the information we've set out to get." She pointed to the note about the silver Camry with the partial plate number. "Cord, how are we doing on an ID?"

"There are thirty-seven vehicles in New York State with plates ending in those four digits, eleven in New York City, three in Brooklyn, one in East New York. It's registered to Ibrahim Habib at 497 Jerome Street. But I checked, and there's no such address."

"So, Aziz is using the same dodge Cruz used." This was like running in quicksand.

"But that part of Jerome Street is very close to the tower on Dumont and Ashford," Vera said. "So, he must live somewhere nearby."

Kim turned to Colangelo. "We should alert the Seven-Four about the silver Camry and have them detain Aziz the minute they see him. Martin, you and Tim head down there, and I'll ask Doug and Andy to join you too."

"Consider it done," Colangelo said. "What else?"

Kim turned to Vitello. "Anything new from…"

"Ballistics confirms that the slugs that killed Bob were fired from the same weapon that killed the two Red Hook officers. And the crime lab got a print from one of the shell casings."

Now, that was big. "Great. Send a copy to Colonel Spiers at Army Intelligence. I'm sure they have Aziz's prints on file. That leaves Coravos."

Bostwick had a suggestion. "We could do the same thing in Greenpoint we're doing in East New York with Aziz—flood the area with cops. We know the cell tower his calls pinged."

She had to think about it. "Coravos has done the most to conceal his identity, probably because he has the most to hide. He's also clearly smarter than the other two. He may have seen us cruising his neighborhood last night, so he's alerted to our interest. Let's hold off for now. I want to talk to Prinz again and find out how much else he knows about Coravos and his pals."

"Won't that give him more time to slip away?" Bostwick asked.

"Maybe, but there's something else that bothers me, and it suggests he isn't going anywhere. That bullshit Rita Henshaw spouted this morning."

Cord snorted. "Looking for cover because her theory of the crime blew up in her face."

"But she knew we'd escorted Prinz out of his building, and she knew the time of day we'd done it. Prinz said he suspected he was being watched. I think he was right and either Coravos or someone working for him tipped off Henshaw."

Colangelo must have known what she was thinking. "She'll never give it up."

Kim ignored the comment. "Martin, you and Tim should take a Stingray to East New York with you. I'll join you after an errand."

"What use is the Stingray to us?" Martin asked. "We don't have a number to use for scanning."

"We may when I get back," Kim replied. "Captain, I need Detective Rydell to join me."

Colangelo met her request with arched eyebrows. "Okay, Kim, but Henshaw will never give it up."

"I guess we'll just see about that."

***

"I'm getting the sense that you and I don't get along," Rydell said as Kim drove across Manhattan toward the *City News* studios near Times Square.

"I like you just fine, Rydell. Just make sure you remember this is my investigation. I don't want any freelancing."

"What's that supposed to mean?"

She stopped at a light. "You need a hearing exam?"

"See, that's just what I mean. What's your beef with me?"

"You know full fucking well what 'no freelancing' means. When we meet who I'm looking for, I want you to do one thing, only. Am I clear?"

"Yeah. What's the one thing?"

"Stand there looking slightly menacing. Do not say anything unless I ask you a direct question."

"So, I'm the intimidation factor? You're the good cop and I'm the bad cop?"

"No, Rydell, I'm the bad cop. You're just the threat behind the bad cop."

They rode another block in silence before Rydell said, "Is that all you think I'm good for?"

Kim found a parking spot. "No, but it's something I believe you can do well. This is a test of your reliability. If you pass, I'll know I can rely on you."

"What makes you think you can't, now?"

She grasped the door handle. "Sorry, we don't have that kind of time. Coming?"

***

Rita Henshaw looked surprised to see Kim. "I expected someone from DCPI, not you."

"Sorry to disappoint you. Can we step outside, please?" Kim turned without waiting for an answer but was not surprised when Henshaw followed. The racket of a jackhammer half a block away made for a nice background.

Excellent, she's expecting a story from this.

Kim led her into an alley next to the studio, where Henshaw saw Rydell standing by the car, arms folded. "What's his function? To beat me up?"

"No, I'm quite capable of doing that myself."

Henshaw froze. "That's not funny, Detective."

"I didn't come for comedy. Seven dead cops are no laughing matter. Neither are two dead teenagers who died solely to throw off the likes of you."

"I don't know what you're…"

"That's not your best play, here." Kim made a small motion with her arm and Rydell closed in on the now quite nervous reporter. "Your report this morning had a serious error. Mr. Prinz was not arrested yesterday."

Henshaw gave a nervous shrug. "So you say now."

Kim pulled a business card from her pocket and handed it to the reporter. "The hand-written number is the direct line to the warden at Rikers Island. Call him. Ask if Felipe Prinz is currently in custody at Rikers. Go ahead, we'll wait."

Henshaw stared back in stunned silence.

Kim pulled out another card. "That's the direct line of the warden at the Tombs. Call and ask him the same question." No reaction. Kim pulled out a third card. "The warden at the Brooklyn Detention Center. Same deal. Go ahead. Start calling. We'll wait."

Henshaw swallowed hard. "What do you want?"

"Two things. The first is for you to admit your story was pure bullshit."

Henshaw shot a glance at Rydell, then back to Kim. "All I have to do is yell."

"Go ahead." Kim nodded in the general direction of the persistent jackhammering. "No one will hear you." She broke into a cold grin. "Life in the big city."

"I… My story was true, based on the facts as I knew them at the time."

"What facts? You got a fucking phone call from someone who I'm certain didn't identify themselves, handing you a line you were just dying to run with."

"I wouldn't say…"

A flick of Kim's wrist, and Rydell stepped closer.

Henshaw paled. "Could you please make him back off?"

"Claustrophobic, are we?" Kim's voice dripped with mock concern. "First, you tell me what steps you took to confirm that fairy tale before you went on the air."

"I… well, I didn't…"

"So, your answer is none. Zip. Nada." She leaned into Henshaw's face. "So, you admit the story was bullllllshit."

Henshaw could only nod.

"Good." Kim's sudden cheery voice unnerved the reporter even more. "Now, for the second thing I want. And it's so obvious, I don't even need to say it."

Henshaw gave tiny, nervous shakes of her head. "I… I can't. I don't even know who it was. He didn't give a name."

"Of course, he didn't. Because he's way smarter than you are. But at least we've established it was a male. High voice? Deep voice?"

"Deep but not too deep."

"Accent?"

"Spanish accent, not too heavy."

Kim flashed another insincere smile. "Rita, darling, you're just a font of information. I'm so pleased."

Henshaw nodded. "But I can't tell you…"

Kim's smile vanished, replaced by a hard glare. "You will give me… the… number… he… called from." Together, she and Rydell backed the reporter against the concrete wall.

"He told me not to." It came out a whisper.

"Now?" Rydell asked.

Unplanned. It must be in his DNA. "That's up to Ms. Henshaw. What'll it be?"

She blurted out the number.

"Wait." Kim took a step back, pulled out her cell, opened the Notes App, and entered the number. "Thanks. One more thing. We never had this conversation."

# CHAPTER SIXTY-THREE

"I know," Rydell said when they returned to the car. "You said no freelancing. Sorry."

Now, Kim could laugh. "It's okay. It was a brilliant touch."

"You can trust me, now?"

Should she? It wasn't like they could repair the damage now.

But it would gnaw at her if she didn't. "Bob Nolan was a recovering alcoholic. You had to know that."

"I'd heard. He never said anything about it, if that's why you're asking."

"It isn't. The night everyone went out for drinks, why did you invite Bob to go along, knowing that…"

"I didn't invite him. Therese Vazquez did. And, between you and me, I was surprised and somewhat irritated because when I invited Therese, I was hoping something would develop."

"Aren't you married?"

"Yeah, but I'm not an extremist about it. I know you won't approve…"

"Not for me to say."

He paused. "Thanks. Anyway, when Bob came along, I didn't think anything of it. Guys on the wagon come out with us all the time and drink ginger ale or club soda or whatever. And it wasn't that I objected to Bob coming, it's just that Therese was kind of mothering him and I knew that would kill any chance I might have had with her."

"Maybe that's why she wanted him along. She's had a bad experience with a hyper-attracted male."

He paused. "I could probably guess who, but I won't. Is the next stop the Castle?"

"Yes. I want to give this to Vera to check out, but I also want to let the captain and the lieu know about our chat with Henshaw."

Rydell glared at her with alarm but said nothing else.

***

Felipe had decided early on that staying stoned a good part of the time was the only way he could survive the boredom of protective custody. His buddy, Yasiel, might have been right about the reasons they'd legalized it, but if it was helping ol' Felipe cope, he wasn't about to argue.

Yasiel. Felipe had decided early on he was fucking nuts, but not early enough. The revolution that Felipe had advocated for years had been his dream, but Yasiel was determined to make it a reality. By the time Felipe had realized what was happening, Yasiel and his buddies had hijacked CHE, leaving Felipe out in the cold.

How fucking unbelievable was that?

Two sharp knocks at the door. He tried to ignore them. Fucking cops always claimed they were "just checking to make sure he was okay", but Felipe knew better, that they were fucking with him.

The door opened.

Shit. Forgot they had the key.

"You got visitors."

He peered at the woman detective—that bitch, Brady. And with her was the biggest fucking goon he'd seen in a long time.

"Shit, Prinz," Brady said, "don't you ever stop smoking that shit?"

"Not if I can help it. You oughtta try it sometime. We could get down together."

"In your dreams."

The goon just glared at him, which struck him as funny.

"All right, Prinz," Brady said, as usual all hard business. "Can you tell me where Coravos lives, and who else from his crew is in your group besides Enrique Cruz and Ibrahim Aziz?"

Whoa, way too much for his head. He waved his arms. "Can you slow it down, Miss Faster-then-a-speeding-bullet?"

"Where does Coravos live?" she asked.

"At his house?" He started laughing again. This was some funny shit.

The goon looked pissed, but Brady was cool. "And where is his house? And don't tell me 'Brooklyn', or I'll sic my partner on you. Or I can release you and allow you to take your chances on the street."

So much for cool. "Somewhere in Greenpoint. I don't know where, but his favorite place to meet it is a little park by the river."

"Could you be a little more specific? The name? The street it's on?"

"Don't know the name, but it's right at the end of Greenpoint Avenue." His buzz was fading.

"What about his other members?"

Damn, this bitch was relentless. "I don't know their names, but they would just show up at protests. I'd say somewhere between five and ten."

***

Kim had spent the ride back trying to decide how much to tell her superiors about her encounter with the reporter. She was certain Henshaw wouldn't say a word to anyone, both because she couldn't know if Coravos could learn of it and because nothing in the encounter could be made to show her in a favorable light.

But if Henshaw ever did go public with it, or even just report it to Internal Affairs, it would mean trouble for Kim. Although most of what transpired could be interpreted as the heat of the moment, Kim's assertion that she could beat up Henshaw herself could only be read as a threat of violence, and her suggestion that any cries for help would not be heard over the other street noise would underline that.

She wouldn't lie to Bostwick or Colangelo. She'd known them both for too long. But if she told them everything, it would put them in the position of having to protect her, and that wasn't right, either. Then again, if she withheld something that came out later, by whatever means, and she hadn't told them, they'd never trust her again.

Rydell turned to her as she turned the engine off, having parked only a few feet from where Bob Nolan was murdered. "You got awful quiet all of a sudden."

"Planning next steps."

"Got it. Before we go inside, I just want to say you did terrific work back there. Ever since you came here, I've been hearing what a great cop you are, but today you showed me just how great. I know you came close to the line. That took balls. If you ever get into hot water about it, I'll back you up all the way."

She gave him a warm smile. "Thanks, Cole."

And then she made her decision.

***

She stopped by the desk Vera was using first. "This is the number of the phone that was used by Rita Henshaw's informant for this morning's story. I need you to dig out every detail on it you can. But most important, I need to know where the call to Henshaw originated, and any towers it pinged either before or after the call."

"I will get on it right away, Brilliant American Lady Detective."

Bostwick sidled up to her. "She gave it up? Without a fight?"

"We need to discuss that."

As they entered Colangelo's office, the lieu cut off any opening statement by Kim when he said, "She got it, Captain."

"Rita Henshaw gave up her informant willingly?" Colangelo's tone left no doubt that he didn't believe it.

"Not right away. I needed to convince her." She recounted the conversation in full.

When she finished, he sat back and said nothing.

"Jesus, Kim," Bostwick said at last. "You kind of went over the line, there, didn't you?"

"I wish you hadn't told us," Colangelo said at last.

"I wouldn't expect a captain with years of experience in Internal Affairs to react that way," Kim said.

"We both served in IAB," Colangelo replied.

"I didn't want you to be sandbagged if this blew up later. I thought you deserved to know up front." But as she reflected, she wondered if anything would come of it. After all, Rita Henshaw was not a suspect in a crime, so it wasn't as if Kim had violated her right against self-incrimination.

The right to protect her source also wasn't violated, since Henshaw didn't know who that was. Besides, it was a right often asserted by journalists but not always upheld in court.

Threatening to beat up a citizen, though, was outside the department's policy guidelines.

"Captain," Bostwick said, having apparently gone through the same thought process Kim had, "what do you think the result would be if that reporter did file a complaint?"

But Colangelo had one more question. "Did Rydell do or say anything you haven't already told me?"

"All he did was stand close. And all he said was, 'Now?' Other than that, nothing."

"What did he mean?" Colangelo asked.

"I honestly don't know. We never discussed it."

Colangelo exchanged looks with Bostwick. "I see. All right, Kim, thanks for letting me know."

# CHAPTER SIXTY-FOUR

Kim walked straight to the conference room, where Vera was adding notes to the marker board.

"Ah, Brilliant American Lady Detective is back." Vera completed a diagram that resembled part of a wagon wheel, with a circle in the center marked with the phone number Kim had gotten from Rita Henshaw, and three spokes leading outward, each ending in another circle marked with a phone number. One of those numbers had an additional note, "ENY".

Kim pointed to it. "Same tower?"

"*Da.*"

"What about the central one?"

Vera sighed. "Some in Greenpoint, but also other parts of Brooklyn, and one in Lower East Side."

"Probably looking for his good buddy, Prinz," Cord said.

Kim agreed. "But that also means he's not hiding out. Vera, can we track his movements, tower to tower?"

"*Nyet.* He turns phone off when not in use."

"Which means he doesn't know when someone is calling him," Cord said.

A positive. "He probably turns it on periodically to check, or maybe he and Aziz have set times to check in. But if Aziz realizes he's about to be picked up, he can't warn Coravos." She glanced at the remaining Stingray, sitting on the table. "Prinz didn't give me much that was useful, but he did mention at least a few other members. Coravos may very well turn that phone on to keep in touch when he's home. And a Stingray can pick it up."

"I agree," Cord said. "I'd be glad to ride with you."

Vera threw down her marker. "*Nyet!* You make promise, you keep promise."

Cord looked so sheepish that Kim had to laugh. "Thanks, Cord, but Martin and I can both handle the Stingray."

"Martin's already out there, scanning with Tim." Cord was able to regain some dignity.

Shit. She'd forgotten. "Then, I'll take Rydell with me. He can drive while I scan."

Cord pulled himself to his feet. "I've got far more practice with these things than you do. I can sit in the back seat and scan, and you can take Rydell with us for added muscle. Vera, I won't even get out of the car."

"And what if shooting starts?" Vera asked.

Kim stepped in. "Cord, it's only been eleven days since you were shot, and only eight since you left the hospital. You shouldn't even be here." But she knew he was right about his experience with Stingrays.

"You said desk work only, no field." Vera sounded desperate. "You promised."

Cord walked over to Vera and embraced her. "Yes, I did. And I meant it. But I didn't foresee this situation. I've got a stake in this, too, having been shot by these bastards. We have a limited window before these guys decide to switch up phones again." He turned to Kim. "You do realize that. And when they do, Coravos won't make the same mistake twice."

She couldn't argue with him.

"Even Martin isn't as experienced with Stingrays as I am. With Rydell riding shotgun, you won't need me if things get rough."

"Let's see what the lieu thinks, because if I agree without telling him, and this goes south, it'll be my ass."

***

"Mr. Mayor," Justin said, "several members of the City Council are asking where you stand on the bill to revoke the special real estate tax abatement for Madison Square Garden. And Joanna Dunbar has called twice asking about it."

The mayor had just ended a call with the owner of that esteemed establishment. "They can't vote on it without my say-so?"

"They're your supporters, sir. They want to make sure they're all in agreement with you, since your stance will be seen considering your election battle with the speaker."

No way to avoid that. "Yes, if I agree with it, I'll be seen as knuckling under to him, and if I oppose it, I'll be labeled as an intransigent, or, worse, insensitive to the needs of... fill in the blank."

"We could use the revenue, sir."

"We could, indeed. But let's take care we don't throw out the window what we take in at the door." When Justin stared at him, he continued, "We collect other taxes from the Garden, namely sales tax and income tax. We also collect taxes from the businesses that surround the Garden. Who knows how much of that we'd lose if the Garden were to relocate outside the city limits?"

"So, you're going to oppose it?"

"As my specific condition will be met, yes, I am. And I'll make a statement to that effect at my press conference tomorrow."

"May I ask, sir, what your condition was?"

The mayor told him. "But that remains between you and me."

***

Bostwick had agreed, with the condition that if Cord started to feel weak or ill, Kim would bring him right back to the Castle. Before they'd left, Kim had asked Vera to keep them informed by text of any tower pings from either number. Vera had nodded but said nothing else.

She had Rydell drive, taking the same route up Graham Avenue to McGuinness Boulevard she'd taken, so that she could handle communications from the passenger seat while Cord stayed in the back operating the Stingray. "Turn left onto Greenpoint Avenue."

"Where, exactly, are we going?" Rydell asked.

"According to Vera, most of the tower pings from the cell number we got from Henshaw were from a cell tower in a little park by the river. Probably the same park where Prinz met Coravos."

Kim's cell signaled a text. It was from Vera. *Call from Greenpoint number to number we don't have. Logged new number from tower in Brownsville.*

"Calling up reinforcements," Kim said as she read the text aloud. *Thanks. See what you can learn about the new number. Did the Greenpoint number ping the same tower by the river?*

*Da. End of Greenpoint Avenue.*

Rydell made the turn onto Greenpoint Avenue.

"Anything yet, Cord?"

"Negative. Must still be out of range."

Text from Martin. *Located cell on Jerome Street. Preparing to pick up suspect Aziz.*

She texted back, *Make sure you have backup before you take him. Let me know how it goes. Good luck.*

They were just approaching West Street, the last cross street before Greenpoint Avenue dead-ended at the park, when Cord called out, "I got a hit. Not in the park itself. It's a bit further north on India Street. Turn right on West Street, then straight three blocks to India Street and make another right. The house will be on the right."

They parked across the street.

"We just gonna sit and wait?" Rydell asked.

"For the moment. I'm calling the Nine-Four for backup. I'm also calling the lieu to have him request an Emergency Services unit. I'm not taking any chances."

# CHAPTER SIXTY-FIVE

The first patrol car from the Nine-Four arrived ten minutes later, pulling up next to them. "You Brady?" one of the officers asked.

"That's me. We believe the guy who's been gunning down cops is hiding inside. I'm waiting for ESU to get here before we go get him."

"I'm Sergeant Grady. Nice to meet you. I've got three other units en route. I suggest we place two of them over on Java Street. You can't tell from here, but some of these houses have yards that connect, and there are spaces leading onto the next block. You got a photo of this guy?"

Kim handed him four copies.

He chuckled. "Nice to see you came prepared."

"Please warn your men to be careful, Sergeant. Coravos is a former army marksman, and we know he has at least one AR-15. He also may have accomplices with him."

"How many?"

"At most, five."

"Kim," Cord said, "he's making a call. Not a number we've seen before."

"Thanks, Cord. Let Vera know so she can check it out." She turned to the sergeant. "That's one less person he could have inside, but it may mean he's calling for reinforcements."

"I'll call in for another ESU outfit. This could get ugly."

***

The mayor stepped up to the podium at City Hall. "Thank you all for coming. As many of you have been reporting, the City Council is now debating a bill to revoke a special property tax abatement that Madison Square Garden has enjoyed for many years. Many of you have asked where I stand on this proposal. While, on its face, it appears to raise additional revenue for the city—and there is no question that the city could use additional revenue—there are several economic factors that the studies Mr. Barnett has made public to support his proposal do not consider. When these factors are added to the mix, the net gain from revoking the tax abatement is considerably smaller than tax gain. For that reason, I ask the Council to defeat this proposal. I promise that I will veto it if passed."

***

Two ESU trucks pulled up, and a lieutenant whom Kim thought looked familiar approached.

"Detective Brady?" he said. "Kim Brady?"

As she stepped out of the car, she remembered. "Lieutenant Zimmerman?"

"We meet again. The last time, I was praying you wouldn't get us all blown to hell and gone. What's the situation?"

"Our suspect, one Yasiel Coravos, is inside that building. We're not sure which apartment. We know he's armed with an AR-15, and I wouldn't rule out other weapons. We think he's alone, but I can't say with absolute certainty. There are yards behind these houses and some access to the street beyond. We currently have officers from the Nine-Four stationed along that street as well as this one in case he tries to run. My bigger concern is if he forces us to go in and get him and he starts shooting."

She showed him an aerial view of the block on her cell from Google Earth.

He studied it. "Very well. I'll deploy two sharpshooters at the edge of the yard from the other street, and two snipers from the roof of this building behind us. We have additional shooters we can set up here at street level. It would be helpful if we could determine where in the house he is."

Kim had an idea. "I've been waiting for you guys to arrive before I engage him." She paused when she received a text from Vera. *He made two more calls. Receiving numbers logged. One more in Brownsville, and one in Kensington. Checking call records now.*

That made three others he'd called in addition to Aziz. "Lieutenant, there is a possibility that as many as three members of our suspect's group may attempt to…"

"I'll call for an additional unit, you call for more backup, and we'll secure the perimeter."

# CHAPTER SIXTY-SIX

It was another hour before the additional units arrived, the perimeter was established, streets were closed to traffic, and the ESU sharpshooters were in place.

Kim dialed Coravos' cell. He refused the call.

She got a text from Martin. *Aziz in custody. Taking him back to the Castle.*

She replied, *Well done, Martin. Coravos may take a little longer. Vera found three more members of their network. Let the precinct cops take him to the Castle, and let the lieu know they're coming. You and Tim bring the Stingray here in case Coravos' buddies are heading this way.*

Zimmerman handed her a bullhorn.

"Thanks." She raised it and pressed the button. "Yasiel Coravos, this is Detective Brady of the NYPD. Your house is surrounded, and all escape routes are blocked. I am going to call your cell again. I advise you to take the call."

She wasn't confident he would answer.

And he didn't.

She raised the bullhorn again. "Mr. Coravos, we can do this the hard way or the easy way. It's up to you. Mr. Aziz has already surrendered to police."

She tried again. He refused the call.

She had a sudden thought of Lodemay, whom she hadn't heard from since her last chess move. This was a chess game of another variety. She raised the bullhorn. "You don't have an endgame here, Mr. Coravos. Enrique Cruz is dead, the man who killed him with a SIG Sauer P210A is now in custody, and this block is sealed off, so your remaining three associates can't possibly help you, if that was why you called them. And if you called to tell them to run, we'll hunt them down the same way we hunted down Cruz, Aziz, and you. Do yourself a favor and take the fucking call."

# CHAPTER SIXTY-SEVEN

He took the call. "A woman cop who talks dirty. The higher-ups won't like that, Brady."

"They can sue me."

"They can do much more than that. And they will when your case against me collapses because you violated that reporter's rights."

"I have no idea what you mean." Although her gut told her this was about to take a dangerous turn.

"Sure, you do. You forced the lovely Rita Henshaw to give you this number. Don't you know police can't force a reporter to give up her sources? What did you do? Threaten to beat it out of her?"

"It's nice to see you're already thinking about your legal defense. I admire a man who thinks ahead. But this isn't a chess game."

"That's the second time you've made a reference to chess. Do you play?"

"Yes."

"I thought so. I like a woman who thinks ahead. I'll bet you play a careful game, especially when playing as black."

"I do. Why?"

"If you think about it, isn't being a cop a lot like playing with the black pieces? You wait for the criminal to make the first move, and afterward every move of yours depends on his moves."

"I suppose."

"You're quite attractive. I'm very glad I didn't kill you that day in the park. I could have. I had you in my sights just after you crossed the finish line, the little police emblem on your shirt right in my crosshairs, your little pigtails wet with sweat."

"They're called low dog ears." Why on Earth had she said that?

To keep him talking about her. And possibly give some clue to his location.

"Do you ever wear your hair that way on the job?"

"Sometimes."

"So, why aren't you wearing it that way, now?"

"I didn't have the time. Been too busy."

"Ah, yes. Tracking me down."

"And Mr. Aziz. He surrendered immediately."

"So you said."

The call dropped.

Text from Vera. *Tower pings on all three other cells show movement toward your location.*

Kim passed the information on to Zimmerman, then answered Vera. *Thanks for the update, Vera. Excellent work. Please text both Martin and me on their progress.*

She returned to the car. "Cole, check the glove compartment for some small rubber bands."

After staring at her as if she were crazy, he checked. "How many do you need?"

"Two."

# CHAPTER SIXTY-EIGHT

When she called again, he answered. "That's much better. The pigtails make you look younger, more innocent."

Whatever floats his boat. "We need to discuss your situation."

"I'd rather discuss you. Do I detect a little gray hair?"

She did have a single gray hair on the left side even she sometimes forgot about because it was so hard to see.

So, how could he see it? "You must have keen eyesight to be able to see it from a distance."

"I do."

He must be watching her through binoculars.

Or a telescopic sight.

She studied the house. He couldn't be in the basement because the line of sight was partially obstructed. "You didn't shoot me in the park because you needed the victims to all be black to support the white ultranationalist false narrative. But you could shoot me now because you've already killed a white detective."

"I didn't kill him."

"No, Aziz did that, but it was all part of the plan, wasn't it?"

A chilling laugh. "I don't know. Was it?"

"I see your point. Another component of your defense."

"And, yes, I could shoot you now. A little more pressure on the trigger."

He was behind an open window. The first-floor windows were all closed. One window was open on the second floor, but a fire escape would foul the field of fire. All three were open on the third. The top of the fire escape blocked the middle window, and a tree blocked the one on the right. He was behind the window on the left.

She stared at it, trying to get a glimpse of him.

"I don't want to, though. Between the pigtails and those lovely eyes… I'd hate to destroy all that."

"There's no reason for anyone else to die, Mr. Coravos. We can end this now, peacefully."

Another chilling laugh. "You think I'm just going to resign? Tip my king?"

The call ended.

# CHAPTER SIXTY-NINE

She pulled Zimmerman over to the car, out of the line of fire. "Third floor, the window all the way on the left."

"How do you know?"

"No time for that. It's where he is. He had me in his crosshairs the whole time I was talking to him."

"I've got a team on the next street ready to go in. They'll need to go slowly, and if he has anyone in there with him, it could get ugly. I'll need you to keep him talking once they enter the house. But please don't stand out in the open like that, now that you know where he is."

"Thanks, Lieutenant, but I've got no choice. He'll smell any change in my posture in a second."

# CHAPTER SEVENTY

Kim waited for the signal that Zimmerman's men were ready to enter the house and that the snipers on the roof had the window in their sights before calling again.

"What took you so long?"

"You're the one who hung up on me. I thought you'd call me back."

"And you're hurt that I didn't?"

Should she?

"Not hurt, exactly, just disappointed."

"Because you thought we were getting along so well."

"That, plus I wanted to ask you about Felipe Prinz."

His tone turned derisive. "What about him?"

"How did you convince him to allow you to infiltrate his group?"

"Easy. I told him things he didn't want to hear, like how he needed us so he could be more effective, as well as things he wanted to hear, such as what a natural leader he was. His problem was that he had a taste for well-to-do white women, which turned into a taste for the capital class lifestyle."

"Which disgusts you, as a true revolutionary."

"Correct, even if you think you're mocking me."

"I'm not."

"That makes me feel better. I will say, though, speaking with and seeing you, I can understand the attraction."

"Then why don't you come down and we can talk face-to-face?"

Zimmerman whispered, "They're outside his door. Keep him talking."

But the call dropped.

# CHAPTER SEVENTY-ONE

"Tell them to hold positions and remain quiet," Zimmerman said to a subordinate.

Kim called Coravos again, but he refused the call.

Another try, another refusal.

She took the bullhorn again. "Mr. Coravos, you need to answer the phone. We need to continue our conversation."

She tried again, but before placing the call, she undid the top two buttons of her blouse.

"Now, that's more like it." His voice was oily, like some lounge lizard hitting on her in a bar. "Lovely cleavage."

"Thank you. Why did you hang up on me?"

"Because you tried to change the rules of the game. You…"

From inside the house came the sound of several shots in rapid succession.

"Men down!" someone called out.

On Zimmerman's walkie-talkie, Kim heard one of the snipers on the roof. "He's not in view."

"Hold fire." Zimmerman turned to one of his men. "Fire tear gas into that window. Now!"

Two cannisters were fired. The shooting stopped.

Kim and Rydell rushed through the front door with several men from ESU.

# CHAPTER SEVENTY-TWO

Kim was halfway up the flight of stairs between the second and third floors when her eyes began to tear. One ESU man was sitting with his back against the wall opposite the door to Coravos' apartment, bleeding from his side while another tended to him. The third crouched by the side of the door.

"Come out, now, Coravos, or you're dead." Kim had her Glock out.

One minute…

Two minutes…

A single shot from outside.

A squawk from the radio of the wounded ESU man. "He's down, but I didn't get a clean shot. Be aware."

"We'll wait until this clears, then check on him."

# CHAPTER SEVENTY-THREE

The smoke had cleared but Kim's eyes were still tearing.

Inside, Coravos coughed.

She stood outside the door and peered in. Coravos was crawling toward a sofa, no doubt looking to use it for cover, dragging the AR-15 with him.

She stepped into the open doorway. "Freeze."

He peered up at her.

"Push the rifle away. Make any other move, and I empty the magazine into you."

Coravos didn't move.

"Going once," Kim said. "Going twice…"

He shoved the rifle a few feet in her direction.

The ESU man got on his radio. "Suspect has surrendered. Need medical teams for two, stat."

Kim kept the Glock pointed at his head. "Yasiel Coravos, you are under arrest for terrorism, murder, conspiracy to commit murder, and conspiracy to commit a terrorist act." And she read him his rights, continuing to keep the Glock trained on his head. "Where are you hit?"

He stared at her but said nothing.

"Oh, now it's the silent treatment? Fine. Bleed to death. It's your fucking choice."

Apparently, he couldn't resist arguing. "I thought you wanted to save my life."

She still didn't lower the Glock. "I did. I was able to arrest you without having to kill you. If you decide to bleed out now, that's on you. Not me."

"Nice logic."

"So, what's it going to be? You want to tell me where you're hit, or would you rather bleed to death?"

"Right shoulder. Your sniper was a lousy shot."

She finally holstered the Glock. "I'd say he did just fine, considering it was area fire."

***

Zimmerman greeted Kim when she returned to the street. "We'll take Coravos to the hospital to have his wound treated. When he's released, we'll turn him over to you for processing."

"Where are you taking him?"

"Wyckoff Heights. We'll let you know his prognosis when we know. In the meantime, I'll keep my guys here with the Nine-Four in case his three associates show up."

"Thanks."

He extended his hand. "Pleasure working with you again, Kim."

She took it. "The pleasure's mine. Unfortunately, I still have a great deal to do."

But when she and Rydell returned to the car, Cord was deathly pale.

"You know, Kim, I'm thinking you and Vera might have been right. Maybe this was too much for me to take on."

"Want me to drive?" Rydell asked.

The day, already a long one, was about to get longer. "Yes."

She turned to Zimmerman. "I need someone to take Detective Washington to the emergency room."

Zimmerman corralled Sergeant Grady. "Have someone take the detective to Wyckoff Heights."

"Thanks." Back to Rydell. "Hand me that Stingray."

# CHAPTER SEVENTY-FOUR

Kim texted Vera with the news about Cord, adding at the end, *He wasn't hurt, it was just exhaustion and possibly dehydration. I'm sure he'll be fine. In the meantime, keep information about the others coming.*

Vera answered almost immediately. *Thank you, Brilliant American Lady Detective. I will forgive him. Kensington appears to be on F or G line, now at 9th Street. Two from Brownsville are together, now at Classon Avenue station.*

She responded to Vera and included Martin. *Thanks, Vera. Keep those updates coming. Martin, all three will arrive at Greenpoint Avenue Station on the G. The first two probably in less than 15 minutes, the third about 10 minutes later. How soon can you meet me there?*

Martin replied immediately. *Coming north on McGuinness now. ETA in 5 minutes.*

She turned to Zimmerman. "I need…"

"Go. The truck and men are at your disposal. I'll keep the perimeter tight just in case."

She waved the sergeant from the Nine-Four over. "I need two patrol cars of your men."

# CHAPTER SEVENTY-FIVE

Knowing the two from Brownsville were together made it easier, as Kim only needed to track one cell phone. They'd track the Kensington guy after they dealt with the first two.

Just as Martin pulled up, the Brownsville pair reached Flushing Avenue. "Good to see you, Martin, Tim. The first two are four stops away. We'll watch for them when they come up out of the subway."

There were two sets of entrances to the underground Greenpoint Avenue station, one on the corner of Greenpoint and Manhattan Avenues with three stairways, and one on the corner of Manhattan Avenue and India Street with two stairways. She and Rydell would take the India Street end, on the theory that it was closest to Coravos' home, while Martin and Tim would take the entrances at the other end. "If I'm wrong and they pop up on your end, just tail them and call my cell. Lieutenant," she added to Zimmerman, "your men will deploy at my end."

Zimmerman agreed, then handed her a wireless headset. "This will keep you in two-way radio contact with my team."

"I don't need to be in the truck to use it?"

"Nope. Just stay within range."

She turned to Rydell. "Okay, Cole, you drive, I'll man the Stingray.

The two stairways into the north end of the station were located on the southeast and southwest corners of Manhattan Avenue and India Street.

"No need to pick a stairwell," Kim said to Zimmerman. "They'll walk westward either way." She had Rydell park on the western side of India Street, about a hundred feet from the corner, while Zimmerman stationed the ESU truck around the corner on Manhattan Avenue.

Rydell was studying the block behind them, a tree-lined street with small apartment buildings and multi-family houses. "Kinda nice neighborhood."

Kim had to agree. It wasn't all that different from where she and Jake lived. She choked down the pang of regret at the thought they may have to leave it. "I just hope we don't disturb it too badly."

As the train drew closer, a text from Vera would signal its arrival at each station: Broadway… Metropolitan Avenue… Nassau Avenue…

"Suspects are now one station away," she said into the headset. "One stop."

"Copy that." Seven voices, ending with Zimmerman's.

Back to the Stingray.

Two minutes… one minute…

Kim's cell pinged with a text from Martin. *Any sign of them?*

She was about to answer when a pulsing dot appeared on the Stingray right at her location. A new text arrived from Vera: *Greenpoint Avenue.* With the window open, she could hear the train pull in.

And pull out.

The pulsing dot stayed.

# CHAPTER SEVENTY-SIX

"They're here," she said as she texted the same to Martin.

"I suggest you stay put until you get a visual," Zimmerman said. "I don't want to spook them and have them rush back down the into the station."

"Copy that," she replied. "Cole, watch my cell for anything from Martin."

"Got it."

She kept watch on the closer stairwell.

A lone woman emerged from the station, while the indicator on the Stingray hardly moved.

A young man with red hair and freckles.

Two middle-aged women.

An elderly woman who paused at the top of the stairs to catch her breath.

Kim's cell pinged with a text.

"It's from Vera," Rydell said. "She says, 'Kensington guy is at Bedford-Nostrand'."

Six stops away.

"Two Hispanic males just exited southeast stairs," a voice whispered in her ear.

On the Stingray, the pulsing dot was moving closer. She peered straight ahead.

There they were, not looking especially threatening, but both wearing cargo pants with bulging pockets. "Suspects spotted crossing Manhattan Avenue, appear to be carrying."

"We'll let them come toward you, Kim," Zimmerman said. "We'll come in behind as you and your partner intercept."

"Roger that, Lieutenant. Losing headset now. Out."

# CHAPTER SEVENTY-SEVEN

Both men reached the near side of Manhattan Avenue.

"Not yet." Kim laid the Stingray on the floor, wishing Zimmerman had provided Martin with a headset as well.

The two men passed the stairway to the station, and four ESU officers fell in step with them a few paces behind. Two more tracked their progress from across the street.

Kim had her Glock out.

Three… two… one…

"Now." She sprang out of the car, assumed a two-handed stance. "Freeze. Police."

The one on the right went wide-eyed and froze.

A blur from the one on the left.

A shot.

The one on the left crumpled, a pistol clattering on the pavement.

Rydell rushed over and knelt on the fallen man's chest to pin him.

ESU rushed in.

Kim grabbed the one still standing and threw him against a brick wall. "Name!"

"Fuck you."

She grabbed a tuft of hair and slammed his head against the wall. "I asked you your name, you piece of shit."

He only moaned in pain.

She patted him down. The bulge in his pocket was a gun. She pulled a pair of latex gloves from her back pocket and leaned hard against him while she put them on.

The gun was another SIG Sauer P210A. "I see this is a popular model with you terrorists." She called for an evidence bag.

Rydell brought one over, having turned the other man over to ESU. "The other one was carrying a Glock 19."

Kim still had her guy pinned to the wall. She grabbed his hair again. "Okay, sonny, what's it gonna be? You gonna tell me your name, or would you prefer kissing the wall again?"

When he said nothing, she slammed his face against the wall.

Blood spurted from his nose.

"Awright! Mendez. Juan Mendez."

"Well, Juan Mendez, you are under arrest for criminal possession of a weapon and conspiracy to commit a terrorist act."

"You might find these handy." Rydell handed her a set of handcuffs.

She was glad Mendez couldn't see the grin, and she cuffed him. "Okay, Juan Mendez, you can get our relationship off to a good start by telling me the name of the third member of your little trio, the one who should arrive here any minute."

"I'm not sayin' nothin' till I get a lawyer."

"My men will take these birds into custody," Zimmerman. "You have one more to catch."

# CHAPTER SEVENTY-EIGHT

"You okay?" Rydell asked as they returned to the car.

She pulled the Stingray onto her lap and entered the number of the Kensington guy. No pulsing dot appeared.

Rydell handed her cell to her. Text from Vera. *Where are you? Kensington man just pinged tower near Nassau Avenue.*

She texted Martin and donned her headset. "Third suspect approaching station. Same drill."

But it wasn't. A crowd had gathered. "Lieutenant, we've got to clear those onlookers."

"No time, Kim. I don't have enough men for that, and there's a danger he'll see us and be spooked."

She turned to study the block behind her. "Cole, turn around and move two hundred feet back. Lieutenant, we're moving further west on India Street. There's a construction site that's walled off. Your men can stay behind that until he passes."

"I don't like it, Kim. Might want to let him get closer to the house."

"He'll see the bunch from the Nine-Four and run."

"Roger that."

Back to the Stingray. A pulsing dot appeared on the screen. "Subject has arrived. Stand by."

Several iterations of, "Copy that."

Sudden thought. "Lieutenant, are the two we have in custody beyond view from the station?"

# CHAPTER SEVENTY-NINE

"Subject Ali is en route to Wyckoff for treatment," Zimmerman replied.

So, that was his name. She'd get the first name later. "What about Mendez?"

The red dot was moving toward them, but Kim didn't see anyone.

Text from Martin. *I think our guy just emerged from the east-side stairwell.*

At least moving back would leave time for her to verify it.

Someone was just arriving on the west side of Manhattan Avenue and the dot was moving closer. "Subject spotted. Hold positions."

"Elvin! Cops!!"

Elvin dashed down the stairs to the station. Martin and Tim set off in pursuit.

"Stay with the Stingray," Kim said to Rydell.

But he was already out and running.

"Or," she said aloud to herself, "I'll secure the Stingray." She grabbed her cell and texted Martin. *Rydell on his way to join you. Keep me posted.*

Text from Vera. *No additional tower pings. What happened?*
Kim answered. *Missed him.*

***

She'd forgotten to check in with Jake, and she had three texts asking if she was all right. She'd seen the news vans at the perimeter the Nine-Four had set up, so he had to know some of what had happened. She texted him now. *I'm okay, nothing but a little irritation around the eyes from tear gas. Got the bad guy and two of his buddies, chasing another. Took Cord to the hospital; exhaustion and dehydration. He'll be fine. Hope you're okay.*

But she wasn't ready for his response.

*I got a call today from an NBA team. They want me to interview tomorrow.*

She waited for him to tell her what team, but he didn't. Fear gripped her. Having apprehended Coravos, Aziz, Mendez and Ali, she was feeling a lot differently about the job and the city. But she'd made her promise, and she would stand by it.

And Jake.

Her cell pinged. *Knicks. Senior Analytics Advisor.*

Another text from Martin. *Lost him. A train pulled in as we reached platform. Wait for next train and chase?*

It was tempting.

But they had Ali to tend to, plus Coravos and Mendez. *No, let him go for now. We'll have Vera keep tabs on him, and maybe we can get something out of the guys we bagged.*

But what she was really doing was cutting her losses.

# CHAPTER EIGHTY

She remained silent on the drive back to the Castle.

Rydell noticed. "Hey, I know it sucks that one got away, but this morning we didn't even know he existed. We bagged the big guy and two of his associates. Three, if you count Aziz."

"But one got away, and who knows how many others. We need to bag them all, or this will be like a recurring injury."

He drove a little further. "My guess is that the captain will be pleased, which means the higher-ups will be pleased." He fell silent again.

"So, what's bugging you?"

He was debating with himself whether to say it.

"Come on, Cole, the suspense is killing me."

That brought a hint of a smile. "Well, that's progress, I guess. You're calling me by my first name."

"You did well today. You were a member of the team."

He made the turn onto Flushing Avenue. "That's what I wanted to talk to you about, only I don't want to appear insensitive, which I know you think I am."

So, that was it. "You want to join our unit as Bob's replacement, and you think I'll be offended because he was my friend."

"Am I that transparent?"

"No, I've just been expecting something like that, especially since you've been helping us ever since… ever since we lost Bob. It's an obvious move, and I doubt there'll be any hesitation about it. I'm not offended."

"Would you be offended if I asked you to mention it to Captain Colangelo? I know you and he have some connection, which I won't speculate about."

She laughed at that. "There's nothing to speculate. He was my lieutenant when I was in Internal Affairs. He felt bad when I got pushed out a year early, and please don't ask me about that."

"I won't."

She considered his request. "Sure, I'll talk to him."

Cole heaved a sigh of relief. "Thanks. It would mean a lot."

***

Bostwick and Colangelo were waiting when they arrived. Martin and Tim arrived five minutes later, and Colangelo gathered them in the conference room for a recap. Kim described the scene with Coravos, the takedown of Ali and Mendez, and her frustration that the last suspect had gotten away.

"I wouldn't beat myself up too much over that if I were you," Bostwick said. "In retrospect, you were spread thinly, even with ESU there. Remember, this began as an operation to apprehend one guy holed up in a house. Then, you added the take-down of Ali and Mendez, and then you had to contend with the arrival of a third person. Not too shabby, considering everything was on the fly. The truth is that Zimmerman should have taken command once Coravos was apprehended and requested whatever backup he needed."

"No one could have predicted the crowed lingering and the need to move further from the station without adequate time to lay everything out," Kim said.

"No," Colangelo said, "but he damned well should have moved Mendez out of there, turn him over to the Nine-Four. They were one lousy block away."

True, but she hadn't thought of that, either. "I want to get photos of Ali and Mendez over to Army Intelligence, Homeland Security, and the FBI."

"Good," Colangelo said.

"How's Cord?" Kim regretted not asking as soon as she'd arrived, but events had moved too quickly.

"He's okay," Vera said. "He'll be home tonight. But no more work for a while."

"Before we go any further," Bostwick said, "Rydell, since you shot Ali, I need both your pieces."

"Lieutenant," Kim said, "Cole's become a valuable member of this team. How will he be able to assist us if…"

Colangelo spoke up. "Come on, Kim, you were in IAB, you know the drill. Any shooting is a mandatory review. Detective Rydell is on Administrative Leave until IAB finishes their review."

Rydell handed over the piece from his shoulder holster, and then the one from his ankle holster.

"Sorry, Cole," Kim said. "Okay, next steps. First, we…"

Colangelo cleared his throat.

"Kim," Bostwick said, "can we have a private word?"

She followed him into his office but didn't become alarmed until he closed the door.

He gestured for her to have a seat. "We have a problem. Rita Henshaw has filed a police brutality complaint against you. Captain Colangelo has arranged to have your hearing fast-tracked to tomorrow morning."

"That's pure bullshit, Lieu, and you know it. I already told you and the captain how it went down." Maybe Sacramento would be better after all.

"Her version is different. She claims you said you'd beat her if she refused to give you the phone number."

"Absolutely not true. I was very aware of the consequences of stepping over the line."

Bostwick held her gaze. "No matter how you look at it, you came damned close."

"Rydell was there. I'm sure his testimony will…"

"I would advise you to consult with an attorney from the Detective's Endowment Association, Kim. Rydell is currently under investigation for the shooting today, which will probably negate his impact as a witness."

This was nuts. "He shot a terrorist who was about to shoot him. We both saw the weapon before he shot, as I…" She saw it. "Oh, that's just great, just fucking dandy. We're both under investigation, so he can't help me, and I can't help him. You know what? I'm going to demand that my IAB hearing be delayed until Rydell is cleared."

"The captain requested the process be expedited so that you'd be back on the case. You know damned well we need to arraign Coravos, Aziz, Mendez and Ali within twenty-four hours of their arrest, and that the clock on discovery, a lousy 35 days, starts ticking at that point."

"Not my problem anymore." She stormed out.

# CHAPTER EIGHTY-ONE

Kim was explaining all the events of the day, including the complaint against her, to Jake when the door buzzer sounded. The voice over the intercom said, "My name is Aiden McManus. I'm an attorney for the Detective's Endowment Association."

She buzzed him in.

He was a short man, no more than 5'6", wearing a gray glen check suit, a starched white shirt, red striped tie, and a fedora that he tipped to her as soon as she opened the door. "A pleasure to meet you, Detective."

He was sixty if he was a day, with a ruddy complexion, a twinkle in his eye, and the hint of a brogue.

"Thank you. I'm pleased to meet you as well, but I haven't even called the DEA yet. I assume this is about the complaint against me."

"It is, it is. I was contacted by a Captain Steven Colangelo a short while ago and asked to take your case as well as the case of your partner, Detective Cole Rydell."

She should have known Colangelo would do whatever he could.

"The good captain explained that you intend to ask for a delay so that Detective Rydell could appear as a witness for you. I've taken both cases so there's no need. I've already spoken to your partner, so let's sit down and map out a plan of attack."

It was impossible to dislike this man. "You mean defense, don't you?"

"I do not." He gestured to the chess set on the snack table with her game with Lodemay. "You play chess? Surely, you attack when you have the black pieces."

***

The mayor picked up the empty coffee mug on his desk and hurled it across his office in Gracie Mansion. The mug landed on the plush carpet and didn't break. "They did what?"

Justin gestured for calm. "I know. It's outrageous. But it's departmental policy to investigate every shooting and every complaint of brutality. Ricky is sure they'll both be cleared quickly. The DEA has already assigned an attorney, McManus, the best they've got."

"I guess we should be thankful Henshaw didn't go the Civilian Complaint Review Board." The mayor had longed to get rid of the CCRB, but it had become an institution.

"I suspect Henshaw knows she has no case, and she couldn't have known Rydell would shoot someone later in the day. I think she did this just to get a black mark on Kim's record."

Which wouldn't surprise the mayor. "What happens if IAB clears her?"

"Assuming they clear it as an unfounded complaint, it still goes on her record, but so does the fact that there was no basis. If instead of it being unfounded, they decide there's insufficient evidence, that's also noted."

"Which they might do to avoid getting roasted on *City News* as being a rubber stamp for bad cops. You say Rick Conti knows all about this?"

"He had to. The four terrorists must be arraigned by tomorrow, and then he only has 35 days to disclose all the evidence the police have, or the case gets dismissed."

"A ridiculous limitation that will be eliminated when the state finally passes its budget."

***

Joanna Dunbar had just finished her evening report and was leaving the studio when she spotted a familiar figure waiting for her. "Justin Cates, as I live and breathe. What brings you here?"

"Wanna go for a walk? I have a story for you."

She laughed at that. Over the years, Mr. Cates had morphed from an irritating shadowy figure who turned up at crime scenes to a trusted source of occasional information, almost always at the behest of his boss. "What does the mayor want me to say?"

But Justin remained serious. "He knows all the facts I'm about to tell you, but he doesn't know I'm here and he might even fire me if he did."

"Won't he figure it out when I report what you tell me?"

"This isn't for immediate use. It's background if you decide to use it for a story down the road." He told her about Kim's confrontation with Rita Henshaw and the complaint to IAB.

"They'll never take her word over Kim's."

"True," Justin said, "but it will go into her record just the same. And there's another twist, something even the mayor doesn't realize. If it's in her record, Coravos might try to use it to say his rights were violated, and without the number, Kim never would have tracked him down."

Was he nuts? "That's absurd."

"Is it? What if a judge like Vickers gets the case?"

Holy shit. He must have picked that up from Rick, who would know.

***

It was nearly midnight. McManus had kept Kim's spirits up while they talked, but now that he was gone and Jake had turned in, she couldn't help turning things over in her mind.

Jake's interview with the Knicks was tomorrow. On Monday, he'd fly out to Sacramento for an interview there. Her IAB hearing would be in nine hours. If it went against her, Sacramento might look better. If it went her way, she'd be praying for the Knicks.

*What I want won't affect the outcome of anything.*

She had to just fight her battle and fight it she would. She made certain the bedroom door was closed, so that she didn't disturb Jake. Then she texted her cousin, Jim. *Are you still up? Because I need to talk to you.*

His response was immediate. *Call my cell.*

And for the next forty-five minutes, they talked.

# CHAPTER EIGHTY-TWO

*Friday, May 2, 8:55 a.m.*

Cousin Jim was waiting for Kim outside the offices of the Internal Affairs Bureau near the Holland Tunnel. He'd already explained that he wasn't qualified to represent her, but she didn't need him for that. Aidan McManus would do just fine. She just needed his presence.

A link to Dad and Granddad.

McManus joined them and they went inside, where the lieutenant who'd replaced Colangelo escorted them to the conference room she remembered so well from her days with IAB. But now it felt alien to her.

Two IAB detectives and a stenographer joined them, and as soon as Rydell arrived, they got down to business.

McManus started it off. "I suggest we take Detective Rydell's case first. It's the best way to escape from the Catch-22 that threatens to catch us."

The IAB lieutenant scowled. "I'm not sure the reference is appropriate, Counselor, but I'll grant your request."

Rydell described the events leading up to his shooting of Suspect Ali. "I had seen a bulge in his pocket, and I saw him reach into that pocket and pull out a handgun. Under the circumstances, My only choice was to fire."

"Didn't Detective Brady already have her weapon out?" the IAB lieutenant asked.

"Yes, sir, she did, but she was covering Suspect Mendez. Since he had a similar bulge in his pocket, I had to assume he was ready to pull his weapon, too."

"I have here a signed affidavit from Lieutenant Zimmerman of the Emergency Services Unit who was on site at the time and witnessed the incident," McManus said. "As you will see, it supports Detective Rydell's statement in its entirety."

He'd been right. They wouldn't need Kim's testimony. His opening gambit had been brilliant.

"We have already stipulated that it was Detective Rydell who fired the shot," McManus continued. "Therefore, I see nothing for the bureau to deliberate. I ask you declare a righteous shoot and allow us to move on to Detective Brady's case."

The IAB lieutenant looked stunned. "That's extraordinary, Counselor. Our procedures…"

McManus interrupted. "If you don't mind my saying so, Lieutenant, this entire case is extraordinary. But if you can give me one substantive reason to delay your decision, I'll withdraw my request."

The lieutenant exchanged whispered comments with the two detectives. "Very well, Counselor. Request granted. Detective Rydell's shooting is declared to have been justified."

Cousin Jim whispered in Kim's ear, "Round One to the good guys."

***

Joanna had pitched stories before to Ed Lyons, the head of the Independent Television Network, but never one like this. She wasn't ready to go with it, yet, but she needed to know if he would back her if she did.

"That's a helluva story, Joanna. When did Detective Brady tell you?"

"She didn't, and she doesn't know I know. I got it from Justin Cates, and before you get angry at the mayor, according to Justin, he doesn't know Justin came to me, or the calculation about how Coravos could use this."

"So, what's the story? What do you propose to do?"

"Nothing, yet. I'm informing you, that's all. I think it's a longshot that we'll be able to use it, but if we ever can…"

"Noted. Let's wait and see what happens."

***

Kim had just finished describing the sequence of events in her confrontation with Henshaw. She'd left nothing out.

"Thank you, Detective. However, you realize your version and Ms. Henshaw's do not align."

Rydell spoke up. "I can verify everything Detective Brady has said. No one ever said they were going to beat her or acted in a violent manner."

"Let's focus on your actual words and deeds." The IAB lieutenant consulted his notes. "Detective Brady, by your own admission, when Ms. Henshaw asked if Detective Rydell was going to beat her up, you replied, 'no, I'm quite capable of doing that myself.' How else can anyone interpret that but as a direct threat?"

"I was stating a fact. I took her comment as a suggestion that, as a woman, I was incapable of defending myself and needed a man to do it for me. Yes, I was asserting that I was physically stronger than her. But please note that I only said I was capable of it. I never said I intended to do it."

He didn't appear to be convinced. "You and Detective Rydell also both backed her against a wall in an alley. She interpreted that as a prelude to a beatdown."

McManus had said to attack. "I have no control over someone else's interpretation. Given what we were asking her to do, I had every reason to expect she might flee rather than give us the information we needed. We were blocking her escape route, nothing more."

He considered that. "Then, Detective Rydell, what did you mean when you asked Detective Brady, 'Now?' What was that supposed to mean?"

To Kim's shock, Rydell laughed in that free and easy way of his. "I didn't mean anything. It was just something I said."

"To pressure Ms. Henshaw?"

Rydell shrugged. "If that's how she took it, fine. It's not as if I was about to sock her one. Let's not forget that this… 'reporter'… was shielding someone who was responsible for seven cops and two civilians being murdered."

McManus inserted himself into the exchange. "I believe Detective Rydell's point was that the police had an urgent need for the information, and they did not exceed department guidelines to get it."

"What about Ms. Henshaw's right to protect her source?"

"Adjudication of that matter is beyond the scope of IAB," McManus said. "The question here is whether Detective Brady exceeded departmental guidelines in obtaining critical information from Ms. Henshaw. As Ms. Henshaw's description of the events have been refuted by both Detective Brady and Detective Rydell, that question must be answered in Detective Brady's favor. I ask she be reinstated immediately."

# CHAPTER EIGHTY-THREE

Cousin Jim gave Kim a huge hug as they parted ways on Hudson Street. "See? You didn't need me."

"Yes, I did." She kissed his cheek. "And thank you so much for coming."

Not surprisingly, Colangelo was waiting for her and Rydell. "I'll give you two a lift back to Brooklyn. We have a lot to discuss.

Kim waited until they were in the car heading to Brooklyn. "Before we get back, Captain, I want to thank you for the scheduling idea. I'm afraid I wasn't thinking too clearly yesterday afternoon."

"Can't blame you for that. You'd already had a helluva day. Glad I could help."

She suspected he might have helped a little more than he was letting on, behind the scenes. But she knew not to ask.

Colangelo continued. "While we've been busy here, Lieutenant Bostwick informs me that all four of our terrorists have been arraigned, so the clock is ticking. I'll need you to get everything together for the DA as quickly as possible."

"I know, we only have thirty-five days. Has anyone interviewed any of our four altar boys?"

"No time. Lauren Davis will be waiting for us at the Brooklyn Detention Center, where we'll interrogate Mendez and Aziz before we hop over to Wyckoff for Coravos and Alvarez."

"Mendez first." She liked the idea of working their way up the ladder, and Mendez was clearly at the bottom and might be the most likely to deal. She also liked the fact that Davis was assigned to the case. A sharp lawyer with seductive good looks and a sharp tongue, she could speak with the patios of her ancestral Jamaica, or with the crispness of the Georgetown Law School graduate that she was.

***

Upon entering the small conference room at the BDC, Kim had to stifle a laugh. Mendez had a large tape across the bridge of his nose, a reminder of the close encounter he'd had with the brick wall during his arrest.

ADA Davis walked in a moment later.

Rydell turned and stared, wide-eyed and mouth agape.

"Whatchoo be lookin' at?" she demanded.

Kim introduced them. "Detective Rydell is with another unit at Brooklyn North, but he's been helping us out on this case."

"He best be keepin' his mind on de case, and not on me."

Rydell remained cowed. And the best part was that Davis wasn't doing this for Rydell's benefit, but for Mendez, on whom the effect was not lost.

Kim took her preferred place across the table from Mendez, with Davis and Rydell on either side of her. Mendez had a legal aid attorney with him.

Legal Aid led off the discussion. "Before we begin, I must protest the police brutality against my client."

Before Kim could respond, Davis leaned across the table at the attorney. "We leavin' that nonsense by de side o' de road. She was tryin' to cuff him, he was resistin' and tryin' to pull a gun on her.

Ain't nobody gonna buy dat brutality stuff." And then she dropped the Jamaican accent. "Are we clear, Counselor?"

Legal Aid shifted in his seat and cleared his throat. "Very well. What is it you'd like to discuss?"

Davis turned to Kim. "Detective Brady, would you care to take the lead in this proceeding?" She might as well have been offering her a crumpet at an English tea.

"Yes, thank you, Counselor. Mr. Mendez, you were intercepted while approaching a crime scene, armed. We have evidence that you were summoned there by Mr. Coravos, who was in a standoff with police. If you provide us with information on the membership and structure of Mr. Coravos' organization and what you intended to do with the pistol we took from you, I'm sure Ms. Davis will take that into consideration when taking this case to the grand jury."

"My client will not incriminate himself," Legal Aid said.

Davis reverted to her Jamaican voice. "We got him cold on conspiracy and weapons possession. Wedder we make dem go away is up to him."

Legal Aid shrugged. "Make us an offer."

Kim addressed Mendez. "Tell us what you know. All of it."

"And," Davis added in her Georgetown Law voice, "depending on how much he tells us and testifies to in court, we can work something out."

Kim had the ball. "Three of you traveled to Greenpoint yesterday. You and Mr. Ali were together. The third individual was about ten minutes behind you and eluded us, thanks to your shouted warning."

"Oops," Davis said. "Dere's anudder charge, obstruction of justice."

Legal Aid waved his arms. "Wait a second."

"Take a chill pill, Counselor," Kim said. "It's the easiest one to deal with." She shoved a notepad and pencil across the table at Mendez. "Full name, any known aliases, address, phone number, and the make, model, color, and year of his car, if he has one."

Mendez stared at the notepad. "He don't have a car." He made no move to reach for it.

"If he gives you what you want," Legal Aid said, "he's placing his life at risk."

Kim exchanged glances with Davis. "This is just for the obstruction charge. If he wants it dropped, he tells us. If he gives us more, we'll give him more. But if he doesn't give us this, this meeting ends here and now."

"Sounds good to me," Davis added.

Legal Aid nodded to Mendez, who said, "His name is Elvin Alvarez, and he lives on East 2nd Street in Kensington." He wrote down the address, e-mail address, and phone number, then shoved the notepad back to Kim. "He don't have no aliases."

Kim pulled out the list she'd gotten from Colonel Spiers. It was the first chance she'd had to check it since before they'd gone to apprehend Coravos. To her surprise, his name was there. So were Mendez and Ali. "You knew these men from your army service?"

"Yeah."

"How many others were in your group besides the four of you and Aziz?" Kim asked.

"Nobody."

Kim stood. "I don't believe you."

"Ooh," Davis said, "Dat not good fo' you, boy."

Legal Aid stood, too. "Hey, he's cooperating. If he says there was nobody else, he means it."

"Bullshit," Kim said. "These assholes thought they were launching a revolution. Coravos was careful to use aliases and burner phones, and he had elaborate plans of attack. Every shooting was well thought out, escape routes planned, timing worked out. He also sent out a call for help yesterday that he believed would hold off ESU, the Nine-Four Precinct, and my detective squad. So don't sit there and fucking tell me there wasn't anyone else." She shoved the notepad back at him.

"No list, no deal," Davis said.

# CHAPTER EIGHTY-FOUR

Kim called Martin and asked him to check Elvin Alvarez for priors. Twice he'd been busted for possession with intent to sell, and once they'd gotten him on a weapons charge. Clearly, the army had not made him the best he could be.

Or maybe they had.

She had Martin print out his mug shot and had them head to Kensington and pick Alvarez up. She called Driscoll to arrange for backup. Meanwhile, they had Aziz to interview. And since he'd killed two police officers as well as Enrique Cruz, Davis was much less inclined to give him a sweet deal.

"I ain't sayin' nothin'," Aziz said.

"Suits me," Kim said.

"Me, too," Davis said. "Three counts of Murder One."

"Three?" his Legal Aid attorney said.

"Sure," Kim replied. "Two police officers, and the third in furtherance of committing a terrorist act."

"Conference over," Davis said.

It was off to Wyckoff Hospital.

While en route, Kim got a text from Jake. *First interview went well. I'll let you know the rest later.*

***

"I don't think we should bother with Ali," Kim said. "I doubt he'll give us anything more than Mendez gave us, and he was about to shoot Rydell, here."

"You'd have made a damned fine lawyer, Kim," Davis replied, "but I must disagree. You're probably right about Ali, but anything extra he gives us will serve to nail Coravos, and he was clearly the leader. What about the list Mendez gave you?"

"Five names matched with a list I got from Army Intelligence, the other two didn't. I've forwarded all seven names to the FBI, Army Intelligence, and Homeland Security."

They found Ali's room first. His Legal Aid attorney was also there.

Ali blanched when Rydell walked into the room.

"Whatsa matter?" Davis asked, "you see a ghost?"

Ali pointed at Rydell. "He tried to kill me."

"If I'd wanted to kill you," Rydell said, "I'd have succeeded."

"I think he should leave," the attorney said.

"He stays," Davis replied. "And if Mr. Ali answers these detectives' questions in a helpful manner, he might win himself a deal. But if Detective Rydell leaves, we all leave and there's no deal."

After a short silence, Kim said, "I guess that's agreement." She recapped what they'd learned from Mendez and showed him the list of names. "Do you recognize any of them?"

"Yeah."

"And they are all members of your group?"

"Yeah."

"Are there any others?"

Ali glanced at his attorney, who nodded.

"I think so, but I don't know their names. Yasiel mentioned Philly and Boston."

Kim made some notes. "And these additional members, would they all have been recruited from units that served in Afghanistan?"

"Yes. Yasiel was a sharpshooter, but he worked for the regimental adjutant. He had a lot of contacts throughout Central Command."

"How did he manage to pull you all together?" Kim asked. "What was his pitch?"

"He arranged for us to meet with leaders in the Taliban, convinced us we were fighting an unjust war to maintain a corrupt system of government at home. And every time someone was killed, it was one more reason to oppose it. Yasiel said the only answer was to combat any enforcement of order as the ruling class defined it."

Time for another angle. "So far, we know that Coravos, Cruz, and Aziz were shooters. You and Mendez were both armed. Were all members of your group armed?"

"Not initially. Everyone had to prove himself on the firing range. Yasiel kept a cache of handguns at his apartment and allowed each cadet, as he called them, to use them for practice. When he was convinced that someone had attained the level of Expert, the weapon was theirs."

"So, why now for the revolution? And why non-white victims?"

"When Come Home Ernesto organized all those demonstrations a few years ago, Yasiel thought he'd finally found a way to launch his revolution. He waited until Felipe Prinz got out of jail and then approached him about joining forces. Prinz was glad to have new members."

"Did they discuss violent revolution?" Kim asked.

"Yeah, that was the point. But then Yasiel pegged Prinz as a pussy, that he was all talk and no action. He told us, 'Fuck Prinz, it's time for action'."

She needed specifics. "Was anyone else involved in the shootings at Prospect Park a week ago last Sunday?"

"No. Yasiel wanted more shooters but decided against it because it was our first operation, and the nature of the event would mean lotsa cops. Next to Yasiel, Enrique Cruz was the best shooter we had. So, two shooters. And they'd have an easier time gettin' out."

Kim thought of Lodemay. "But someone saw Cruz enter the park. It's how we were able to track you all down. Was Aziz the best shooter after Cruz?"

"Yeah. After that, there was Alvarez, Mendez, and me. But none of us were as sharp."

***

Before they entered Coravos' room, Kim said to Rydell in a soft voice, "Stand as close to him as you can."

Rydell feigned shock. "Won't that violate his rights?"

Davis covered her mouth to stifle a laugh. "I think I like this guy."

"Yeah," Kim said. "He kind of grows on you."

An attorney was waiting with Coravos. He immediately greeted Lauren. "Ms. Davis, I don't believe we've met. Grant Walker. I'm representing Mr. Coravos." He turned to Kim. "You must be Detective Brady."

"And this is Detective Rydell." She made a quick note of his name on her cell.

"I hope we can work something out," Walker said.

Kim ignored the comment and directed her attention to Coravos. "We recovered the AR-15 you used to try to kill several police officers. Once our ballistics people examine it, which they are doing as we speak, they will match it to the slugs you used to kill two detectives a week ago Sunday. We have statements from your accomplices detailing how you recruited members to your group back in Afghanistan and fomented rebellious activities here."

"You need direct evidence to support accomplice testimony," Walker said.

Rydell moved closer to the IV line running into Coravos left arm.

Coravos caught it. "What's he doing?"

Rydell shrugged. "Nothing."

Davis took over. "We've got you cold on the two murders in the park, the attempted murders yesterday, conspiracy to commit murder and conspiracy to commit a terrorist act. Plus, accessory on all the other shootings, because you were the boss of the whole thing."

Rydell was staring intently at the drip of medication from the bag into the tube.

"Get away from that." Coravos was growing anxious.

Rydell shrugged. "It's weird how this works. And it's all sealed, so no air gets in."

"I don't think he likes you, Mr. Coravos," Kim said.

Rydell was still staring at the IV. "Why do they keep air out?"

"Because if air gets into the bloodstream, it can cause a blockage, perhaps a heart attack." Kim said it as if trying to be helpful.

Rydell nodded. "Oh."

"This has gone far enough," Walker said. "Get him out of the room."

"I'll do no such thing." Kim turned to Rydell. "Please step away from that. You're making Mr. Coravos nervous, and you know we don't want to do that. After all, he only tried to kill us all yesterday."

Davis directed her comments to Coravos as if nothing had happened. "Usually, I interview prisoners to get a deal, like Mr. Walker wants, so that we don't go to trial, which is long and expensive for the state. And I'm under a lot of pressure." She turned to face Walker. "You see, the feds want this case. They want to try your client for terrorism and treason. In fact, Detective Brady has been working with them on this case, sharing what she learns with them, and they've been sharing what they know with her."

"That's how I found out about his meetings with the Taliban when he was in Afghanistan." Kim watched for the look of shock on Coravos' face, and she wasn't disappointed when it registered. "Oh, you didn't think they knew? Well, they did."

Davis continued talking to Walker. "So, here's my offer because that's what I've been tasked to do. Two counts of murder one for the shootings in the park, five counts of accessory to murder one for the other police shootings, one count of accessory to attempted murder one for the wounding of Detective Washington in the park by Mr. Cruz, and one count of accessory to murder two for the ordered killing of Enrique Cruz." She turned to Kim. "Did I get everything?"

Kim bit her tongue and nodded.

Walker nearly exploded. "What the hell kind of deal is that?"

Davis shrugged. "I dropped the conspiracy charges and terrorism charges."

"We'll take our chances at trial," Walker said.

Davis laughed. "You don't have prayer at trial."

As soon as she and Rydell were back in the car, she texted Cousin Jim. *I need a piece of information on a lawyer. His name is Grant Walker, and he's definitely not a Legal Aid guy. I need whatever you can find on him.*

# CHAPTER EIGHTY-FIVE

Kim stopped at the Castle to update Bostwick and sign out. Just before she signed out, Susan Garmin walked in. "I need to speak with you."

"Okay. I'm on my way home. If you are, too, we can take the B38 bus together. It stops right outside."

"Thanks. It's about my brother."

Kim accompanied her outside. "Is he all right? He owes me a chess move, and I've been getting concerned."

"Thank you. No, he's not. A few days ago, he called me. He said you'd told him he should, and that he should see a doctor about his symptoms. He'd started to exhibit many more symptoms than just delusions. He was having searing headaches, dizziness, even nausea. I got him to a doctor, and he's been diagnosed with advanced Glioblastoma." She started to cry.

Kim patted her arm. "I'm so sorry. What's…"

"He's in Sloane-Kettering. They've scheduled the surgery for tomorrow morning."

The bus pulled up. Once seated, Kim said, "Is there anything I can do?"

Susan shook her head. "You've already done more than anyone else ever did. You've been his friend."

"And I'll continue to be…"

"You don't understand. The chances of eradicating the tumor are very slim. He might not even survive the surgery."

"I'll be praying for him. And for you."

***

Jake greeted her with a hug. "I guess they reinstated you."

She held the embrace. "They did." The kiss was delicious.

"Does that mean I should cancel my trip to Sacramento?"

It pulled her up short. She'd promised, but now…

She'd promised. "I think you should take whatever you think is the best opportunity. How did today go?"

"After the interview, I was about to leave when the owner invited me to join him and the senior management of the team for lunch. They knew all about you and praised you as a great detective. They knew you'd run the half-marathon and then dealt with the shooting. We talked a lot about basketball, about the game…"

"And about analytics?"

"That hardly came up at lunch, although we'd talked about little else during the interview. I told them you were as much a fan of the game as I was, but you liked the college game better these days."

"You said that?"

"Sure. It's true, isn't it? Anyway, after lunch, the owner said he couldn't think of two better people to welcome into the Knicks family."

"Wait… you mean… they…"

"They offered me the job, Kim. Assistant General Manager for Analytics."

She gasped. "Assistant General Manager? Did you take it?"

"I told them I had to talk to you, first. Should I keep that appointment in Sacramento?"

She jumped back into his arms.

****

It had been a long, hard day, but now she was staring at the chessboard, brooding over the text she'd gotten an hour earlier from Cousin Jim.

*Grant Walker is a senior partner at Carson, Weller, and Walker, a Park Avenue firm. He's their top criminal law guy. Listed with Superlawyers since 2018. My guess is he don't come cheap.*

"Hey." Jake came up behind her and wrapped his arms around her waist. "What's up? I thought you'd be thrilled."

She told him about Lodemay. "Our game never got beyond the third move."

"Looks drawish."

She chuckled.

"It's almost midnight. You running tomorrow?"

"Yes. And then I have Bob's funeral at St. Patrick's, and I need to go in."

He turned her around to face him. "No, Kim. You haven't taken a scheduled day off, or even an unscheduled one, since before the shooting in the park. You're coming to bed, sleeping until seven, then running before the funeral, after which you will come home and chill. Tomorrow night I am taking you out to dinner to celebrate. *Capice*?"

"Capice."

# CHAPTER EIGHTY-SIX

*Saturday, May 3, 12:55 p.m.*

Bob Nolan had no immediate family, just a couple of cousins who were glad to have the department handle the arrangements.

The commissioner spoke briefly, followed by Captain Colangelo, both of whom praised Bob's years of service. Kim spoke last.

She didn't want to speak, because she wasn't sure she couldn't get through it without becoming emotional. Jake had suggested she write out what she wanted to say beforehand, and she'd taken his advice.

But as she stepped up to the pulpit, she left the written remarks in her pocket. "For the past seven years, I've been proud to call Bob Nolan my partner. He was as good a cop as I've ever known, an insightful investigator, and a loyal and supportive partner. But to me, he was more than that; he was family."

Her throat tightened, and she took a deep breath. "In his early days on the force, he had partnered with my father and remained friends with him until he died."

Another deep breath. "I first met Bob eight years ago, during my first tour in Homicide at Manhattan South. My partner there, Mike Resnick, who I'm glad to see is also here today, had been

Bob's partner earlier in his career and suggested Bob would be helpful in our investigation. And he was. When I was later transferred to Brooklyn North, I was thrilled to gain Bob as a partner."

She paused again, knowing this was the hardest part. "Bob led a solitary life. Police work was everything to him. He sometimes joined my husband and me for holiday dinners if we had no other engagements. He was always supportive, always brave..." She wasn't sure she could go on. "He didn't deserve to..."

She couldn't go on. She returned to her pew, next to Captain Colangelo, who placed a hand on her shoulder.

***

"You okay?" It was Mike Resnick.

"I am, now."

Colangelo approached. "You were great, Kim."

"I didn't feel great. I felt like I had to rush it all out before I fell apart." She turned back to Mike. "So, when's your retirement party?"

"Won't be one, at least not yet. I've been offered a spot at One-PP on the commissioner's staff. Sounded like a good transition into retirement."

"That's great, Mike. You deserve it. We'll keep in touch." Because they hadn't been since she left Manhattan South.

Colangelo rolled his eyes but said nothing. He knew how she liked to work.

# CHAPTER EIGHTY-SEVEN

*Wednesday, May 7, 8:05 a.m.*

Kim had just completed a speed-training run over at Brooklyn Bridge Park, sprinting two-minute intervals with jogging breaks in between. It was one of her favorite workouts. As she walked the last block along Monroe Place as part of her cooldown routine, she spied a familiar figure leaning against his car in front of their place.

"Since when do you walk at the end of a workout?" Justin asked.

"Ever since I read that it was an excellent way to help prevent injuries. What brings you over this morning?"

"I've missed you. So has Ricky. He was just saying last night that ever since he made Executive ADA, he doesn't get to see you too often. We've talked about getting together for dinner sometime. Maybe now's the time. We could celebrate Jake's new four-year contract with the Knicks."

She froze. "How do you know about that?"

Justin froze, too, as if he realized he'd said something he shouldn't.

She leaned against his car, next to him. "The Knicks only announced that they'd hired him. MSG never makes the terms of the contracts with their staff public." Oh, no.

"I will tell you the whole story, Kim, but you must promise to withhold judgment until I'm finished. Will you do that?"

Did she have a choice? "Go ahead."

He explained how the owner of MSG had approached the mayor about protecting the tax abatement, and how the mayor had decided to proceed. "I know what you're thinking, Kim; that he did this to keep you close to him, within range, so to speak. I suspected that, too. But that's not it at all. He did it because he was afraid that if Jake was forced to move to another city, it would cause tension between you two. He also felt he owed it to Jake to do him a solid. It's his way of closing the door on his feelings for you."

"Are you saying he's no longer attracted to me?" That was too good to be true.

"I don't think he'll ever not be attracted to you. But he knows he can't do anything about it, and he shouldn't try. You think the reason he didn't go to the Vickers dinner was that he can't stand the judge. It's true, he can't, but he's too much of a pol to pass up an event over personal dislike. He passed it up because I told him you'd be there, and he thought avoiding you was the best thing to do. Considering how you looked that night, I agree."

***

By now, Kim had brought Ken Taylor, Colonel Spiers, and Homeland Security up to date on Coravos and his group. Colangelo called her and Bostwick into his office for an update.

"Other members of the group remain at large," she said when she'd finished. "So, we probably need to keep Prinz in protective custody."

"I don't agree," Bostwick said. "According to Ali, he, Alvarez, and Mendez were the best marksmen, but Coravos didn't trust them to handle any shooting until he was in danger. We can only conclude that anyone else out there is even less capable. What's more, we have Ali's statement, corroborated by Alvarez, who has been in custody since Saturday, and the direct evidence we've gotten on all the shootings. So, what, exactly, are we protecting Prinz from?"

Kim couldn't argue with that. But she had an additional thought. "This business about Coravos' big money lawyer bothers me. How is he affording this?"

"Why would that concern us?" Colangelo asked.

"Because neither he nor any of the others we have in custody have regular jobs, yet Coravos could afford to keep them all armed, to pay for target practice for God knows how many members at shooting ranges, and a network of burner phones. This is a bigger operation than we suspected, and it wasn't until that high-priced lawyer walked in that it occurred to me."

"So, what do you want to do?" Bostwick asked.

"We've already looked over his limited finances and found nothing. I'd like to expand that. Maybe talk with Prinz to see if he knows what Coravos' source of income was. Who knows, maybe Prinz was being cut in for some."

"What kind of income do you expect to find?" Colangelo asked.

"I don't know. Whatever it was, it had to be illicit. Maybe someone in Narcotics knows something."

Bostwick snorted. "Even if you're right, Prinz would never admit it. He's too cozily tucked up in that hotel downtown."

She turned to Colangelo. "What if I used him remaining in protective custody as a chip for information?"

Colangelo stared out his office window and thought about it. After a couple of minutes, he turned back to Kim. "Talk to him. Tell him he's being released from protective custody and why. If he balks, then go ahead. But we can't waste too much time extending this investigation. That 35-day clock is already running."

"I've already sent all our notes and transcripts over to the DA's office, so we're covered on that. Anything else I uncover won't affect that. And if Lauren Davis has another conference with Coravos and his attorney, I can raise it there."

"Okay but talk to Davis before you do."

***

The air in Prinz's hotel room was clear, but his eyes were not as he stared at her.

"Geez, Felipe, every time I see you, you're more wasted than the last."

He laughed a little harder than necessary. "Hey, baby, there's worse ways to spend the day. Besides, what else I got to do here every day?"

"Funny you should mention that. We have Coravos and his henchmen in custody, so there's no need to keep you locked up here. You're free to go."

He staggered back as if she'd slapped him. "Holy shit."

"I should think you'd be pleased. We got all six. Well, five. As you know, they took care of Cruz, themselves."

"You think there were just six of them? Are you shitting me?"

"If you know of more, give me the names."

"I don't fucking know the names. And why the fuck is it that every time I see you, it's a fucking buzz-kill?"

"Why should that be? What's so terrible about getting your life back?"

"What life? Do you know how many guys he's got?"

"I'm all ears."

"I told you, I don't know. But this guy's got power behind him someplace."

"I think you're bluffing. Because if you know that much, you know more. You might even know where his money comes from."

He fell silent.

Bulls-eye. "Tell me, Felipe, now, or you're back on the street."

"You gotta promise me you'll keep me protected, first."

"This isn't your game, and you don't make the rules. You give me information, and I will evaluate it. Keep quiet, and we check out now. Your choice."

"I don't know the specifics, but I know he's been dealing."

"Dealing what?"

"Smack. I don't know much, but at least two of the guys you nailed were dealing with him, mostly at high schools. Since they legalized weed, it's no longer cool for kids. So, smack is back in style."

"Which two guys?"

"Alvarez and Mendez."

"And how do you know this?"

"Coravos tried to recruit my group for distribution. But I told him no, because you guys are always looking at us, anyway, all it would take is one bust to kill the whole group. It was a sore point between me and him."

"And you'd be willing to testify to this?"

"Yeah."

"Okay, Felipe. You've won yourself a stay of execution. We'll investigate Aziz, Alvarez and Mendez, and if it checks out, we'll talk about extending your protection."

***

There was only one problem: Kim had no contacts in Narcotics. Upon her return to Wilson Avenue, she made a bee-line for Colangelo's office.

"Okay," he said when she'd briefed him. "Search the apartments of Ali, Aziz, Alvarez and Mendez and see if you turn up any drug paraphernalia. Meanwhile, I'll check with some people I know in Narcotics and see if they have anything on Coravos. If either exercise turns up anything, you can re-interview our choir boys."

His phone rang. "Colangelo… Yes, she's here… Right now?… Okay."

"What?" She already had a sinking feeling of something going wrong.

"Change of plans. Send Stransky and Brogan to check the three apartments. Well, four. Give Coravos' place another look. You need to head on over to the courthouse and meet with Rick Conti. Walker's filed some motion, and Conti needs your help."

Oh, no. Not Let-em-run Ron.

# CHAPTER EIGHTY-SEVEN

"I should have known," Judge Vickers said as Kim entered his chambers with Conti and Davis.

Walker was already seated.

She took one of the remaining seats. "I was just thinking the same thing." But she said it without a hint of humor.

"Be careful, Detective," the judge replied. "You're here at my sufferance."

But if what Rick had told her downstairs was true, she had little sufferance of her own left. She said nothing.

The judge nodded to Walker. "Proceed, Counselor."

"Your honor, you have my motion to dismiss in front of you. It has come to our attention that Detective Brady obtained information leading her to my client by illegal means. She brutalized Ms. Rita Henshaw into revealing my client's cell phone number. Without that information, the police would never have located him. Their discovery of him is therefore fruit of the poisonous tree, and the charges against him should be dismissed." He handed the judge another document. "This is a copy of the complaint Ms. Henshaw filed with the police department regarding the incident."

"Your honor," Rick said, "the Internal Affairs Bureau has already dismissed the complaint as unfounded."

"That's true," Walker said, "but just because the department white-washed the incident, that doesn't change the fact that Ms. Henshaw was forced by police to disclose information provided to her in the course of newsgathering. It was therefore protected, and she had a right not to disclose it."

"In the 1990 Amendment to the State Shield law," Rick said, "the legislature codified the test established by the Court of Appeals in the *O'Neill* case two years earlier: that the privilege may be overcome when the materials sought are: highly material and relevant, critical or necessary to the maintenance of a party's claim or defense, and not obtainable from any alternative source. I've asked Detective Brady to join us to speak to the facts of the situation."

"Very well." The judge was clearly not pleased.

"Your honor, to begin with," Kim said, "Ms. Henshaw was never harmed or threatened with harm, which is why IAB cleared Detective Rydell and me of any violation of law or procedure."

"Your word against hers," Vickers said.

"And you have decided you believe her version without even listening to mine, even though I've taken the same oath you have, to protect the laws of this state, and she has not? Is that justice?"

He only glared at her.

She continued. "The facts, as they relate to the requirements of the Shield Law, are these. I did not seek the content of Ms. Henshaw's conversation with Mr. Coravos, or his name, because I already knew those. I sought only the number of the phone he had used to call her. And that number was highly relevant and material to my investigation. It was critical to the people's case against him because, without being able to arrest him, there would be no case. And since it was a number of a throwaway phone, it was not obtainable from any other source."

"The three-pronged test of *O'Neill* is met, your honor," Conti said.

Vickers thought it over. "I agree. Defendant's motion to dismiss is denied."

# CHAPTER EIGHTY-EIGHT

"Good work," Bostwick said when Kim returned to the Castle and reported the outcome. "I can't believe ol' Let-em-run didn't explode when you challenged him."

"He knew I was right. He was letting his ideological bias get in the way."

"Didn't Lauren Davis say anything? I'd love to see her let loose with her Jamaican shtick on him."

"Lauren's too smart for that. She'd never overstep Rick, who's her boss, and she'd never play it any way but dead serious with a judge. Judges see only the Georgetown Law side; perps and their attorneys get the Jamaican bit." Back to the case. "Anything from Narcotics?"

"I called the guy I know over there, and he said he didn't recognize the name, but said he'd get back to me. Rydell called in just before you walked in. Aziz's apartment came up clean. He should be back shortly. Martin is checking out Mendez and Ali, while Tim is checking Alvarez. I must say, Rydell has been a real help."

Great, it was the opening she needed. "Is there any chance we can bring him over to our unit? He'd be a great replacement for Bob."

"Sort of robbing Peter to pay Paul, isn't it?"

"He's a good detective, Lieu, and he seems a lot more focused since he's been working with us."

Bostwick considered it. "You two didn't appear to hit it off at first. What happened?"

"I think I was reacting to Bob's death. That hurt a lot."

"Past tense?" It came out as a whisper.

"Well, yes, it still does. But I obviously misjudged Cole. We've gotten used to each other. And, while Bob was a first-grade detective, Rydell is second-grade, so, a budget savings."

Bostwick guffawed. "You checked that out? Shit, you are serious. Okay, I'll talk to the captain about it."

*** 

Joanna Dunbar knocked on Ed Lyons' office door. "I have an idea for a series of special reports I'd like to run by you."

"Have a seat."

"Since I've come to ITN, the thing I've been most impressed with is how you stick to the principle of editorial views not interfering with reportage. Even though we're local, we stand out even against the big-name national news channels. So, it occurred to me that we could run a series of reports of cases in which ideological bias has tainted news coverage in a big way. And we could start with the situation I told you about last Friday. Henshaw and *City News* could have derailed the case against those guys. Judge Vickers nearly threw the case out and let them go."

Lyons pondered it before responding. "You got that from Justin Cates, who could only have gotten it from Rick Conti. What do you think would happen if that got out?"

"My idea is simply to highlight the misinformation aspect."

"I understand that. But it comes down to you wanting this station to attack a rival station for their editorial policies and reporting. They would then do anything they could to attack our credibility, including how you got information about proceedings in a judge's chambers. Conti would be exposed for leaking it to Cates, who leaked it to you, and the city would lose a quality ADA. Your friend, Detective Brady, would also be caught in the fallout. I don't suppose you've run your idea by her."

"No, I haven't."

"We're as respected as we are because we don't get into squabbles with other networks. We leave it to the public to see people like Rita Henshaw and the stations that employ them for what they are. Most news stations cast their reportage to fit the opinions of their viewers. We don't do that, and it's what makes us stand out in the field. We're not going to change what has been a successful approach."

# CHAPTER EIGHTY-NINE

*Thursday, May 8, 7:35 a.m.*

Bostwick had already called to tell her the searches had turned up nothing, but that Rydell had gone to the BDC and interviewed Aziz again. Aziz had confirmed that Coravos was dealing.

Kim and Rydell now joined Bostwick in the conference room. Lauren Davis was there, too. The case board had become jammed with notes, and there was precious little room remaining.

Kim's cell buzzed with a text from Josh Lewin at Homeland Security. *It's possible Coravos is working with drug cartels in Colombia or Mexico. We are investigating, along with the Drug Enforcement Agency and the FBI. Suggest you proceed with prosecution on the charges you've already filed. We'll continue to investigate and file charges if we see fit.*

"That's a relief," Davis said after Kim read the text aloud. "The last thing I'd want would be to go back to Vickers and ask for a postponement."

Colangelo walked in, and from the look on his face, Kim knew it wasn't good news.

The commissioner probably wants me on the carpet.

"I'd best be getting back," Davis said. "I'll let Mr. Conti know we're not pursuing a drug angle on these guys."

Kim braced herself as she watched Davis go.

"Okay," Colangelo said. "I'm glad I have all three of you in one place. Detective Rydell, Lieutenant Bostwick has requested that I transfer you to his unit, permanently. I've approved that transfer."

Kim heaved a sigh of relief.

Rydell burst into a broad grin. "Thank you, Captain."

"It was actually Kim's suggestion," Bostwick said. "So, if it's okay with you, I'll assign you two as partners."

"Fine with me," Rydell said.

"Great," Kim added. "You had me scared for a minute, there, Captain. I thought there was bad news."

He turned serious. "There is. Once we interrogated Coravos' accomplices and got information, we decided it wasn't safe to have them all together at the BDC. We transferred Coravos to Rikers Island."

"Rikers?" Kim didn't like where this was going. "Why not the Tombs?"

"That was my suggestion, but Corrections thought Rikers was the better choice. I got a call a few minutes ago. There was a melee in the mess hall this morning. Coravos was stabbed and killed."

Shit. "Well, Cole, I guess we have our first assignment. Let's get up there. Captain, has Corrections come up with any leads on their own?"

"None. Up there, they have their hands full even on a good day. Do the best you can."

As they were getting ready to leave, Kim got a text from Susan Garmin. *Hello Detective Brady. I just wanted to let you know my brother passed away last night. He never regained consciousness after the surgery. If it's all right with you, I'd like to stop by your headquarters tomorrow to give you something he left for you.*

What could he have left? *I usually get in a little before eight. But to save you the trip, I'll be glad to meet you by the B38 bus stop at Cadman Plaza. I'm there about 7:15.*

Her response was immediate. *Thanks. I'll see you there.*

***

They didn't get back to the Castle until five. Kim couldn't remember a more frustrating investigation. No one had seen anything, heard anything, or knew anything. No one knew what had started the brawl. It was said to be spontaneous, although most of the guards they'd interviewed thought otherwise.

The warden was the very portrait of impotent frustration. "We have too many prisoners and not enough guards, and that's with the state's insane law on no-cash-bail. The people who are pushing to close this place down have no clue how to deal with the overload."

His best guess was that one of the cartels had someone inside who had taken Coravos out.

Ken Taylor agreed. "It looks like he might have been playing the cartels off against the revolutionaries, but there's no way to know what his goal really was."

One door left to nail shut.

***

To Kim's surprise, Prinz was straight when she arrived at his hotel in downtown Manhattan.

"Shit, what do you want now?"

"Pack up, Prinz. You're busting outta here."

"What about Coravos?" There was no mistaking the alarm in his voice.

"Dead. Killed this morning at Rikers. His co-conspirators are in jail awaiting trial, and the cases against them are air tight. Pack your bag. My partner and I will drive you home."

Once in the car, Rydell drove.

Prinz sat in the back. "Why are you guys being nice to me?"

"We just wanted a final chat," Rydell said.

"Final?" There was no missing the alarm in his voice.

Kim chuckled. "Geez, Felipe, have you been binging on gangster movies? He meant 'final' for this case. Now that Coravos is gone, and he clearly had you scared shitless, I thought you might feel comfortable telling me stuff you held back earlier."

"Like what?"

She turned harsh. "Cut the shit, Felipe. You know what."

"Okay, okay. He wanted to use CHE as a kind of distribution network for smack. He said he had an endless supply, and that dealing could fund anything we wanted to do, even forming a well-armed attack force. I told him there was no way I'd want our folks to do any of that shit, that we already had you guys looking at us every time something went wrong in the city. I also said that most of our members weren't cut out to be hard-core criminals."

"Including you?" She didn't make it an accusation.

He turned red. "Well, yeah. And that was the problem that he and I always had. He thought I was soft, but it wasn't that. I knew what I wanted, and it wasn't what he wanted. That's why he never told me about the shootings in advance. He was afraid I'd turn on him."

Rydell snorted. "You'd never turn on someone like that. You'd be too scared. You and Coravos were alike in one way—both for yourselves, first and second, and fuck everyone else."

# CHAPTER NINETY

*Friday, May 9, 7:12 AM*

"Hello, Detective."

Kim took Susan Garmin's hands in hers. "I'm so sorry."

"He never mentioned this to me. I just found it when I went to his apartment to clear out his things. It was sitting on the keyboard of his computer." She handed Kim a business-size envelope. On it, in an uneven scrawl, it said, *To Queen-Knight Detective Kim Brady. To be opened only in the privacy and security of her own castle. Not THE Castle.*

She had to smile. She couldn't remember having mentioned the nickname, but, like many other things, he managed to find out somehow. "Thank you. Was he very afraid before the surgery?"

"No. I think he knew he wasn't going to make it." Her eyes glistened as they met Kim's. "In a very strange way, I think he loved you. I'll never forget your kindness to him."

***

Later in the day, Lieutenant Driscoll came by to meet with Kim, Bostwick, Colangelo, and Lauren Davis to review everything they had. Davis was convinced that the remaining four conspirators would take deals. The FBI would continue to search for any missing group members, but no one was confident they'd be found.

***

Mindful of Lodemay's request, Kim waited until she arrived home to open the envelope. In it, she found another note in the same scrawl that had adorned the envelope.

*Dearest Queen-Knight,*
*4. Bg2.*
*If you are reading this, I have gone home to Our Lord and will not be able to finish our game. I'm sorry because you would have been a worthy opponent. The last time we spoke, you said I had been very helpful to your investigation. I thank you for honoring me that way.*

*I know you never believed I was Jacques de Molay, or even descended from him. But you accepted me, which was a greater gift. In return,*
*I have enclosed something to remember me by. I have had it for far longer than I can remember.*

*May the blessings of the Lord be with you,*
*Your obedient servant,*
*Jacques de Molay*

She reached into the envelope and pulled out what appeared to be an ancient coin. After studying it, she logged onto her desktop and did a search for French medieval coins, just to prove to herself that it was a fake, a prop for Lodemay's fantasies.

She soon found the same coin, with a square knight's cross on one side and on the other, a square with crescents on opposite ends. It was described as a denier, from the medieval French County of Marche, minted sometime between 1199 and 1249.

Lodemay's coin showed signs of wear but was in better condition than the one she found online appeared to be.

Like it had been well cared for.

# AFTERWORD

In April of 2025, New York City Mayor Eric Adams, facing a strong primary challenge, decided to run for re-election as an independent. His announcement was made several months after I had written about Raymond Brandt doing the same thing for much the same reasons, thus providing us with a classic example of life imitating art.

In May of 2025, the New York State Legislature repealed the onerous requirement that prosecutors submit all evidence in discovery to defense attorneys within thirty-five days, thereby taking the pressure off Kim and her team.

# ACKNOWLEDGEMENTS

I am blessed to have two wonderfully dedicated beta readers in Jan Foley and Ray Lodato. They have been a part of my writing since the first Kim Brady book, *Past Grief*. I'm also deeply grateful for the support from Elena Hartwell and Tosca Lee at International Thriller Writers, and fellow writer James L'Etoile. None of the Kim Brady Mysteries would have seen the light of day without the fabulous work of Reagan Rothe and his team at Black Rose Writing: David King, graphics designer extraordinaire, Justin Weeks, the king of sales, and most recently Mary Ellen Bramwell, the editor who steered me right on this novel.

Thanks to my good friend (and fellow hockey fan) Jim Brady for lending me his persona to serve as Kim Brady's cousin. He first volunteered while I was writing *Proving A Villain*, and in so doing helped me to fill a major plot hole. Anyone who would like to appear in a future Kim or Dan mystery can email me at ejl.author@gmail.com.

Most of all, a special thank you to my beloved wife and alpha reader, Cindy. Forty-nine years of marriage to me earns her a special place in the pantheon. Her suggestions on my writing are delivered with a unique mixture of love and the assurance that accepting her comments assures no one gets hurt.

# ABOUT THE AUTHOR

Edward J. Leahy is a retired tax accountant and IRS agent with degrees in government and politics and an MBA in Public Accounting from St. John's University. He is a Maxy Award Finalist and has published four other novels in the Kim Brady series and two in the Dan Brady series. He lives in Jackson Heights, Queens, with Cindy, his wife of forty-nine years, where he enjoys running, writing, chess, music, and photography, as well as dining out in the many restaurants New York has to offer.

# OTHER TITLES
# BY EDWARD J. LEAHY

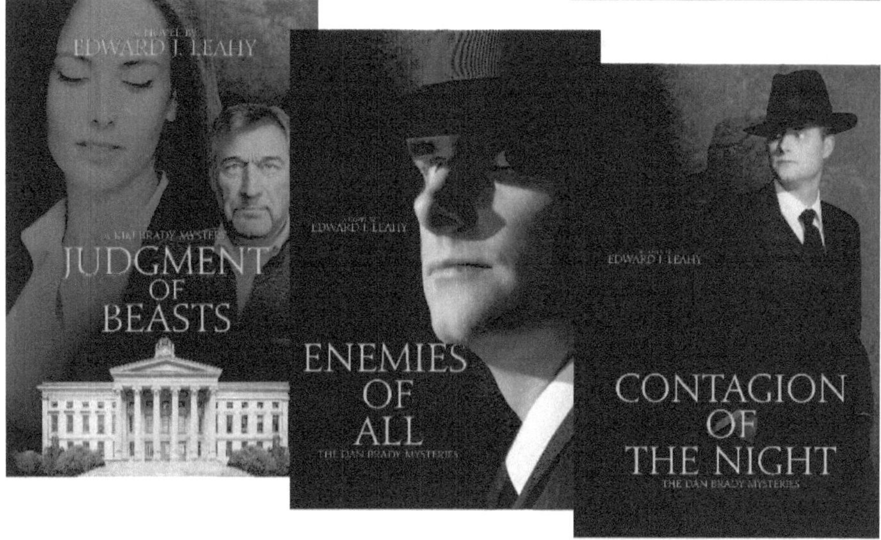

# NOTE FROM EDWARD J. LEAHY

Word-of-mouth is crucial for any author to succeed. If you enjoyed *A Tempest Dropping Fire*, please leave a review online—anywhere you are able. Even if it's just a sentence or two. It would make all the difference and would be very much appreciated.

Thanks!
Edward J. Leahy

We hope you enjoyed reading this title from:

www.blackrosewriting.com

Subscribe to our mailing list – *The Rosevine* – and receive **FREE** books, daily deals, and stay current with news about upcoming releases and our hottest authors.
Scan the QR code below to sign up.

Already a subscriber? Please accept a sincere thank you for being a fan of Black Rose Writing authors.

View other Black Rose Writing titles at
www.blackrosewriting.com/books and use promo code
**PRINT** to receive a **20% discount** when purchasing.